PONY  CLUB
SECRETS

TWO BOOKS IN ONE!

Mystic and Blaze

The Pony Club Secrets series:

PONY CLUB SECRETS

Mystic and Blaze

Mystic and the Midnight Ride

and

Blaze and the Dark Rider

STACY GREGG

HarperCollins *Children's Books*

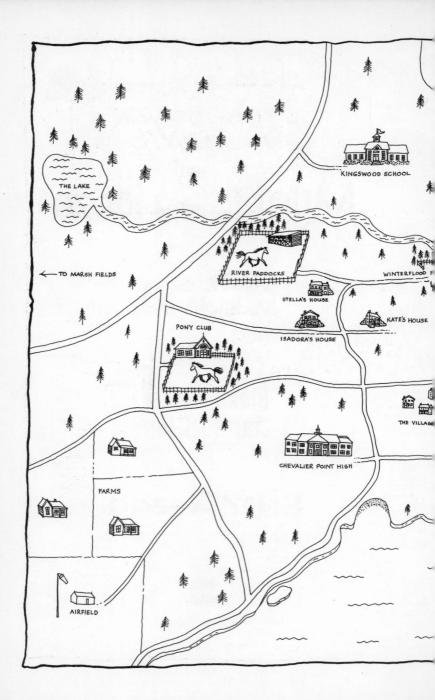

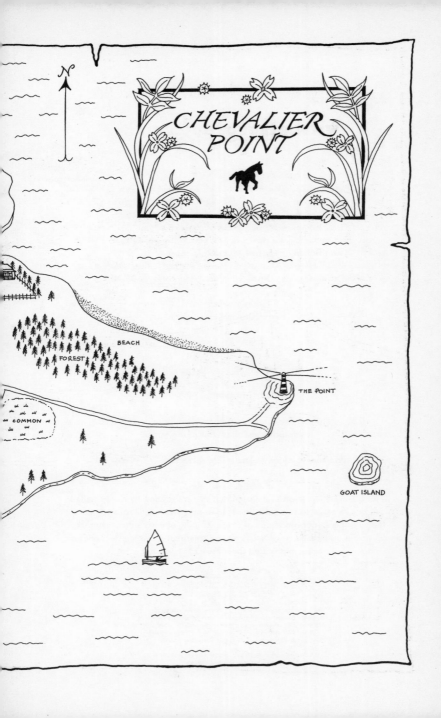

www.stacygregg.co.uk

Mystic and the Midnight Ride first published in paperback in
Great Britain by HarperCollins *Children's Books* in 2007.
Blaze and the Dark Rider first published in paperback in
Great Britain by HarperCollins *Children's Books* in 2007.
First published as a two-in-one edition *Mystic and Blaze* in
Great Britain by HarperCollins *Children's Books* in 2009.
HarperCollins *Children's Books* is a division of HarperCollins*Publishers* Ltd,
77-85 Fulham Palace Road, Hammersmith, London, W6 8JB.

Visit our website at:
www.harpercollins.co.uk

1 3 5 7 9 10 8 6 4 2

Text copyright © Stacy Gregg 2007

ISBN-13 978-0-00-731363-1

The author and illustrator assert the moral right to be identified
as the author and illustrator of the work.

Printed and bound in England by Clays Ltd, St Ives plc

Mystic and the Midnight Ride

For Venetia

CHAPTER 1

Please, please let it be sunny tomorrow, Issie had prayed as she went to bed the night before the gymkhana. But when her alarm clock woke her at quarter to six the next morning and she ran to the window there were grey clouds covering the sky. Still, there was no sign of rain and when she listened for a cancellation on the radio nothing was mentioned, so she headed out into the pre-dawn light to prepare Mystic for his big day.

Stella and Kate were already down at the River Paddock. Stella was busily brushing out Coco's tail, while Kate was sectioning out Toby's neatly pulled mane so that she could start plaiting it into tiny knots along the top of his neck.

"You'd better hurry." Stella smiled. "Tom said he'd be here by seven to help us load them into the truck and take them to the show grounds."

Grabbing Mystic's halter out of the tack room, Issie set off across the paddock. The grass was wet with dew and her riding boots were soaked by the time she reached the spot where Mystic was grazing. The pretty dapple-grey was chewing up great chunks of fresh spring growth and barely bothered to raise his head to acknowledge her.

"Here, Mystic," Issie called hopefully, hiding the halter behind her back with one hand and holding her other hand out towards the pony.

She had forgotten to bring a treat to tempt him with, but perhaps she could bluff the gelding into believing she had a piece of carrot or apple in her empty fist.

No such luck. Mystic had spotted the halter. He gave a deep snort of surprise, shaking his mane and trotting off to the other side of the paddock.

"Oh, Mystic, no! Not today!" Issie cried in despair.

Of course these things always happened at the worst possible moment. Like today. Issie was nervous enough about riding at her first gymkhana. Now she was running late – the others were nearly ready to plait up their horses and she hadn't even started grooming. Even at this distance Issie could see that Mystic had got himself into a right state from rolling in the long paddock grass. There were chunks of dirt matted into his silvery mane and his hocks were stained bright green.

"Come on, Mystic," Issie begged. She bent down, picked a handful of grass and offered it hopefully to the little grey pony. Mystic swivelled his ears towards Issie. He took one step forward, then another. Even though he was knee-deep in grass, the small bunch in Issie's hand was too good to resist. Issie walked quietly up to his side and slid the halter rope around his neck. Then she eased the halter over Mystic's nose and quickly buckled it up behind his ears. Success!

"Who's a naughty pony then?" Stella giggled as Issie led Mystic up to the fence and tethered him next to her Coco.

"It's not just Mystic," Kate insisted. "I spent ages

catching Toby this morning. It's this spring grass. It's making them all act like crazy colts!"

"Do you hear that, Mystic? I bet you wish you were a colt again, eh boy?" Issie laughed.

Mystic wasn't a young horse. Issie had known that when she bought him. Back then she been told that the grey gelding was eighteen. But it was hard to tell the age of a horse. Her pony-club instructor Tom Avery reckoned that the little grey might actually be as old as twenty-five which was positively ancient in horse years.

The pony's dapples had faded over the years from the dark steel of a young colt to a soft dove grey. Mystic's back was slightly swayed too, from years of riding. Still, he was a beautiful pony, only fourteen hands high but he held himself so proudly he seemed bigger. His eyes were dark smudges of coal in his pale face, and they had the calm depth of a horse that has lived a little. Mystic certainly knew his way around a showjumping or cross-country course.

Issie sighed as she examined her horse's hindquarters. "Oh, Mystic, why aren't you a nice dark colour like Toby and Coco? Keeping you clean is twice as much work."

"Don't be so sure," Stella said. "You can't see the grass stains on Coco, but check this out." She gave the chubby little brown mare a friendly slap on the rump and a circle of white dust appeared where her hand had been. "See? I've been grooming for hours now and I can't get rid of it."

Coco turned around to see what Stella was up to and gave her a sniff, nuzzling the girl with her velvet-soft nose. "No, Coco. I don't have any carrots," Stella giggled, "but if you win a ribbon today I promise you can have as many carrots as you want." Coco nickered happily. It was a deal.

Stella and Kate were perfectly suited to their horses, Issie thought. Blonde and blue-eyed Kate was as lanky and long-limbed as her rangy bay Thoroughbred, while Stella, with her bunches of red curls and pale complexion dotted with freckles, was small and bubbly – the same personality as her chocolate-coloured mare.

Stella was Issie's best friend. They had been best friends since the first day of primary school when they realised that not only did they both love horses, they also loved to draw. Even now, art classes were still a competition between the two of them – although their third form art teacher was less than impressed that all they ever wanted to draw was horses.

Issie grabbed a rubber band out of her grooming bucket, using it as a hair tie to secure her long, dark hair out of her face while she worked. Then she dipped her hand back into the bucket of brushes again, this time producing a stiff-bristled dandy brush, and got started on Mystic's hocks, furiously scrubbing away at the mud. She gave Mystic's two white hind socks a brisk scrub with a damp brush to remove the last of the marks, then set about bandaging his legs for the trip. It may only be a few minutes down the road, she figured, but Mystic might still injure his legs in the horse truck if they weren't padded for protection.

The Chevalier Point Pony Club grounds were within riding distance of the River Paddock – about half an hour away at a steady trot. But the stretch of road that you had to ride to reach the pony club was treacherous. The club grounds were just off a busy main road, which made them a nightmare to reach on horseback. Most drivers had no idea of the danger they were causing as they raced past at top speed, never bothering to slow down in case they spooked the horses that were confined to the narrow grass verge on the side of the road.

On rally days, Issie usually rode to pony club the long way, using a series of quiet backroads to reach the grounds, avoiding the main road as much as possible. But today, she wouldn't have to worry about the roads at all. Tom Avery was loading their ponies into his horse truck to drive them to the gymkhana so that they would arrive fresh and ready for the big event.

Issie had bandaged Mystic's tail to keep it clean and was about to start with some last-minute mane-pulling when she heard the stern voice of her pony-club instructor booming out across the paddock. "Come on, girls, I thought you'd have them rugged up and ready to go by now."

Issie turned around to see Avery striding towards her, a tall striking figure in crisp white jodhpurs and long black boots. His face was set in a serious expression underneath the mop of thick, curly brown hair. He held a riding crop in one hand, which Issie had never seen him use — except to thwack against the side of his boot when he was making a point. She guessed he carried it mostly to make himself look meaner.

Sometimes Stella would imitate Avery when he wasn't around, whacking her crop against her leg and barking in a commanding tone, "Come on, chaps, get their hocks under them!" Issie and Kate would hoot with laughter at this impersonation, but the fact was that all three girls had enormous respect for their instructor.

Avery had once been a professional eventer – until he took a bad fall at the Badminton Horse Trials which finished his career for good. He didn't talk much about those days, but Issie knew he had competed against the best riders in the world. He had even been on the same team as Blyth Tait and Mark Todd. But since his accident he didn't ride at all.

Now he worked for the International League for the Protection of Horses, rescuing horses and ponies that had been mistreated and abused by vicious owners, and in his spare time he gave lessons to Issie and the other riders at Chevalier Point.

Hardly a glamorous life for him, Issie thought. After all, Chevalier Point wasn't exactly the most exciting place on earth. It was a small town, perched on a peninsula of land. Issie's mum was fond of saying that there were more horses there than people. Which may have been true. Certainly, if you loved horses then Chevalier Point was the best place in the world to live. With its flat green fields and rolling hills it was perfect horse country.

"Let's get them loaded," Avery instructed the girls. "We've got no time to waste."

"Toby looks great in his new rug," Issie said as Kate led him towards the ramp of the truck. The handsome bay wore a blood-red woollen blanket. Coco, too, was dressed up in her show rug made of navy-blue netting.

Wearing his plain old canvas paddock rug, Mystic didn't look anywhere near as grand. "Don't worry, boy, you look good just as you are," Issie reassured him, worried that her pony's feelings would be hurt if the others got all the attention. Mystic seemed happy enough with Issie's praise. There was a definite spring in his step as he walked up the truck ramp, as if he knew he was on his way somewhere exciting.

Toby whinnied a greeting to Mystic as Issie tied the little grey up in the stall next to the big bay Thoroughbred. She gave each horse a hay net to play with for the five-minute trip and knocked on the window that separated the horses from the passenger cab of the truck to let Avery know they were ready to go. The overcast skies had cleared, the sun was out and they were on their way.

CHAPTER 2

Clouds of dust rose up from the truck tyres as Avery turned off the main road and down the gravel drive that led to the Chevalier Point grounds. Ahead of them were the pony-club gates, hemmed by a line of tall magnolia trees. Beyond the magnolias was another paddock gate and then a series of large plane trees ran like a leafy spine down the middle of the three paddocks that made up the club grounds.

On warm summer days riders could loll about in the shade of the plane trees while their horses rested. It wasn't going to get that hot today. After all, this was the first gymkhana of the season. Still, Avery pulled the horse truck up in the first paddock under two of the biggest trees so that they would be shaded from the glare of the sun.

They unloaded the horses and set to work braiding manes, stencilling chequerboard patterns on to rumps and oiling the ponies' hooves.

Issie had never seen so many riders at Chevalier Point before. The gymkhana was open to all riders in the district, and Issie tried to pick out which riders were from the various clubs by the colour of their jerseys and ties. The Chevalier Point club uniform was a navy jersey with a bright red tie and Issie could see two riders dressed in Chevalier Point colours riding towards her from the far field where the showjumps had been set up.

"Hey, dizzy Issie!" the rider at the front called to her as he cantered closer. "About time you got here. Ben and me have already walked the showjumping course."

Dan and Ben were Chevalier Point Pony Club members. Dan had a flea-bitten grey gelding called Kismit, while Ben rode a grumpy Welsh pony called Max.

"Are the jumps very big?" Issie asked nervously.

"Huge!" Dan teased her. "And you've got to ride fast too, if you want to beat the clock. The best time with no faults wins." He was grinning from ear to ear. Dan was a speed demon. He and Kismit would be the ones to beat in the jumping ring today.

No time to walk the course now, Issie decided. It was nearly time for the first event. She would have to check out the jumps with Stella and Kate during the lunch break.

"Hello, Kismit." Issie reached out a hand to pat the slender grey on the nose. "I suppose you've been promised extra carrots for dinner if you go fast today?" She smiled at Dan.

"Hey! I don't need to bribe my own horse to win." Dan grinned back. "Anyway, we're going to fill in our entry forms now. Do you want to come?" he asked.

Issie was about to say yes when she heard her mother calling her name.

"Isadora! Isadora!" Mrs Brown cried out as she strode across the field towards her. Issie groaned. She couldn't stand the way her mother insisted on using her full name. Isadora. It sounded so snobby and girly, not at all the sort of name for a serious horse rider. Sure, Avery called her Isadora sometimes too, but only when he was telling her off during a riding lesson. Apart from that, everyone else, even her teachers at school, called her Issie.

"I've filled in your entry forms," Mrs Brown explained. "Doesn't Mystic look wonderful?" She gave the grey gelding a very nervous pat and held on to the reins, extending her arm so that she was standing as far away from Mystic as possible while Issie did up the girth.

Everyone said that Issie was exactly like her mum. It was true that they were both tall, tanned and lean with long dark hair. But Issie didn't think they were alike at all. How could they be when Issie loved horses so much and her mother didn't even like them?

Issie wished her mum would give riding a try. Maybe if she could experience for herself the thrill of cantering across open fields with the wind in her hair, she'd finally be able to understand why Issie adored riding so much. But her mum was way too scared to even sit on a horse, let alone canter one.

"What's your first event?" Mrs Brown asked, still reluctantly hanging on to Mystic's reins as Issie finished adjusting her stirrups.

"Paced and Mannered. We're due in the ring any minute now," Issie told her. She gave Mystic a stroke on his dark, velvety nose and her mum gave her a leg up.

"Come on, boy," Issie murmured softly, leaning low over Mystic's neck, "let's show them what we can do."

In the ring, several horses were trotting around warming up. Dan and Ben were already there. A girl that Issie didn't recognise rode in on a skewbald with a peppy trot, a young girl on a chubby chestnut mare following behind her. The chestnut pony had a vicious temper. Her ears were lying flat back against her head – a warning to other horses not to get too close.

The prettiest by far in the ring, thought Issie, was a golden palomino with a star on her forehead and high, lively paces. "Wow! Isn't that palomino gorgeous," Stella said, reading Issie's mind as the two riders sat at the edge of the arena checking out the competition. "I wonder who that rider is? I've never seen her here before but she's wearing our club colours…"

The girl on the palomino had golden hair, almost the same colour as her pony, tied back in two severe plaits. She wore a tweed hacking jacket over her club jersey and had a sour expression on her face.

"I know who it must be," Kate said as she rode up beside them. "That's Natasha Tucker. Her family have just moved here. I bet she's joined Chevalier Point Pony Club!"

The three girls were still eyeing up the palomino with envy, when it suddenly spooked at a plastic bag blowing across the ground. The girl with the sour expression jerked back in the saddle, wrenching on the reins and jagging the little pony sharply in the mouth with the bit. Regaining her seat, she raised her riding crop in the air and brought it down hard on the pony's golden flank. "Stand still you brute!" she squealed.

Issie was stunned. "I can't believe she just did that!"

"Don't worry," muttered Stella, "the judge saw it too and she can't believe it either. Paced and Mannered? More like bad manners! There's no way she's going to get a ribbon for that behaviour. And neither will we for that matter if we don't get in the ring pretty quickly. Come on! The event is about to start."

"Trot on!" ordered the judge, a sturdy woman in blue stockings and a matching straw hat, standing in the middle of the arena. The riders obediently trotted around in a circle.

Issie urged Mystic into a trot and tried to look her best. Heels down, hands still, head up, she chanted to herself as she rose up and down to the rhythm of Mystic's trot.

"Canter!" called the judge. Mystic cantered eagerly around the ring, ears pricked forward, tail held high. Unfortunately his canter was a little too keen. As he got closer to the chubby chestnut mare in front of him she flattened her ears and lashed out with her hind legs. Mystic squealed and shied to one side. Issie let the reins slip and had to grab a handful of mane to stay on his back.

"Halt!" commanded the judge. But there was no hope of that right now. Issie snatched the reins back up but it was too late. Everyone else had stopped their horses and Mystic was still doing an ungainly trot around the ring. She sat down heavy in the saddle and finally he came to a halt. Too late, though – the judge had been watching her mistakes.

When the winners were called into the centre of the ring Issie knew she didn't stand a chance. Kate rode out with a grin on her face and a red ribbon tied around Toby's neck. Behind her was the skewbald in second place and a boy on a brown pony came third.

The haughty girl with the palomino hadn't got anywhere either. As the riders left the ring she barged past Issie and Mystic in a huff. "Get your stupid horse out of the way," she snapped. Then she halted the palomino and turned in the saddle to glare at Issie. Her face was so bitter it looked like she'd been sucking lemons. "It's all your fault anyway," she continued. "If your horse hadn't run wild in there and scared Goldrush I would have won this dumb event. You obviously have no idea how to ride. You shouldn't even be here."

Issie opened her mouth to protest her innocence, but it was too late. The sour-faced girl turned the palomino again and set off at a canter, leaving Issie reeling in shock and anger.

"What was that all about?" Stella rode up to join Issie.

"Well, Stella," Issie said sarcastically, "it looks like I just made friends with the new girl."

As Issie reached Avery's truck she was still deep in thought, mulling over all the things she should have said to nasty old Natasha instead of just sitting there with her mouth hanging open. Then she heard Natasha's shrill voice again. This time, thankfully, she wasn't yelling at Issie. She was talking to someone on the other side of the truck where a silver horse float was parked behind a matching silver sports car.

"Mum, I hate this horse," the girl wailed as she slid off the palomino's back and threw the reins to a tall blonde woman wearing black sunglasses.

"Natasha Tucker!" scolded her mother. "Do you know how much money we've spent on that horse?"

"I don't care!" Natasha barked. "She's useless!"

"Sweetie, please just try to ride her for the rest of the day," her mother sighed. "It seems like every horse we buy for you simply isn't good enough. Give Goldrush a chance."

"All right," Natasha muttered. She was staring at

the ground, kicking the dirt with her riding boot as she sulked. "All right then. But I really can't be bothered. I mean, she's a useless horse. And why do I have to ride anyway? Why won't you buy me a snowboard?"

"Natasha," her mother said firmly, "we've already bought you a jet ski and a pair of rollerblades and a mountain bike, and you don't use any of them. Now, you told us you wanted a pony, and we've paid a small fortune for Goldrush, so you can jolly well get out there and ride her."

With a dramatic sigh of resignation Natasha turned away from her mother and mounted the palomino again, giving her a sharp boot in the ribs as they headed back towards the arena.

Issie couldn't believe it. Was Goldrush just another toy that this girl was getting tired of playing with? How could Natasha Tucker not love the beautiful palomino? And was this awful spoilt brat really the newest member of the Chevalier Point Pony Club?

CHAPTER 3

"Forget about Miss Stuck-up Tucker," Stella giggled. The two girls were sitting on a tartan rug that had been thrown down on the grass next to Avery's truck, noshing into the pile of sandwiches that Issie's mum had prepared for their lunch. "Finish up your sandwich and we'll go grab Kate and walk the showjumping course with Tom."

The showjumping course was laid out at the far end of the club grounds. Avery was already there waiting for them.

"The key to a clear round," he advised them as they set out on foot towards the first jump, "is never take any fence for granted. Especially the first one. Many a rider has a refusal at the first jump because they're too busy thinking about what comes next."

The girls followed along as Avery walked between the fences, describing the various obstacles and advising where the ponies should take off and land. Standing beside the third fence, a parallel rail painted in blue and white stripes, Avery measured the jump against his body. The rail was almost as high as his waist. "These fences are a decent size," he said. "You'll need to be thinking at all times. Keep your horse well-rounded with lots of power in the hindquarters. If you allow them to flatten out you'll never make it over these jumps."

Avery charted out the rest of the course, taking slow careful steps and measuring the strides needed between each fence. "When you're riding I expect you to follow exactly in my footsteps," he told Issie as he walked the line between the fences. "Don't be tempted to cut corners," he said. "Better to risk time faults than to have a refusal."

As they headed back to the truck to saddle up, the girls stopped at the judges' tent and collected their competition numbers, which had been written in black felt tip on to fabric squares that they tied on over their jerseys. Issie was number twenty-two, the last to go. An advantage, she decided, since she could watch the other riders and learn from their mistakes.

"Your first showjumping competition, eh? You must be nervous." Dan gave Issie a grin as he rode up to join her at the side of the show ring.

"Nervous?" Issie tried to act cool even though her tummy was churning with butterflies. "No way! Mystic has done this sort of thing a million times before. I'm pretty relaxed," she said airily.

"Still, hadn't you better go over a few practice jumps?" Dan said, teasing her. "Maybe your problem is that you're a little too relaxed."

Dan was so confident, so self-assured. Issie couldn't stand it any longer. She stared up at him with her hands on her hips. "You think you're so cool, don't you, Daniel Halliday? Well how about a little bet? The losing rider has to groom the winner's horse for a week."

As soon as Issie had opened her mouth she regretted it. What was she saying? Dan hadn't meant to be mean or anything. He only teased her because he liked talking to her, she knew that. She also knew that he was a better rider than she was.

Still, she figured, even losing wouldn't be so bad. She was more than happy to groom Kismit – and hang out with Dan.

Dan removed his helmet, pushing back his blond hair with one hand and then reaching that same hand out to her. "I could use a good groom," Dan smirked. "Let's shake on it."

"Number twenty, Natasha Tucker on Goldrush, please enter the arena," the announcer called over the loudspeaker.

With only three competitors to come, the showjumping course had claimed its fair share of victims. In fact, so far there hadn't been a single clear round. Now it was the turn of Chevalier Point's newest rider to try her luck.

Natasha cantered Goldrush into the ring, pointed the pony towards the first fence and gave her a swift slap with her whip. Goldrush gave a surprised snort and leapt forward, rushing the fence and catapulting Natasha back in the saddle. It wasn't the best start, but somehow Natasha managed to hang on and re-settle herself for the second fence, which Goldrush took with a perfect stride.

One by one, the golden pony took each fence after that without a hitch. As they cleared the final fence, a serious oxer, the crowd let out a cheer. The first clear round of the day. With a fast time too – three minutes and five seconds exactly.

Issie couldn't watch Dan as he entered the ring to begin his round. It wasn't that she was too nervous to watch him; she would have loved to. But she had to warm Mystic up over the practice jump and get him worked in so that he would be ready when her turn came. She rode to the far end of the field and cantered him back and forth over the low crossed rails, all the time half-listening to the loud speaker to hear how Dan was doing. It would be dreadful to lose to Dan, she decided, but much, much worse if they both lost to Natasha.

Issie arrived back at the ringside just in time to see Dan clear the final fence. Kismit took the rails cleanly, then gave a high-spirited buck to signal the end of a clear round, nearly unseating Dan as the pair rode between the flags to finish.

"A clear round in two minutes and forty-four seconds for competitor twenty-one, Dan Halliday," the voice over the loudspeaker announced. "That time puts Dan Halliday in the lead. Would the final competitor, number twenty-two Isadora Brown, please enter the ring."

As the last rider to go, Issie thought to herself, at least she knew where she stood. With only two clear rounds before her, all she needed to do was go clear too and she would win a ribbon. But if she wanted to beat Dan's time? Then she would have to ride faster than she had ever done before in her life.

"Let's go, Mystic," she breathed into the little grey's ear as she leant down low over his neck. Then she squeezed her legs around his plump belly and trotted into the ring. As the judges' bell went to signal the start of the round, Mystic tossed his head and Issie pressed him on into a canter. Her nerves disappeared as she kept her mind focused on clearing the first fence. She sat down heavy and urged Mystic on. He leapt it boldly and fought against her hands to get his head. "Steady boy," Issie cautioned, holding him firmly and looking to the next fence. Again they took it cleanly and Issie's confidence grew with each jump.

They were gaining speed now, until it seemed to Issie as if she were flying. The grey gelding fought against the bit to go faster still and Issie was forced to hang on tight to the reins to keep Mystic under control.

By the time they rounded the corner to face fences six and seven – a double combination – Mystic was in full stride and too strong for her to hold back. Issie found herself on a sharp angle as the headstrong pony rushed the fence and had to put in a last-minute stride to adjust himself. His hind legs went thwack against the top rail of the first jump and Issie could hear the crowd gasp and hold their breath as the pole rocked in its metal socket. Would the rail fall? She couldn't look, she must concentrate on the next fence ahead of her. She tensed, expecting to hear the crash of the rail falling behind her, but instead she heard a cheer rise up from the crowd. The rail hadn't fallen. She was still clear.

Over the next fence and there she was with just one

jump between her and a clear round. As they neared the big oxer she felt butterflies rise in her tummy and tried to calm herself. "Trust your horse, Issie," she commanded herself out loud. She gave Mystic his head and sat deep in the saddle. The dapple-grey took off perfectly and soared over the rails, landing cleanly on the other side. Clear round!

Mystic was flecked with sweat and snorting from his efforts as the pair left the ring. Issie slid to the ground and threw her arms around his neck giving him a hug and inhaling the sweet smell of warm, damp horse sweat. *It must be the best smell in the world!* Issie thought, breathing in deeply.

"Good lad, Mystic. Well done! A clear round!" she murmured to her pony, her face still buried deep in his grey mane.

"Hey, hey," Dan called as he rode over to her, "what are you doing? Get back on your horse – you'll have to ride into the ring in a minute to get your ribbon!"

But which ribbon? With three clear rounds, Issie's time was crucial now. Had she gone fast enough to beat Dan?

"Competitor number twenty-two, Isadora Brown, a

clear round in two minutes fifty-six seconds," the announcer called. "The winner is Dan Halliday on Kismit. Second place goes to Isadora Brown on Mystic, third Natasha Tucker on Goldrush. Would all riders please come back into the ring to collect your prizes."

As Mystic trotted into the arena, Issie felt like she was in a dream. It didn't matter that Dan had beaten her. She had won her first ribbon. Mystic seemed to know it too; as the three riders cantered around the ring in a lap of honour he bristled with pride, flicking his tail and arching his neck.

"You are totally the best pony ever, do you know that?" Issie told Mystic as they rode back to Avery's truck. "Just the best," she repeated again proudly as she pulled the little grey up to a halt. OK, so she'd lost her bet with Dan and she'd have to groom Kismit for a week – she didn't care. Second place. And a clear round! How fantastic was that?

Issie was just about to dismount and give Mystic yet another hug when she heard someone crashing about on the other side of the silver horse float.

"Stop that! Stand still, damn you!" Natasha Tucker's voice was raised in a high-pitched squeal. She had been trying to take off Goldrush's tack but the pretty palomino kept dancing nervously as the girl tried to undo her bridle. "Stop it!" Natasha shouted again, this time giving Goldrush a slap across the neck with her riding crop.

As the whip cut hard into her flesh the palomino reared up, jerking the reins out of Natasha's hands. Natasha stood there helplessly as Goldrush planted her front legs back on the ground, standing on top of the loose reins and tangling them around her legs.

Caught in the reins, Goldrush went wild with terror. The mare tried to back up to get free, but found herself pressed up hard against Toby and Coco who were tied to the truck beside her.

What happened next came so suddenly that Issie didn't have a chance to stop it. She watched as Goldrush kept backing up into the other horses, kicking out in terror with her hind legs. Then Toby gave a snort and pulled back hard against his halter rope. The knot gave way and his lead rope came loose. Coco, too, had worked her way free from her tether. Now, all three horses were loose and heading for the paddock gate.

It was then that Issie noticed that the main pony club gate was still open – someone must have forgotten to shut it as they had driven in to park their horse float.

"Hey! The gates. Shut the gates!" Issie yelled.

As the horses bolted through the first paddock gate and headed for the main gate, Issie saw people running after them, trying to divert them from the exit. *It's no use,* she realised. *They'll never catch up with them on foot.* But maybe she could reach them on Mystic.

She wheeled the little grey around and clucked him into a canter, leaning low over his neck. The horses were through the gate now and already clattering along the gravel driveway that would lead them to the deadly road.

In full gallop now, Issie and Mystic rounded through the gate behind them. "Come on, boy, we've got to beat them to the road." Issie dug her heels into Mystic's sides, urging him on even faster. Mystic was gaining on the horses but as they got closer to the intersection where the roads met, Issie realised they weren't going to make it in time. She would have to ride out on to the road after the horses and try to herd them back again.

The clatter of gravel became the clean chime of metal horseshoes hitting tarmac as the horses struck the main highway. There was the honk of a car horn as two vehicles sped past, one of them narrowly missing Toby.

Issie quickly checked for more traffic then followed the runaway horses out on to the road. She pulled Mystic around hard in front of Toby and waved an arm at him, spooking the big bay and directing him back down the gravel drive, back towards the pony club.

If she could get Toby to lead the way, maybe the others would follow. It was their only chance. Two cars had already nearly hit them. How long could their luck last?

Suddenly the deep low boom of a truck horn sounded off behind her. Issie heard the sickening squeal of tyres and smelt burning rubber. As the truck rounded the corner towards her, everything suddenly seemed to go into slow motion.

To Issie it seemed as if Mystic was turning to face the truck, like two stallions set to fight. The grey horse reared up suddenly, throwing her backwards with such force that she flew clear of the oncoming traffic, landing hard on the shoulder of the road. There was a sickening crack as her riding helmet met with tarmac, the peak splintering as it took the full force of the blow.

Groggy from the fall, Issie tried to stand up, to move, but her vision blurred and she could taste blood in her mouth. In the distance came the screech of tyres again and then the most hideous sound she had ever heard, the sound of a horse screaming. Through the sirens and the traffic noise she could make out a voice calling out her name, and then everything faded to black.

CHAPTER 4

Issie could hear hoofbeats. In the pitch black she saw the blurry grey shape of a horse galloping towards her. Just out of her reach, the horse reared to a stop. His nostrils flared, and he pawed the ground impatiently, flicking his head and nickering to her. Then, as suddenly as he had come, he wheeled around and galloped away again. Mystic? It had to be. Issie tried to yell out to him but she couldn't speak. What was happening to her?

"I think she's coming round," a voice broke through the blackness.

Then another voice, softer, calling her, "Isadora. Isadora. Wake up."

And there she was, lying between the cool white sheets of a hospital bed, looking up into her mother's eyes.

"My God, Isadora! You gave me such a scare." Mrs Brown had tears in her eyes as she hugged her daughter tightly. The embrace was so strong, Issie found it hard to breathe and had to gasp for air. As she took a deep breath her chest ached and she let out a squeal of pain.

"Do your ribs hurt?" A woman in a white coat was leaning over her. Issie nodded yes.

"Isadora, my name is Doctor Stone," the woman said. "I don't think your ribs are broken. I suspect it's just bruising. We'll be sending you down to x-ray shortly to check. But first I need to ask you a few questions, just to check that you're OK. You had a bad fall and you may be suffering from concussion." The doctor held up her hand. "How many fingers am I holding up?"

"Three," said Issie. She was surprised at how wobbly her voice was. "And what day is it?" Doctor Stone asked as she checked Issie's eyes with a little torch light. "Umm… Saturday?"

"Excellent." The doctor was making notes on her

43

chart now as she talked. "How old are you, Isadora?"

"Twelve," Issie had to think for a moment, "but I'll be thirteen soon."

Doctor Stone gave her young patient a concerned look. "Now, I want you to think carefully, Isadora. I want you to try to remember the last thing that happened to you. Do you know why you're here?"

Issie shut her eyes and tried to think. What had happened to her? She remembered the sound of a truck horn, and the way Mystic had reared up, as if to protect her from the huge steel vehicle that was bearing down on them. Then nothing, nothing but the tarmac rushing up to meet her, that inhuman scream and then the blackness.

"Where is Mystic?" Issie felt a wave of panic sweep over her. "Mum, is Mystic OK?"

Her chest ached sharply as she tried to sit up. "Isadora, please try and stay still until we can get those ribs x-rayed," Doctor Stone said firmly. She turned to Mrs Brown. "I don't think we'll need to keep her in overnight. If the x-ray comes out OK, she can be discharged this evening."

"But what about my horse?" Issie was cold with

horror as she spoke. Her mum kept ignoring her questions about Mystic. Something was wrong. Mrs Brown had turned her head away from her now. At first she couldn't speak. Finally, she faced her daughter and took her hand. Her words came softly but in Issie's ears they were like crashes of thunder.

"Isadora, there was nothing anyone could have done. The truck…" Her mother's voice trailed off for a moment. "…Isadora, Mystic is dead."

"No!" Issie felt hot tears running down her cheeks. She was shaking, gasping once more for breath. "No!"

"I'm sorry, honey." Her mother was still clutching her hand, and she was crying too. "Stella saw it all from the side of the road. You and Mystic saved the other horses, you know. If you hadn't gone after them and herded them back up the driveway, who knows what would have happened. But then the truck came…" Mrs Brown stroked away her daughter's tears. "You know, I think Mystic was trying to save you too. When he reared up and threw you clear of the truck, it saved your life. So it wasn't just the other horses he saved. He saved you."

"Isadora," the doctor interrupted, "I'm just going to

give you a sedative. It'll take away the pain and let you relax for a while."

Issie nodded vacantly. She didn't really hear what the doctor was saying, and she could no longer feel the pain in her ribs. Instead, it was her heart that ached. An ache that consumed her entire soul. Mystic was dead.

Issie barely even noticed the sting of the injection that Doctor Stone gave her, but she began to feel its effects almost immediately. She felt woozy, and her muscles went limp. Through half-closed eyes she could see her mother sitting beside the bed holding her hand, then she drifted off, back into darkness, back into black sleep.

Her mother was still sitting by the bed two hours later when she opened her eyes again.

"How are you feeling, honey?" Mrs Brown ran her hand softly over her daughter's forehead, smoothing back her dark hair. Issie's complexion, usually a light olive colour just like her mum's, was so drained and pale she was almost the same colour as the hospital sheets.

"I've telephoned your dad," Mrs Brown told her, still stroking her hair as she spoke. "He said he would fly up to see you, but I told him it would be OK, that you were likely to be going home tonight. Still, he was very worried about you."

"Sure he was," Issie said. Since her mum and dad divorced three years ago it seemed like she hardly even existed. Her father had remarried and had a whole new family in another city now and it had been months since she saw him last. What made her mum think that just because she'd been in an accident he would come running?

"Anyway, he sent you these." Mrs Brown lifted up a pot of yellow chrysanthemums and plonked them down on the table by Issie's bed.

"Issie," Mrs Brown took her daughter's hand, "when you're ready to talk about what happened to Mystic…"

"Mum, I don't want to. Not yet…" Issie was trying hard not to start crying all over again. She looked down at the bed clothes, refusing to meet her mother's eyes. "Can't I… can't we just go home now? I just want it all to be over."

"I'm sorry, I hope I'm not interrupting?" Doctor Stone entered the room. "Only we really need to get Isadora down to x-ray now."

Mrs Brown sighed. "Of course. We can talk later when we get home."

Two hours later, the x-rays had been taken and Doctor Stone's diagnosis was confirmed: no broken bones, just some bruising, slight concussion and a large swollen lump at the front of her head where the peak of the helmet had connected with the road.

Issie was getting dressed to go home when she heard a knock. "Can we come in?" Stella and Kate stuck their heads around the corner of the door to Issie's room. Issie gave them a weak smile and the two girls entered the room and sat down beside her bed. Kate looked pale with shock and Stella's freckled face was flushed hot pink from crying.

"How are Toby and Coco?" Issie wanted to know.

"Well, Toby has gone lame. But it's nothing serious. The vet thinks it's a stone bruise from galloping on the gravel but he should be OK in a week or so." Kate managed a grin.

"And Coco is just fine. She threw a shoe, but she wasn't hurt," Stella continued. "In fact, that run is probably the most exercise she's had in years!"

"If you and Mystic hadn't caught up with them..." Stella sighed. "Well, it was just the bravest thing I've ever seen." She looked down at her shoes for a moment and then back at Issie. "I mean, I know there's nothing I can do to bring Mystic back, but Kate and I were thinking... if you wanted to, you could ride Coco and Toby any time you like. We could even work out a roster. You could have Coco on Mondays and Tuesdays and ride Toby on Wednesdays..." She paused as Issie began to cry.

"Oh, Issie, I know it's not the same as having your own horse but..."

Issie shook her head. "It's not that. Don't you see? I don't want another horse. Not after what happened to Mystic. I couldn't... I'm never going to ride again."

That night, home from the hospital, Issie found it hard to sleep. When she did finally close her eyes, the vision of the grey ghost horse returned. There was the pounding of hooves, and then once again the horse appeared and reared to a halt just out of Issie's reach.

This time she could see his face more clearly. The smouldering charcoal eyes, the velvety nostrils flared with tension. It was Mystic. She was sure of that now. She held out her hand and the horse whinnied gently, lowering his head so that the tip of his nose traced just above the ground as he stepped towards her. Issie knew that the lowered head was part of "horse language". It was Mystic's way of saying, "I know you. I trust you. You're part of my herd."

She spoke softly to him now, "Easy, Mystic, easy, boy. It's me, boy…" Her hand reached out and Issie felt a shock of wonder as her fingers touched the silver tussock of his mane. The sensation of the coarse, ropey hair against her skin was totally real. This horse was no ghost! It was as alive as she was. Why, if she only reached out her other hand and grabbed on to his mane, she was sure she could swing herself up on to Mystic's back and ride him. Ride him just as she had done before the accident had ruined everything. She reached out a hand, but Mystic stepped backwards and pawed fitfully at the ground with his left front hoof. Then he turned again and galloped off, the silver stream of his tail disappearing into the blackness.

"I know it sounds stupid," Issie told her mum at breakfast the next day, "but it was as if he was real. I mean, I know it must have been a dream, but it didn't feel like a dream. It was like Mystic was really there, right in front of me. I even touched him!"

"Oh, sweetheart," Mrs Brown took her daughter's small, tanned hand in her own, "you had a bad fall and you've been through a terrible experience. It's only natural that you'll be pretty shaken up for a while. But you have to face up to what has happened. I know it hurts and you miss Mystic. But you're lucky to be alive."

Mrs Brown smiled gently as she reached over and poured out a cup of hot chocolate for Issie and a fresh cup of tea for herself. "Your father and I have discussed the best thing to do about this…" Mrs Brown looked down at her cup of tea. She paused, unable to get the words out. "Isadora, I know how much you love horses. And I know what happened wasn't your fault. You were very brave to do what you did. But, well, your father agreed with me on this…" Mrs Brown finally looked her daughter in the face.

"Issie, I can't let you have another horse. It was so terrifying when you were in that hospital bed and I didn't know whether you would even wake up. I couldn't go through that again. I am your mother and… oh, Issie, you have to understand I can't risk something else happening to you. I know that you want to get another horse and—"

"No, Mum, you don't understand!" Issie felt hot tears well in her eyes. How could her mum even think she would want a new horse? All she wanted was Mystic. She wanted her horse to come back to her. How could she explain to her mother that Mystic was more than just some pony to her? That he had been her closest friend, the one soul that she could confide all her secrets to, because he would never betray her. A kindred spirit who she could trust totally and love absolutely. The most important thing in her life. The truth was, she couldn't explain it to her mother, or to anyone.

Issie took a deep breath and kept her eyes on the bowl of cereal in front of her. "I don't care anyway." Issie could feel the tears running down her cheeks; she wanted to stop crying but she couldn't. She wiped her cheeks roughly with her sleeve and faced her mother. "I said that I was never going to ride again, and I meant it."

CHAPTER 5

"You know Lisa Jones?" Stella was chattering away and looking absent-mindedly for a book in her school bag as they walked into Mrs Carter's classroom for fourth period maths. "Well," Stella continued, "her family moved to the Hawkes Bay and she had to go to this new school. I think it's called Iona College. Anyway, it's very posh and they get to ride horses at school. Can you believe it? Horse riding is actually a school subject! So instead of doing a stinky old maths class, you could go riding instead. Lisa grazes her horse there and she's allowed to go and check on him at lunchtimes, and they even have proper stables with loose boxes to keep them in. I mean, that would be so cool, wouldn't it?"

Issie just nodded, and headed for the back of the classroom, taking her usual seat at the far corner of the room. She was sick and tired of hearing stories about horses and how much fun they were. It seemed like ever since she told Stella and Kate that she wasn't going to ride any more, the pair of them had been trying to come up with new ways to get her interested in riding again. OK, she knew her friends were just trying to help, but she wished they would leave her alone.

Stella leaned over from her desk and whispered to Issie, "Hey, Kate and I were thinking that after school, if you're not busy—"

Issie groaned and cut her off in mid-sentence, "Stella, I don't want to go riding. Not this afternoon. Not ever!"

"OK, OK, get over yourself," Stella sneered back. "What I was going to say is that me and Kate, well, you know how Kallista Field has a pierced belly button? Well, they do piercings at Lacey's chemist shop and we were thinking of getting them done too."

Of course Issie knew all about Kallista Field. There were always stories about the young dressage rider in

PONY Magazine. Issie even had pictures of Kallista up on the wall in her bedroom. Kallista wasn't just a good rider, she was also tall and beautiful with long blonde hair. And she had a pierced belly button. Issie had seen it in photos and she had to admit, it did look pretty cool.

Stella kept on talking, "Kate says she still can't decide whether to get one or not. But we were talking to Louisa Bull – she's really cool, she's a fourth former but I know her because she's in my house – anyway, she has one and it looks so fab and she says it didn't hurt much at all." She poked Issie in the tummy and grinned. "You would look so good with one, Issie. So what do you say? Are you in?"

Issie winced and pulled up her jersey to look at her naked belly button. It was an innie, not an outie, a small, delicate whirl in the middle of her olive-skinned tummy. She imagined the piercing gun clamped over it, driving a steel ring through her skin.

"I don't know…" Issie muttered. "Mum wouldn't be too keen on it…"

"It's OK," Stella insisted. "I asked Penny and she said she would take us, so you don't need to ask your mum."

Penny was Stella's older sister. She was much older than Stella and was in her first year at university. The two sisters both had the same curly red hair and freckles – and the same naughty streak too. If anything, Penny was even wilder than her little sister. And Stella always wanted to do what Penny did. Penny already had her belly button pierced – and her tongue!

"Come on," Stella was whining. "Your mum won't even notice. We'll all do it together. It'll be fun."

Issie took her hand off her stomach and tucked the thin cotton of her school shirt back into her skirt, smoothing it down flat. She had always wanted to get a piercing. Even plain pierced ears weren't allowed at Chevalier Point High. But a belly button? Who would ever notice it underneath your school uniform?

OK, so her mum would kill her if she found out. But who cared? Besides, why shouldn't she have some fun and do something exciting for once? She was so tired of feeling this way, tired of being numb and depressed. Maybe Stella was right. It would look pretty cool to have a belly-button ring like Kallista.

"What sort of rings are there?" Issie sighed.

Stella let out a squeal of delight. "Yay! I knew you'd

say yes! This is going to be great! There's plain silver ones, or you can get ones with a stone in them," Stella continued. "I was thinking of getting maybe a purple stone like an amethyst but you can get whatever you want." She looked at Issie's screwed-up face. "I swear. Honestly. It doesn't hurt!"

A couple of hours later, Issie wished she had never taken Stella's word for it. There she was, lying flat on her back on the thin white chemist shop bunk bed, looking down at her skin stretched taut under the clamp of the piercing gun. There was a felt-tip dot on her belly button where the ring would pierce the skin, and a woman with too much make-up on was busily daubing her tummy with antiseptic solution.

"Now take a deep breath and breathe out as the needle goes through," the woman instructed. Issie looked away from the gun, trying not to think about it as she sucked in a deep lung full of air. As she breathed out she felt a sudden rush of pain.

"There. You're done." The woman smiled. Issie

looked down at her newly decorated navel. It was red and tingling. "You'll have to keep it very clean for the first couple of weeks while it heals, and whatever you do, don't take the ring out," the woman instructed, passing Issie some antiseptic to take home with her. "And try not to wear clothes that rub on it and irritate the site."

"I can't believe you two went through with it!" Kate shrieked as the three girls came out of the chemist into the bright sunlight to meet her.

"What? I can't believe you chickened out on us!" Stella teased her back.

"I didn't!" Kate insisted. "I never said I would get one. I only said I was thinking about it." She leaned down and peered closer at Issie's red, swollen belly button and pulled a face. "Eugh! Does it hurt?"

Issie looked pleased with Kate's reaction. "Not really," she lied. In fact, she could feel her tummy button all hot and throbbing where the ring had gone through.

"You know," Stella began, "when Louisa Bull had hers done she told me that it went all infected and she woke up one morning and, oh, this is really going to

gross you out, her mum had to take her to hospital
because—"

"Stella! I thought you told me that Louisa's belly
button looked really cool?" Issie yelped. "What
happened?"

"Nothing happened!" Penny snapped. "Stella! She
didn't go to hospital, she just went to the doctor and he
gave her some ointment to put on it and sent her home
again. Stop exaggerating and making up horrible stories."

Penny pulled up her own t-shirt to show them her
belly button. It had a silver ring with a green glass leaf
dangling down from it. "Look, I've had my piercing for
two years now and it's fine," she reassured Issie.

"I was just joking!" Stella insisted, grinning
mischievously. "Hey, Issie, let's go back to your house
and try on clothes. I need to find a tank top that will
show off my tummy button."

The Browns had lived in the same house ever since Issie
was little. It was a two-storey wooden home, surrounded
by rambling, overgrown gardens. From Issie's bedroom

upstairs she had a view down over the big back lawn to the grove of trees at the end of the garden.

The view inside Issie's bedroom, however, was one big mess. The girls had spent the past hour trying on everything in Issie's wardrobe and the place looked like a stall at a jumble sale. There were pairs of jeans and shoes thrown all over the floor, and the bed was stacked so high with piles of clothes that you could barely see Stella and Kate, who were flopped down in the middle of it all on top of the duvet.

Issie stepped out of the wardrobe. She had stripped off the light-green pleated skirt and white shirt of her school uniform and was wearing a purple floral crop top and dark blue camouflage pants. She stood in front of the mirror to admire her new look. For once, her skinny boyish figure was working to her advantage. The pants hung down so low on her hips they exposed her stomach, showing off the freshly pierced navel.

Issie stared at her tummy button. It was still swollen and red, and even though she would never admit it, she was a little worried about what she had done. Stella's story had scared her. What if the piercing really was turning septic? The skin around the ring did actually look all red and raw and it was hurting a lot more than she had thought it would.

Issie shrugged off her fears. At least Stella had been right about one thing, she thought, that silver ring did look pretty cool. It suited her, the slim metal circle resting perfectly against her tanned belly.

Issie was wiggling the ring and gazing at her reflection when she suddenly noticed the other two girls staring at her. Feeling embarrassed to suddenly be the centre of attention, she struck a ridiculous supermodel catwalk pose, pouting and throwing her head back, one hand on her hip, the other raised to blow a kiss to an imaginary camera.

The two girls fell about on the bed laughing. Stella was snorting so hard she was almost choking and Issie collapsed on to the duvet next to her in a fit of giggles.

As she lay there panting with laughter she realised this was the first time since the accident that she had been able to forget about Mystic and have some fun.

"Wait, wait!" Stella leapt up and grabbed a pair of sunglasses off the dressing table. She put them on, along with a pair of foolishly high heels that Issie had borrowed out of her mum's room, and began strutting up and down the bedroom. "Who am I?" she asked giggling. "I'll give you a clue," she added, clearing her throat and talking in a mock posh voice. "I want a new pony! I want to go snowboarding! I'm a spoilt brat!"

"Oh, don't..." Issie tried to stop laughing so that she could get the words out. "...we shouldn't make fun of Natasha. It's mean."

"That's easy for you to say!" Stella snapped. "You haven't had to put up with her at pony-club rallies for the past month. Honestly, she is such a snob she won't even speak to Kate and me! At lunchtimes she ties her horse up at the other end of the paddock and refuses to even come near us."

Stella looked distracted for a moment, then she bent over and examined her stomach. "I hope this ring doesn't get caught on my jodhpurs when I'm riding." She frowned.

Then she noticed Issie throwing her a sulky look.

"Oops. Sorry, Issie. I keep forgetting that you don't want to talk about horses." Stella smiled. "I guess I just can't believe it, really. I know you feel awful about what happened to Mystic. But it was an accident. And, well, I don't mean to be harsh, but Mystic was really old. So at least he didn't have much longer to live anyway."

Issie couldn't believe what she was hearing. She was used to her friend's lack of tact. Stella had a habit of saying the wrong thing at the wrong time. But this was a bit much even from her. How would she feel if it was Coco that had died? Issie was trying so hard to hold back the tears that she felt too choked up to say anything. She wanted to say that Mystic was special. That he was her horse and that he may have been old but he had a young spirit that refused to give up. She wanted to tell her two friends how she still saw him every night. A silver ghost horse, too real to be just a dream. So real he felt like flesh and blood. Somehow Mystic was still there with her. She just wished she knew why.

The phone in the hallway rang. "I'll get it," Issie squawked, keen to escape this dreadful conversation, and the horrible feeling of tears welling up yet again in her eyes. She ran down the corridor, sliding on the hall rug as she made a grab for the receiver. It was Tom Avery's voice on the other end of the line.

"I've been trying to get in touch with you since this morning." Avery sounded serious. "Listen, Issie, something has come up. Can you meet me down at the horse paddock tomorrow morning at around eight?" He paused. "And bring the key to the tack room with you."

When Issie asked him why, Avery became even more mysterious. "I need you to help me with something, that's all," he said, hanging up before she had a chance to ask any more questions.

Before Issie went to bed that night she set her alarm clock and laid out her favourite old faded blue jeans and a pair of boots to wear the next morning. She hadn't spoken to Avery at all since the accident. And now this. Why was he being so mysterious? And what did he need her help for?

She sat down on the bed and pulled up her pyjama top to have one last look at her newly pierced belly button before she went to sleep. "Oh, well," she muttered to herself, wiggling the little silver ring with her index finger, "nothing could surprise me now."

But she was wrong.

CHAPTER 6

The pony-club paddocks were deserted when Issie arrived, except for the horses dotted about the field, grazing in the morning sun. Avery was nowhere to be seen, so Issie climbed over the fence and unlocked the tack room.

Standing in the tack room, she felt a rush of emotion as she looked at the hook and saddle horse where she had kept Mystic's things. His leather halter and canvas paddock cover were still hanging there, but the saddle horse was bare. When Mystic had gone under the truck, her beloved Stübben saddle had been destroyed too. Not that it mattered, Issie reminded herself. She didn't need a saddle because she wasn't going to ride ever again.

As a further reminder of her vow, up there on the wall next to the empty saddle rack was a photograph. It was her and Mystic; taken the day that she had first brought the dapple-grey here to his new home. It must have been the end of winter, because Mystic's coat was thick and fluffy with winter growth. His mane was long and flowing; it obviously hadn't been pulled in months. His eyes were dark and steady, staring straight at the camera. And there she was with him, the wind whipping her long dark hair across her face so that her eyes were barely visible. She had one hand on Mystic's wither and the other holding his lead rope. They made the perfect team.

"There you are!" Avery's voice behind her made her jump. "Come on out for a moment, I've got something to show you. Oh, and bring that halter. You're going to need it."

Issie emerged into the sunlight to see Avery's horse truck parked outside the gate. He climbed back into the cab again and gestured for her to swing the gate open to let him drive through.

As Issie closed the gate behind him, she watched Avery ease the vehicle alongside the loading ramp. When he pulled the truck to a stop, she could hear the uncertain shift of hooves against the matting floor. There was a horse in there! Of course! Why else would Avery tell her to bring a halter with her. But which horse? She looked out across the paddock to see Toby and Coco both grazing peacefully at the far end of the field. It wasn't them on the truck then, but... The stamp of hooves became more restless and the high-pitched nicker of a horse could clearly be heard from inside the truck.

Avery leapt down from the driver's seat and strode over to her. "Good, good," he said. "All set then? Let's go!" He began to unbolt the doors. "Issie you go in and put her halter on. We'll put her in the pen by the tack room for the time being."

"What? What are you talking about?" Issie didn't understand.

"Oh, right. I'm sorry." Avery smiled. "It's a horse, Issie. And I want you to have her." He held up his hand to stop her cries of protest. "Look, I didn't mean to spring it on you like this. I understand how much it hurt you to lose Mystic. And maybe it is a little soon to expect you to get back into the saddle again. But I had no choice. You know about my work with the International League for the Protection of Horses, don't you?"

Issie nodded.

"It's my job to investigate reports of horses that are being mistreated or badly looked after by their owners. And if those horses are being neglected, then it's also my job to take them away and find new homes for them. People can be unbelievably cruel," Avery continued, shaking his head, unable to disguise the disgust in his voice. "Can you even imagine, Issie? No grass to eat, just dirt to live on. A paddock no bigger than a cattle pen. When the horse protection league found this mare, she was... well, you'll see for yourself in just a moment what sort of a state she is in.

"Issie, I know it's not fair to ask this from you. This mare is in a delicate condition. She's very sick, one of the worst cases I've ever seen." Avery's face was grim. "She needs round the clock care from someone who really understands horses if she's going to pull through. Even then she may not survive... And I know you're still hurting from losing Mystic. But when I saw her I knew that you were the one to take care of her. To love her. Because she'll need someone like you, someone who truly loves horses, who has a way with them, to bring her back to life."

A faint, nervous whinny came from behind the door. "Now, come on," Avery looked at her intently, "what do you say?"

Issie knew that there was nothing she could say. She just nodded to Tom, and stepped to the side so that he could open the door and let her in.

In her worst nightmares, Issie had never seen anything like the sight that was now before her. In the centre stall of the truck stood a chestnut mare. At least Issie supposed she was a chestnut. The pony's coat was so covered in mud, and worn thin in great patches, that you could hardly tell what colour she was at all. From beneath the caked mud, her ribs stuck out sharply through her skin. Her rump, rather than being rounded and firm, was hollowed out where the muscles should have been. And the pony's legs were covered in mud sores. But it was the pony's expression which upset Issie most of all. The little mare wouldn't even raise her head to look at Issie, and when she finally did look her way, her eyes showed pure terror. As Issie got closer the mare let out a long, low snort of fear. But she didn't attempt to back away. It was as if her spirit was so broken she didn't care what happened to her any more.

"Easy now, girl," Issie cooed as she put the halter on. The chestnut mare flinched away from her hands as Issie fastened the halter buckle, but she was too weak to put up much of a fight. "Easy now," she murmured again, stroking the length of the mare's slender neck. Underneath the dry mud on her legs Issie could make out four white socks, and down the mare's dainty face ran a white blaze.

"What's her name?" Issie asked Avery as she tried to cluck the mare into moving forward and out of the truck stall.

"Doesn't have one, I'm afraid," Avery said. "At least, we don't think she has a name. We never did track down the people who did this to her. We're trying to trace the owners so that animal cruelty charges can be laid against them, but it's not easy. So… no owners and no name."

"I think we should call you Blaze," Issie whispered to the mare, "after that pretty white blaze that's running down the middle of your face."

"Hey, hey, wait a minute," Avery smirked, "you can't just go ahead and name this horse." He paused. "Unless, that is, unless you're willing to keep her?"

"Oh, Tom," Issie sighed, "of course I'll keep her. Like you said, I don't have a choice, do I?"

"You understand the rules of the ILPH, don't you?" Avery asked. "If a horse comes into our care we can appoint a guardian for that horse. But that's all you will ever be to Blaze – her guardian. You don't own her, so she's not yours to sell. If you ever change your mind about her or can't look after her you must return her to the League and they'll find a new home for her."

Issie nodded, then turned to the chestnut mare. "Do you hear that, girl? I'm your new guardian. And I'm going to take real good care of you. Come on now, come out and see your new home."

Issie led Blaze down the truck ramp and her heart nearly broke as she watched the little mare, all wobbly on her feet, gingerly putting one hoof in front of another.

She tied the chestnut to a fence rail. It had been hard to really examine her in the truck. Now, in the bright sunlight, she stood back and took a long hard look. She was definitely a pony, not a horse; Issie guessed she stood somewhere between fourteen and fourteen-two hands high. And there was no doubt that she was well bred. Even in such pitiful condition the mare showed signs of her Arab bloodlines. The classic dished nose and finely pricked ears gave her away. As did her legs, slender and delicate like a ballet dancer's.

In the sunlight the mare's coat was darker than Issie had first thought, a deep liver chestnut. Her mane and tail were a light shade of honey, almost flaxen blonde. Looking down at her legs, Issie could see that she did indeed have four white socks. In fact, the two hind socks were almost stockings – running all the way right up to her hocks, while the white blaze which began as a large star on her forehead continued in a slender streak all the way down her face to her velvety nostrils where it finally tapered away.

"She's beautiful, Tom," Issie breathed softly.

"We'll have to keep her in the pen for a couple of days or so, I'm afraid," Avery said briskly. "She's too weak to be let loose to graze with the other horses at this stage. If they took to her she'd never survive the fight. I'll try and sort out the grazing so she can have a paddock to herself in a day or two and in the meantime you'll have to start bulking her up on hard feed and hay."

Avery looked concerned. "We're talking about more than a physical problem with this mare though, Issie. It's her mind that needs the most care. She's been through a lot. Whoever owned her must have abused her terribly. She doesn't know how to trust people any more. And it's going to take a lot of work and patience to win back that trust.

"Might as well get to work on the physical stuff straight away though, eh?" Avery pointed to Issie's grooming kit and gave her a knowing grin. "I'll bet there's a decent coat under all that mud, so get to it! I've got to dash. You need to spend some time, to know her better. And," Avery added, "of course you'll need to talk to your mum about things too – but I'm sure she'll be fine about it, won't she?"

Issie was about to respond to this and point out that, actually, her mum wouldn't be fine about it at all. But Avery wasn't listening.

"Excellent then! Right. I'm off. I'll check up on you both next week."

And with that, Avery backed the truck out of the gate and left Issie standing there open-mouthed.

Issie stood there for a moment longer, watching the truck as it became smaller in the distance. Then she turned back to the horse and reached for her bucket of grooming brushes. As she lifted the dandy brush towards Blaze to scuff off the dried mud, the pony let out a terrified snort and pulled back hard against the rope, her eyes wild with fear.

"Easy, girl, I'm not going to hurt you," Issie murmured. She put the brush down and reached her hand up to stroke Blaze's neck and calm her down. But the mare wasn't having any of it. She backed up, straining against the rope, her ears flat back against her head.

Issie felt terrible. She knew Blaze wasn't acting up on purpose. It was simply that the poor horse had been so badly abused in the past she was scared of being touched. Issie realised it was only natural that Blaze would be scared of her too, but it still hurt.

Once more she moved slowly towards the horse, and Blaze backed even further away, letting out a low, long snort of terror.

"Blaze! How can I brush you if you won't even let me get near you?" Issie pleaded, close to despair. Then she had an idea. In the tack room there were three large bins of hard feed for the horses, the first two filled with oats and chaff and the third with pony pellets. Issie grabbed a handful of these and walked back over to Blaze.

This time the nervous chestnut didn't back away. She sniffed the air, then stretched out her long, elegant neck as far as she could without actually stepping forward. Food. She could smell it all right. But was she brave enough to take it? Still not moving a single hoof, the mare craned her neck even further, then used her rubbery lips to stretch out and snuffle up the pellets out of Issie's hand.

"Good girl, Blaze," Issie murmured, reaching her

hand out once more to stroke the horse. Blaze let Issie's fingertips graze against her mud-coated neck before she backed up once again, heaving with fear.

"Easy, girl, it's OK," Issie said, backing away herself, admitting defeat. She went back to the tack room a second time, but when she emerged again she wasn't carrying a handful of pellets, but a slice of hay. Stuffing the hay into the hay net in the far corner of the pen, she managed to get close enough to Blaze to unclasp the lead rope from her halter so that she was free to go and feed.

"I think we've done enough for one day, hey, girl?" Issie spoke gently to the mare. But inside she wasn't feeling so great about her first meeting with her new horse. How was she expected to feel when Blaze wouldn't even let her pat her?

She stood and watched as the mare nervously ate her hay. One thing was certain: this wasn't going to be easy.

CHAPTER 7

"Issie! Issie! I've got to talk to you..." Stella was panting from the effort of trying to catch up with her friend as she entered the school hall. It was Tuesday, assembly day, and they were late as always.

"Quick," Stella grabbed Issie by her school jersey as she caught her up, "let's sit up the back so we can talk."

She pushed through the herds of Chevalier Point High students trying to find seats and made a beeline for the back benches, dragging Issie along behind her. "Here!" Stella squeaked, claiming two spaces on a bench at the far end of the hall by throwing herself down and using her bag to mark a place next to her for Issie.

"So," she grinned as Issie sat down, "I know you don't want to talk about horses any more, but this isn't just about horses. It's like a mystery or something…" She paused for dramatic effect, lowering her voice to a whisper. "There's this new pony grazing at the pony-club paddocks and no one knows who it belongs to!"

Issie tried to speak, but before she could open her mouth Stella was rambling on again. "You should see this horse, Issie, she's beautiful. Part Arab I think, well, she looks like an Arab anyway. She's sort of a dark chestnut colour with a pale mane and tail, and white socks, totally gorgeous. She's really skinny and stuff but apart from that she's, like, the most amazing horse you've ever seen." Stella paused for just a minute to take a breath and then started raving on again.

"I've asked everyone at the pony club and no one seems to know who owns her. Kate thinks maybe she belongs to Natasha—"

"No she doesn't!" Issie snapped, fed up with Stella's chatter. "She belongs to me. She's mine."

"What?" Stella squealed. Instead of shutting her up it seemed that this news had her more excited than ever before.

"Why didn't you tell me? Issie! Where did she come from? How could you possibly afford her? Did your mum cave in and buy her for you after all? What's her name?"

"Her name is Blaze," Issie muttered under her breath. She could see Mrs Savage, the fourth form dean, glaring at her now. If they kept on talking during assembly then she and Stella were bound to get detention. "And Mum doesn't even know about her. I can't tell you any more now. It's too complicated. I'll explain after assembly – at lunch break."

At lunchtime, Issie was on her way to the tuck shop to get a fruit pie when she was almost tackled from behind. "Gotcha!" Stella giggled, her arms around Issie's waist. "Now, come on. Tell me what's going on. I'm not letting go until you do."

And so Issie told Stella the whole story – how Avery had found Blaze in a terrible state and brought her to Issie, who had agreed to take on the chestnut mare and nurse her back to health.

"And the worst thing is, she just doesn't trust people," Issie said. "Avery said I can ride her soon because she's putting on weight, but I don't want to rush things... It took me a week before she would let me brush the mud off her! She's been so scared, Stella!"

"Oh, Issie, how dreadful!" Stella's eyes brimmed with tears. "Poor Blaze. She must have been so badly mistreated by her old owners. That's why she's being so difficult. I'm sure you'll make friends with her if you just keep trying. You can't give up on her. She needs you."

Stella was buzzing with excitement. "I can't believe you've been keeping Blaze to yourself all this time too! We've got to go and find Kate and tell her all about it. She's been dying to discover who owned the mystery horse. We'll both meet you at the paddock after school."

When Stella and Kate arrived later that afternoon Issie had already caught Blaze and was tying her to the fence, preparing to groom her.

"She's beautiful!" Stella was breathless with admiration. It was the first time the girls had seen Blaze up close and even cool Kate was impressed.

"She's got wonderful conformation," she admitted as she ran her eye over the mare's elegant arched neck, "and what a gorgeous face with that fantastic white blaze! Blaze is the perfect name for her."

"You're right, Issie, she must be part Arab," Stella agreed. "Look at her lovely dished nose. I wonder if she has breeder's papers?"

"I don't know," Issie said. "We don't even know who her old owners were, so there's no way of finding out what her bloodlines are."

"Who could be so cruel, treating a horse like that?" Kate shook her head. "Does Avery have any leads to find the old owners?"

"Not yet," Issie said, "but he's reported it to the police so they might come up with something. Anyway," Issie turned to Blaze, "you're safe with me now, girl; I'm going to take good care of you."

"Well," Stella said, "I think it's time for Blaze to meet the boys." She turned to Kate. "Come on, let's go catch Toby and Coco and do some proper introductions."

The two girls grabbed their halters out of the tack room and set out across the paddock, leaving Issie alone again with Blaze.

"Good girl," Issie cooed, reaching out to stroke the mare on her neck. But Blaze made a low snorting sound and quickly backed away. Issie knew better by now than to be disappointed by the mare's behaviour. It was nothing personal; she understood that. Blaze's last owners were cruel to her, so why should she trust anyone?

Issie had been taking it slowly with the mare, trying to gain her trust. Now, as she moved towards Blaze, she didn't pick up a brush straight away. Instead, she reached out an open hand and stroked her wither. The chestnut leapt away at first, but as Issie tried again and again she finally stood still, letting the girl run her hands gently across her glossy neck, back over the wither and down her front legs, feeling tendon and fetlock, then back up again and along her rump and hindquarters, softly talking to the mare as she went.

All the time, Issie kept her gaze low and never looked Blaze in the eye. The stroking was something she had learnt in Avery's natural horsemanship classes.

Avery had also told her to keep her eyes down – horses are prey animals, and being met by the stare of a human predator was liable to spook them.

By the time Issie lifted up the dandy brush, she was thrilled to see that Blaze was almost relaxed under her hands. In fact, once Issie had scuffed the caked mud off her hocks and began to work on her with the body brush, the mare even seemed to enjoy the feeling of the soft bristles against her skin. When Issie took a thick, damp sponge and ran it down the white stripe in the middle of her forehead, Blaze gave a grunt of pleasure and lowered her head against Issie, using the girl as her scratching post, rubbing up and down against her.

"Hey," Issie giggled. "Cut it out!" But inside she was pleased to see Blaze acting so friendly with her. She was starting to trust her.

"Hey, Issie," Stella said as she led Coco up, tying her to the fence next to Blaze, "do you know those men?"

"What men?"

"Over there," Stella said, "in that white van. There are two of them. They've been sitting there watching us ever since we arrived. I thought they must have a flat tyre or something, but they haven't got out of the van to fix it. They're just sitting there staring at us. It's kinda creepy."

Issie put down her hoof-pick and turned around to take a look. Sure enough, there was a white van parked out on the kerb of the road. Two men sat silently in the front seat.

"What are you looking at?" Kate led Toby over to join them.

"That van over there," Stella said, pointing towards where the two men were parked.

Suddenly there was the sound of an engine revving up, and the white van did a quick u-turn back up the street and was gone.

"Well, they sure left in a hurry!" Kate was puzzled. "Who were they anyway?"

"Never mind," Stella chirped, "let's ride." She looked over at Issie who was still combing out Blaze's mane. "C'mon Issie. Are you going to tack her up or not?"

"I… I don't think she's ready to be ridden yet," Issie said. Although she knew that the *truth* was she wasn't ready yet. She was still nervous about getting up on the chestnut mare for the first time, and she certainly didn't want to do it with Stella and Kate watching her.

"Besides," Issie added, "Mum doesn't know I'm here and I'd better get home before she starts to worry."

"Issie, why haven't you just told her?" Kate was shocked.

"I will, I will. I'm just waiting for the right moment," Issie said.

The problem with this secret, though, was that it never seemed like the right time to share it. Every afternoon as she cycled home from the horse paddock Issie imagined herself telling her mother all about Blaze. But somehow, by the time she arrived home, her resolve to share her secret had faded. *Not just yet*, she thought. *Soon. When I've nursed Blaze back to health and we've made friends. Then Mum will have to let me keep her.*

And Blaze was getting healthy fast. In the short time that she had been at the River Paddock, the slender chestnut had put on condition at such a pace that her ribs no longer showed and her coat had lost its stark quality and was beginning to shine a deep burnished gold.

But it was the change in Blaze's mood that mattered most. When Issie arrived at the River Paddock late one afternoon after school she found the mare with her head over the fence of the pen looking almost pleased to see her.

It had been three weeks now since the chestnut mare had been gifted into Issie's care. Now when Issie tethered her to the fence paling, the mare didn't flinch or jump under her touch. Her confidence in Issie had grown. She had begun to trust her.

"What do you think, girl? Shall I take you for a ride?" Issie buried her face in Blaze's thick flaxen mane. She never thought she would want to get back on a horse after what happened to Mystic. But when she looked at Blaze now she suddenly felt this deep, strong urge. She wanted to ride again.

Then she suddenly realised – what was she going to ride her with? Mystic's saddle had been crushed in the accident. And since her mother still didn't even know that Blaze existed, she could hardly ask her to buy her a new one! "Looks like we're going bareback for now, girl." Issie smiled at Blaze.

She could use Mystic's old bridle. It had a simple Eggbutt snaffle bit; just right for Blaze. But before the chestnut mare could wear it, it would need some adjustments. Her pretty Arab face was much smaller, more dished than Mystic's solid features. Issie moved the cheek straps up a couple of holes and adjusted the cavesson noseband to match. Then she eased the bridle over Blaze's head to check the fit. Perfect.

Issie grabbed her old spare helmet out of the tack room and, leading Blaze by the reins, she guided her out of the pen and positioned the mare so that she was standing parallel to the fence. Then she climbed up on the railings and threw herself lightly on to her back.

As soon as Issie mounted Blaze the thought struck her: *What if this mare is actually unbroken? What if I'm sitting on a wild horse who has never had a rider on her back before?*

Her fears disappeared as Blaze accepted her weight and the feel of the bit in her mouth.

"Let's go, girl!" Issie clucked the mare on and gave

her a dig with her heels. Blaze snorted and shot forward at a smart high-stepping trot, which almost rocked Issie off her back.

As Blaze trotted briskly on, Issie found herself sliding around. Riding bareback could be slippery. Without stirrups Issie couldn't rise to the trot, and the bouncing made it almost impossible to stay on.

Holding on to a handful of mane, Issie wrapped her legs firmly around the mare and tried not to jiggle like a jelly as she trotted on. Steering was nearly impossible and it was all she could do to point Blaze towards the entrance to the dressage ring.

Too late she realised that the chestnut was going too far to the left. She tried to pull Blaze to a halt, but the sudden tug on the reins made her bolt forward, missing the entrance entirely. Instead of slowing down, Blaze broke into a canter and headed for the gate that led to the far paddock.

"It's OK," Issie told herself, "the gate is shut. She's bound to stop." But Blaze showed no signs of slowing down, in fact her canter increased in speed. Issie found herself completely out of control, her hands tangled in the flaxen mane as she struggled to stay on board.

"My God! She's going to take the gate!" Issie couldn't believe it. The gate between the two main paddocks must have been at least one metre twenty high and Blaze was racing at it in full canter, completely ignoring Issie's frantic tugs on the reins. With her head held high, Blaze was fighting the bit, and Issie didn't have the strength to haul her back.

A few strides out from the gate, Blaze gave a proud toss of her head, freeing herself from the reins, and then leapt. The chestnut mare arched tidily through the air, clearing the gate with room to spare, and Issie lost her grip on the mane and began to slide. As Blaze landed lightly on the other side of the fence Issie landed too – heavily on the ground with a thud.

The long grass helped cushion her fall. Still, she felt a jolt of pain in her shoulder, and it took her a minute to get her breath back.

As she got up and wiped the dirt off her jodhpurs Issie was shaking and tears of anger and frustration welled up in her eyes. She should never have been so cocky, she realised. After all she'd never ridden Blaze before. She had no idea what this horse was capable of. And yet there she went, as bold as brass, climbing on board and trotting off as if she were the world's best rider. Well, she had paid the price for it. She straightened up, giving her limbs a shake to check that everything was in working order, and looked around for Blaze, who already had her head down munching a patch of long grass as if nothing had ever happened.

Why had Avery given her this horse? It was obvious that Blaze was too spirited for her to ride. She had overestimated herself. She should never have given up on her vow.

"Maybe I'm really not meant to ride after all," she sighed, reaching for Blaze's reins. She led the mare back to the pen on foot, not willing to suffer another fall on the way home. Then she unbridled Blaze, gave her some feed and refilled the hay net and cycled home, her head stuck in a cloud of gloomy thoughts.

She should have known better than to take on this horse; she realised that now. Blaze was moody and unpredictable, not at all what she was used to. If only Mystic were still alive. With Mystic, it had all been easy, she had known what to do. The little grey had been so sweet, like her best friend. With Blaze, it was like she couldn't do anything right. In fact, the mare didn't even seem to like her!

Was it too late to change her mind, she wondered, and give the horse back to Avery? Issie knew the answer. Avery would probably take Blaze back but he would be so disappointed in her she wouldn't be able to stand it. No, she had to stick at it. Things would get better with Blaze. They had to.

CHAPTER 8

"Isadora! Wait! What is that sticking out through your shirt?"

It was a quarter to four. Issie had just charged in through the front door to make herself a sandwich and change into her riding gear before heading out to see Blaze. She hadn't counted on running into her mum. Or that her new body piercing would be so visible through the thin white weave of her school shirt.

"Ummm…" Issie wasn't sure what to say. Lying to her mother would probably just make things worse. Best to tell the truth and get it over and done with. "It's a belly-button ring. I got it done a couple of weeks ago," Issie admitted.

"What? What were you thinking? Let me see it!" Mrs Brown made Issie pull up her shirt to show her navel, still red and puffy from where the ring had pierced the skin. "Oh, Issie! Why didn't you talk to me before you had this done? Look at it! It could get infected!" Mrs Brown was furious.

"It's only a belly-button ring, everyone's got them these days," Issie stood her ground.

"You know very well that you don't charge off and do things like that without talking to me first," Mrs Brown countered. "Honestly, Isadora. Since your father left it hasn't been easy looking after you by myself. But at least I always thought I could rely on you to behave like a grown-up. And now you go off and do this! I'm really disappointed in you."

"It just sort of happened," Issie tried to explain. "Stella was having hers done and—"

"Stella! I might have known." Mrs Brown was livid. "And I suppose if Stella was jumping off a bridge you'd be racing off to do that too, would you?" she snapped. "For God's sake, Isadora, I thought you had more common sense. I hope you checked the equipment they used was sterilised? Heaven knows what diseases you could get from this. Where did you get it done?"

"At Lacey's chemist. Penny went with us."

Mrs Brown calmed down a little. "Well, even so, that doesn't automatically make it safe. There's still a chance that you could get an infection or blood poisoning. Have you been putting antiseptic on it?"

Issie nodded quietly.

"Isadora, I just wish you would talk to me before you race off and do these things, OK?" Mrs Brown fretted. "There are some decisions that are too important to make on your own."

Issie took a deep breath. Now was obviously not the time to tell her mother about Blaze. After all, if she thought Issie was irresponsible getting her belly button pierced without her permission then how would she feel if she knew her daughter had gone ahead and agreed to look after a new pony without even asking her?

Mrs Brown gave her daughter a stern look. "You realise I should probably punish you for this, don't you? It looks like you'll be spending your time after school helping me out at the office so I can keep an eye on you."

Issie's blood ran cold. This couldn't be happening. If her mum dragged her in to work with her every afternoon then how on earth was she going to get to the horse paddock to look after Blaze? With just a few weeks of school left before the summer holidays, Issie had been counting the days until she was free to spend more time with her horse. Until then, she could only sneak away for a couple of hours each day after school. And now she wouldn't even be able to do that!

"No, Mum!" she squeaked. "Please don't. I won't ever do anything like this again. I promise. I was going to ask you first, only Stella made me go there straight away and… oh, Mum, please don't ground me, please!"

"Well," Mrs Brown considered, "I really don't know…" She furrowed her brow and let out a deep sigh, examining her daughter's pleading face. "OK, OK. But I don't want to see you walking through that door with any more body piercings, is that clear, young lady? I want no more surprises out of you."

"Oh, thanks, Mum!" Issie gushed, giving her a hug before bounding up the stairs.

Five minutes later she reappeared again in a sweatshirt and jeans.

"Where on earth are you off to now?" Mrs Brown asked.

"I won't be long," Issie said as she headed for the door. "I'm, umm… going down to the paddock to help Kate pull Toby's mane."

"All right, but be back in time for dinner. No later than seven, OK?" her mother yelled after her.

No more suprises? What would happen if her mum found out about Blaze? Issie thought about how she had lied to her mum. She felt bad not telling her about Blaze, but the time wasn't right. Not yet. For now, the horse had to be her secret.

Kate and Stella were in the tack room when Issie arrived at the River Paddock. "I can't find them anywhere!" Stella was grumbling as she rummaged through a pile of numnahs and old blankets on the floor.

"Find what?" Issie asked.

"The keys to the paddock gates," Stella said. "You know how we always keep a spare set here in case we need to undo the padlock and get the horses out? Well they're missing. And not only that, when I came down to the paddock this afternoon the tack room was wide open – and I could have sworn I locked it last night!"

"Maybe another rider was here after you and they left the tack room open?" suggested Kate as she straightened up the messy pile of horse blankets that Stella had strewn everywhere.

"Anyway," Stella sighed, "the keys to the paddock are gone. What are we going to do? I wanted to go ride out today."

"Let's saddle up," Kate said briskly. "We don't even need to leave the River Paddock. We can head down to the back paddock and take a ride through The Pines."

The Pines were a glade of tall pine trees at the far end of the back paddock. In winter the ground there was boggy, but in summer it was perfect for riding. A dirt track ran between the trees, scattered with pine cones and covered in a thick blanket of dark brown pine needles, which filled the air with their fresh scent.

The Pines had been Mystic's special place. Issie had

loved cantering him through the cool of the trees on a hot summer day. But she wasn't so sure about Blaze. The path between the trees was narrow with low branches over it, hard to navigate on such a headstrong mare.

"Ummm, I don't think Blaze is ready for that," Issie had to admit.

"Oh, go on, it'll be OK," Stella insisted. "We'll go at the front so she can follow us."

The three girls set off at a trot towards the far paddock, Stella and Kate posting up and down, while Issie bounced along bareback. The weeks spent without a saddle had done wonders for Issie's seat and even at a quick trot she felt secure on Blaze's sleek back. As they got near The Pines she even forgot her fears and felt a surge of excitement at the idea of cantering through them again.

The back paddock dropped away down a grassy slope to the trees and the girls trotted down until they reached the path into The Pines. "Ready to canter?" Stella shouted back as she kicked Coco on, leaning forward and standing up in her stirrups so that her weight was out of the saddle.

Issie waited for Coco and Toby to go on ahead before clucking Blaze on to canter. But the mare was suddenly struck with fear at being left behind by her new friends. When Issie urged her on into a gentle canter, she sprang forward as if she was a racehorse in a starting gate, not at a canter, but in full gallop.

"Blaze, stop it, girl! No!" Issie pulled back hard on the reins, but Blaze was having none of it. She had set the bit between her teeth and was off.

At a canter The Pines were easy enough to ride through, but at full gallop with no saddle? Impossible. Worse still, as Blaze strained against the reins, her speed increasing, she began to gain quickly on the horses ahead of her. There was no way the path was wide enough for Blaze to pass the other horses – she would crash into them for sure.

"Out of the way!" Issie yelled to the riders ahead of her. "Blaze is out of control. She won't stop!"

In front of her, Kate and Stella had heard the sound of hoofbeats before they even heard Issie's cries. Now, they urged their horses on. There was no room for them to pull over to the side of the path, and no time to stop. The best option was to ride hard and try to make it to the opening at the other end of The Pines before Issie caught up with them.

The fiery Arab was still ignoring Issie's attempts to slow her down, lost in the pleasure of her own speed. Her strides ate up the ground in front of her, and she was gaining quickly on Toby and Coco.

"Whoa now, girl!" Issie fought to keep her balance and grabbed up a handful of mane with the reins, pulling back as hard as she could. Blaze gave a rebellious snort and kept on running. In front of her, Coco was heaving with the effort of keeping up the pace, her coat flecked with sweat.

At a gallop the three horses emerged from the pine trees into the green clearing on the other side, and as Toby and Coco moved quickly out of the way Blaze powered forward, still in full gallop.

It wasn't until Issie had reached the far end of the paddock that she was finally able to slow the mare down a little, first to a canter, then a trot and finally a gentle jog. Even though her sides were heaving from the run, Issie had to keep a tight hold on her horse to stop her from bolting off again.

"Steady, girl, good girl, Blaze," she breathed, her

arms trembling from the effort of hanging on to the reins. Her heart was beating like a drum in her ears.

"That was amazing!" Kate yelled out as she rode towards her. "I've never seen a horse run like that. Toby's an ex-racehorse and Blaze even gave him a run for his money."

"Good on you for staying on her back at that speed!" Stella was obviously impressed. Issie, however, was less pleased.

"This is the second time she's got away on me." Issie was shaking. "I just can't control her. It's like she goes crazy the minute I get on her back."

Issie had been expecting sympathy from her friends, so she was shocked when Stella barked at her instead, "You're being silly, Issie! Everyone knows you're a natural rider. That's why Avery chose you to take Blaze on. OK, so she's being difficult. I'm sure all she needs to sort her out is a little bit of proper schooling. Talk to Tom. After all, he gave her to you. So why don't you ask him for a little help?"

Stella was right, of course. Issie had been trying to struggle on alone. What she really needed was some advice. "I'll ask Tom if he'll meet me at the paddock one day next week when the holidays have started to give me a hand." Issie nodded. "He'll know what to do."

Still, deep-down she doubted that anyone could really help her ride this spirited mare. Was Blaze too much horse for her to handle?

In the darkness of her bedroom that night, Issie had the dream again. It always began in the same way. The rhythmic sound of hoofbeats seemed to thunder out from the blackness and then the horse appeared like a silver mist in the gloom. As he came closer Issie could make out the misty outline of his body, the proud arch of his neck crested with a thick mane, and the long sweep of his elegant silver tail which trailed almost to the ground. The horse gave a soft nicker and came closer. He was just a few metres away now and Issie could see him clearly at last. It was Mystic. His dark-rimmed eyes looked at Issie intently and he was still for a moment. Then he pawed the ground and gave an agitated shake of his mane, before breaking into a high-stepping trot and heading straight for her.

Mystic came to an abrupt stop right in front of Issie. She reached out a hand to touch him, but before she could get near enough Mystic went up, rearing on his hind legs so that his front hooves thrashed the air above her. At the same time he let out a terrible long, low squeal – the noise a stallion might make if he was rounding up his herd against danger. It was a sound so deep and piercing that it woke Issie up with a start. She sat bolt upright in bed, her heart racing, her pyjamas damp with sweat.

Even now, wide awake, she could still hear Mystic's shrill squeal ringing in her ears. And then she heard something else. Not a squeal, but the drumming of hoofbeats. It sounded to Issie as if the noise were coming from just outside her bedroom window. Without hesitating she leapt up and raced to pull back the curtains, squinting out into the darkness.

She stood quietly at the window and held her breath as she tried hard to listen again. Nothing. The night air was completely still. Her eyes had adjusted now and she could see that the back yard was empty. Reluctantly, Issie let the curtain drop from her hand, moved away from the window and slipped back under the covers and into bed. It was all a dream, she told herself. But as she drifted back off to sleep she could have sworn she still heard the sound of hoofbeats somewhere out there in the darkness.

CHAPTER 9

"Why, Issie! She's looking brilliant, isn't she?" Avery was obviously thrilled at the sight of the chestnut mare.

Blaze was a different horse from the one that had arrived at the River Paddock one late spring morning. She had blossomed under Issie's tender care. She had put on condition so that her ribs no longer stood out so much, and her liver chestnut coat, previously patchy and dull, had been groomed until it gleamed like precious metal.

"I've been giving her a mix of oats, crushed barley and chaff to fatten her up a bit, and a dose of linseed oil to put a shine on her coat," Issie said proudly.

"Fantastic!" Avery enthused as he ran a hand over Blaze's rump, checking on her condition. "Well done. But I can see why this mare has been giving you trouble. Arabs are notoriously hotheaded sorts, and if this girl has been getting pepped up on a diet of oats and the like she's probably got too much energy for her own good. Now that she's in better shape we'll have to cut out the oats to calm her down.

"Now," Avery said, looking around, "let's get started. Where's your gear?" Issie reminded Avery that her saddle had been destroyed in the accident with Mystic. "Well," Avery considered, "not to worry. We won't be needing a saddle for this lesson anyway." He cast a glance at his watch. "At least you're here," he grumbled and reached out a hand to give Issie a leg up. "Where are the other two? I told them to be here at precisely two o'clock—"

The sound of hooves on gravel interrupted him.

"Wait for us!" squeaked Kate, trotting briskly along the road towards the fields.

"We're really sorry we're late!" Stella added. Her chubby little mare was heaving with the effort of keeping up with Kate's rangy Thoroughbred.

"Well, it looks like you've more than warmed these two up," Avery snapped. "Come on then. Let's spend a few minutes in the arena getting them to accept the bit and then we'll pop them over a few jumps and check out your positions."

As they entered the arena Blaze took the lead. "Issie," Avery said, "you change the rein and keep her moving at a steady walk, then when you get into the far corner ask her to move into a trot. Keep plenty of leg on her and keep your hands nice and still."

"You two," he gestured to Kate and Stella, "follow along behind Blaze. Come on, girls! I want to see these ponies paying attention."

As they worked the horses in around the arena, Avery busied himself in the middle of the ring, setting up trotting poles and cavalletti. "Right. Kate, you take the lead now and go over this combination that I've set up," Avery instructed. "The rest of you follow along behind Kate, leaving a decent space between you."

Kate and Stella went on ahead, taking the trotting poles with ease. But as Issie circled Blaze to follow them the mare tossed her head up, avoiding the bit and looking wild-eyed at the rails.

"Keep her steady, Isadora," Avery said.

But it was no use. Blaze simply wasn't paying her any attention. She took the trotting poles with an ungainly bound, then raced at the first cavalletti, throwing Issie back and almost unseating her. Landing off balance, Issie clutched on to the mare's mane as she stopped dead in front of the last jump, then changed her mind and bunny-hopped across it. Issie lurched forward, still hanging on as Blaze took the jump. But as they landed she couldn't keep her balance any longer, and flew over her horse's head.

Hitting the ground with a thud, Issie tried to relax, knowing that it was better to let her body absorb the impact. Still, she felt herself gasping for air as the wind was knocked out of her, and it took a minute or two before she could get her breath back and stand up. By the time she was on her feet, Avery was heading towards her, leading Blaze by the reins.

"Are you OK?" he asked as he reached her. "Yeah, I'm fine, just totally embarrassed," Issie wanted to say. Instead, she just nodded.

"Well, too many oats certainly have made Blaze a bit hot." Avery smiled at her. At least he didn't think she fell off because she was a useless rider!

Issie brushed herself down and tried to calm her nerves with a deep breath as Avery offered a hand to give her a leg up.

He turned to Kate and Stella: "Girls, I know you were looking forward to having a lesson but I think we need to focus on Blaze today. Why don't you unsaddle and then you can come back over to the arena and watch us?"

He turned to Issie: "We need to take things back to basics with Blaze," he told her. "I know you've been along to one or two of my natural horsemanship classes in the past, but with the problems you've been having with Blaze, I think it's time for some special advanced lessons."

He took the mare by the reins and looked at his pupil. "You can dismount now," he said.

Issie was confused. "But, I thought… I thought you just said we were going to do some more work…"

"A natural horseman knows that if you want to be a good rider, the first step is learning to handle your horse while you're still on the ground," Avery replied. "Then once you have your horse's trust and respect you can do anything you like. Now take Blaze into the middle of the arena. We'll play some training games with her that will get her listening to you, and then we'll get started on the real work."

If you happened to see Issie that afternoon playing her natural horsemanship games you would think she looked pretty silly: jumping up and down in front of her horse, waggling her arms and legs like a crazy puppet on a string; doing star jumps in front of Blaze with a pair of plastic shopping bags billowing in her hands, followed by another set of star jumps, this time with a raincoat in one hand and an old umbrella in the other. There were moments when it all seemed so ridiculous that even Issie fell about laughing.

But Avery would glare at her and remind her that this was serious business. "These games are designed to make Blaze 'bombproof'. Do you know what that means?"

"I think so," Issie said. "It means a horse who behaves well no matter what."

"Exactly. We want Blaze to have so much faith in you that nothing can scare her."

And with that, he gave Issie a leg up on to Blaze's back. "That's enough groundwork. Time for you to put your faith in Blaze for once," he said. Avery reached up and undid the throatlash and noseband, lifted the reins forward over Blaze's ears and then slipped the bridle off her head.

"But... what are you doing? How am I supposed to ride if she hasn't got a bridle on?" Issie squeaked.

"You don't need one," Avery insisted. "Just hang on to a handful of mane and sit there. We're going to let Blaze steer. She can go anywhere she wants. I just want you to sit tight and let her have her head."

Avery stood with his arm around Blaze's neck, calming the mare while Issie got comfortable. She gripped a thick hank of mane in her hands and wrapped her legs tightly around Blaze's sleek body.

"No, no, don't grip up with your legs. Relax a little," Avery instructed. "If you relax, your horse will relax too. Now, I'm going to let her go and I want you to just sit there. That's right. Stay perfectly still and let her decide for herself where to go." He kept talking as he released his grip on Blaze. "Horses are used to being told what to do by their riders. So naturally, if you ask one to think by itself for a change, suddenly their brains start to work and, well, who knows what could happen."

"I could fall off again, that's what could happen…" Issie muttered.

"The rails of the dressage arena will keep her from going too far," Avery pointed out. "Now, just sit there and relax totally."

Issie tried to relax but it wasn't easy. Blaze was all excited by the weight of a rider on her back. Her ears were pricked forward and her head was held high. She launched herself into a high-stepping trot and let out a shrill whinny as she charged down to the far end of the dressage arena. Issie forgot about relaxing and concentrated on hanging on as Blaze turned sharply and trotted back up the side of the arena.

"She's doing well," Avery coached. "She's just starting to understand that she can do whatever she likes. In a moment she'll calm down and start walking." Issie wasn't so sure. Any minute now, Blaze could realise that she was free and take a flying leap over the rails of the arena instead, dumping Issie in the process. The trot had now become a canter and Blaze seemed confused by the combination of the weight on her back and no bit in her mouth to control her. She gave a snort and shook her head.

"Stay calm, she'll settle down." Avery insisted.

And he was right. Blaze stopped cantering all by herself, slowing down to a gentle jog. She trotted on, snorting and breathing heavily through her nostrils. "That blowing means she's nice and relaxed," Avery said. "Now try to guide her with your legs, make her trot from one side of the arena to the other."

Issie gently touched Blaze's left side with her leg and felt the mare startle underneath her. She hadn't expected the horse to charge forward so suddenly.

"That's good," Avery reassured her. "Blaze is so alert you only need to give her the lightest of aids. Try again."

This time Blaze responded perfectly as Issie pushed her gently forwards, trotting smoothly across the ring.

"And back again," Avery commanded.

Again, Blaze obeyed perfectly and Issie began to feel the thrill of controlling this wild, high-spirited mare with nothing more than the lightest touch. Riding free, with no saddle or bridle to bind them, she felt as if she were almost a part of the magnificent chestnut Arab beneath her. For the first time since Mystic's death she felt that wonderful feeling again – the sensation that she and her horse were one and the same, the perfect team.

"Now circle around to the end of the ring," Avery continued. "And you can take Blaze over that jump that I've constructed for you."

Issie felt a tingle of nerves. One time at pony club they had knotted their reins and jumped with no hands over a low fence. But never without a saddle or bridle. How could she possibly control Blaze?"

"You won't have to control her," Avery read her mind. "Just let her go and stay with her. Blaze loves to jump; she'll do all the work."

The jump Avery had constructed was made out of forty-four gallon drums lying on their side, topped off with a red and white striped rail. Issie had jumped that high before – but never bareback and certainly not without a bridle to steer with. She stared at the jump, her stomach churning with butterflies, as Blaze circled around it.

"Don't look down at the ground," Avery shouted. "Look up and over the fence, otherwise Blaze will refuse to jump. That's it! Now stay relaxed and turn her towards me."

At the sight of the jump, Blaze's ears pricked forward and she broke into a canter. "Good girl, steady girl." Issie tried to stay relaxed, guiding her horse on and keeping her steady with her legs until she had almost reached the fence. Then she took a fistful of mane in each hand and held her breath. Blaze didn't just jump the fence – she flew over it. Issie felt the surge of power as the mare sprang lightly into the air, and the thrill of landing cleanly on the other side of the fence. They had done it!

"I can't believe it! She jumped it!" Issie gave Blaze a huge slappy pat on her neck. "It was like flying." She had a grin from ear to ear. Stella and Kate, who had been watching the whole thing, were clapping and whooping on the sidelines.

Blaze, too, was buzzing with pleasure. She pranced lightly from side to side, obviously keen to take the fence again.

Avery held the mare still as Issie dismounted. "Well

done, you two." He smiled at his pupil. "That's what natural horsemanship is all about. A horse and rider working as a team. Remember," he told her, "if you have a good seat you don't need to rely on a saddle or bridle. You know Vaughn Jefferis? He's one of New Zealand's most famous eventing riders – he has a fantastic seat – and he learnt to ride bareback. It took four years before his dad finally realised he was serious about being a competitive rider and bought him a saddle. That's why he has such perfect balance when he rides a cross-country course – he's totally in touch with his horse."

Avery looked at Issie. "Your riding has improved more than you realise over the past month since you've been riding Blaze. You two make quite a team now." Avery continued, "In fact, I think you're both ready to come along to the rally this weekend."

"Really?" Issie was shocked; it seemed too soon to take the mare on a pony-club outing, but if Avery was convinced that she was up to it…

"That's settled then," he said briskly, turning and walking off towards his truck. Then he span on his heels to face Issie: "Oh, and one more thing – when you arrive at the club grounds on Sunday, meet me at the horse truck. I've got a surprise for you."

"Another surprise?" Issie squawked. What on earth did Avery have in store for her this time?

CHAPTER 10

As she rode Blaze through the gates of the Chevalier Point Pony Club grounds Issie felt a twinge of embarrassment. It was only a rally day, but even so, all of the ponies would be nicely turned out, with their gear polished and oiled. And here she was riding without even a saddle!

Not only that, Blaze was still totally unpredictable. What if she decided to act up and Issie found herself falling off in front of the whole club? A million thoughts were racing through Issie's head – none of them good. After all, the last time she rode here had been a disaster, a disaster that had ended with Mystic's death.

"Stay calm or you'll pass your nerves on to your horse," Issie told herself firmly. Certainly Blaze seemed happy enough as they entered the grounds. Issie trotted her up to where the horse floats were parked and headed to her usual tethering spot under one of the massive plane trees. It was going to be a scorcher of a day and the big plane would shade Blaze from the heat of the sun.

The smell of privet flower filled the warm morning air. It was still early, around nine a.m., but already there were over a dozen riders here, tacking up their horses and preparing for the rally.

Issie dismounted and slipped Blaze's halter on over the top of her bridle, tying her to the nearby fence. "I won't be gone long, girl, I promise." Issie gave Blaze a quick pat on the neck and headed for the clubrooms. There was time to grab a cold Coke out of the drinks machine before the rally began.

As she reached the clubroom steps Issie looked back over her shoulder to check on her pony. Blaze seemed happy enough. She was standing peacefully under the trees with eyes half closed in a doze, resting one hind leg and swatting the summer flies away with her pale golden tail.

Issie was so busy looking at her horse that she didn't notice another girl racing down the steps as she was going up them. The two of them ran headfirst into one another and a mug of tea went flying.

"Watch where you're going, you stupid cow!" snapped the girl.

Issie looked up and saw Natasha Tucker, her white riding shirt soaked with tea, her face set in a vicious scowl.

"I'm so sorry!" Issie said.

"My shirt is ruined," Natasha snipped. "Calvin Klein! Ruined."

"I'm really sorry," Issie apologised again. "Have you got something else to wear for the rest of the day? We could try rinsing it off under the tap by the horse trough—"

"Yeah, what-ever." Natasha rolled her eyes, obviously losing interest in the whole conversation. "I'll give it to Mum; she can sort it out. Say..." she peered at Issie carefully, "don't you ride that old grey pony? That's your horse, isn't it? But I thought he was..."

"Hit by a truck. Yes..." Issie felt her lips start to tremble. She was determined not to let the thought of

Mystic upset her. She didn't want to lose it in front of Natasha. She wouldn't understand.

"He was killed in the accident," Issie said matter-of-factly. "I'm riding a new horse now." She pointed to Blaze who was standing under the trees with her rump towards them.

"What? That skinny bag of bones!" Natasha said. "She doesn't look up to much."

"Actually," Issie felt her blood boiling, "she's got an amazing jump in her. I was riding her the other day and we went clean over the gate between the two paddocks where I graze her. And she hasn't even been properly schooled yet. I'm sure she'd make a great showjumper with a bit more work."

Issie didn't mean to boast but she just couldn't help herself. She couldn't stand the way Natasha was so smug. Besides, she wasn't exactly fibbing – Blaze did jump over the gate. Issie just didn't mention the fact that it was all Blaze's idea and all *she* did was fall off.

"In fact," Issie continued, "I plan to train her up as an eventing mount. I'll be competing on her shortly."

"Oh, really?" Natasha smirked. "So you'll be riding

at the Chevalier Point one-day event next month, I suppose?"

"Oh, definitely. We're in training for it now," Issie lied.

"Me too," said Natasha. "Goldrush's last owner rode her to area trials and I expect to do the same, so this will be a warm-up competition for us..."

Natasha had been staring distractedly at Blaze while she spoke. Now she turned back to Issie. "Where's your saddle?"

"What?"

"Your saddle," repeated Natasha. "I don't see one on your horse. Where is it? You're not planning to ride her bareback at a one-day event are you?"

Issie didn't know what to say. It was no use lying about it because the rally was about to get underway and Natasha would soon see the truth for herself: that she didn't have a saddle, or any other gear for that matter.

"I, umm... the thing is..."

"Actually Isadora has two saddles. One for dressage and another for jumping and cross-country. We just weren't sure which one to tack Blaze up with for today, were we, Issie?" Tom Avery smiled as he stepped out of the clubrooms and stood beside the two girls.

"So what do you reckon, Issie? Shall we put the dressage saddle on her this morning then swap to the jumping saddle after lunch?"

Issie just nodded. She couldn't believe it. Tom to the rescue!

"Come on. I've got your tack in my truck; let's get her ready." Avery bounded down the stairs towards his horse truck and Issie gratefully followed, relieved to be getting away from Natasha.

She finally caught up with Avery just as he reached the truck. "Tom, thanks so much for covering up for me," Issie gasped, "it's just that Natasha is such a, well, a snob, I suppose, and if I'd told her that I really didn't have a saddle—" Tom cut Issie off in mid-sentence.

"Covering for you? I don't know what you're talking about, Isadora. I was telling Natasha the truth. I've got both your saddles right here in the cab. Can't have you riding bareback at a pony-club meet now, can we?"

Avery opened the front door of the horse truck, and there on the passenger seat of the truck cab sat two saddles. "Remember the other day I said I had a surprise for you?" Avery reached in and grabbed the nearest one. It was made of soft black leather, and had the deep seat and straight-cut flaps of a traditional dressage saddle. "It's a Bates Maestro," he said, handing it to her so that her arm slid through the gullet. "It used to be my eventing saddle. I've ridden dressage tests in this saddle in all the big competitions around the world – at Burghley, Badminton and Lexington. It'll be a tiny bit big for you, I suppose, but it has adjustable kneepads which will help, and we can alter the stirrups, of course. It should fit Blaze just fine. As should this one..."

Avery reached across the seat and lifted out the second saddle. It was made of dark tan leather and seemed more well worn than the first saddle; the kneepads were scuffed a little and there were sweat stains on the padding underneath. *Not surprising*, thought Issie – this was clearly Avery's cross-country saddle.

"This one was made especially for me." Avery stared at the saddle proudly. "It has a flat seat and the first time I rode a cross-country in it I swore I would fall off, but it's actually very comfortable compared to those old-fashioned deep-seated models. It's not ideal for the showjumping phase, but it does the trick.

"It's just the sort of saddle you'll be needing," he added, "if you're going to be riding Blaze at that one-day event."

Issie was stunned. Avery must have heard her entire conversation with Natasha, including all her boasting about entering the one-day event.

"I'm not really entering..." Issie began.

"But of course you are!" Avery boomed. "You've got the saddles. You've got the horse. What else do you need?"

"But I've never even ridden Blaze over a proper fence yet!" Issie protested.

"Nonsense," Avery said, "you said yourself she has a big jump in her. And from what I've seen I'd say this mare is no novice jumper. It looks to me like she's been well-schooled already in the past. All you need to do is bring out the best in her again.

"The one-day event isn't until the end of the season, so you've got nearly two months to train. You've already got her well fed and her fitness is improving. You'll have to commit yourself to training solidly every day from now until the event, of course, but you can do it. Now let's get this saddle on Blaze and see how it looks, shall we?"

For Issie, the rest of the day passed by in a sun-filled blur. There were around fifty riders in the Chevalier Point Pony Club – the best ten riders of the club being chosen to train with Avery. Issie was thrilled when she was singled out along with Kate, Stella, Dan and the dreaded Natasha to join Avery's group.

The morning was spent schooling the horses and Issie was amazed at her own progress. The weeks without a saddle had actually done her some good and she had developed an independent seat. Still, having a fabulous new saddle certainly helped and Blaze behaved like a perfect angel, trotting around the ring with her neck flexed and on the bit. Her paces seemed so light it was as if she didn't touch the ground, but floated around the arena.

It was nearly two in the afternoon by the time lunch break came, and Issie was exhausted and starving. She had just taken Blaze's bridle off and loosened her girth a little so she could relax, then thrown herself down on the long grass under the tree, when Dan appeared.

"Hey, no slacking off!" He grinned. "You're my new groom, remember?"

"What?" Issie didn't understand.

"We made a bet," Dan said, "at the gymkhana, remember? The loser had to groom the winner's horse for a week. Well, I'm ready to take you up on that now."

"I can't believe you!" Issie was shocked. "After all that happened to me that day you actually want me to come over and brush down your horse! God, Dan, you're so insensitive!"

"Hey, hey..." Dan's smile was gone. "I was just kidding, Issie. Honestly. I really came over to see if you want to join us for lunch. Mum's made a giant bacon and egg pie – it's too big for even me and Ben to finish off. And there's stacks of sandwiches and banana cake and..."

"I'd love to." Issie smiled, feeling foolish about her outburst. "Just let me tie Blaze up and I'll be right there."

On the grass beside the Halliday's horse float Dan's mum was laying out the picnic. "Isadora! It's so good to see you riding again!" Mrs Halliday smiled. "Where's your mother today?"

"Ummm, she had too much work on and couldn't make it," Issie said, silently thinking to herself that this must be her day for telling whopping great lies. First she fibbed to Natasha about entering the one-day event, and now she was lying to Mrs Halliday about her mum. The truth was, she still hadn't told her mother about Blaze. She had been too scared to mention it. And now, well, the longer she left it, the harder it seemed to confess that she had started riding again. And with her mum away at work all day, and no school for the rest of summer, it was easy for Issie to slip away each day to school Blaze without being found out.

"Would you like a slice of pie or a sandwich?" Mrs Halliday offered.

"Oh, Mum, give her both! It's been a tough day." Dan laughed, standing up and dusting off his jodhpurs. "I'm going to the drinks machine. Anyone else want anything?"

Issie shook her head and watched as Dan walked off to the clubrooms to get a drink. She watched as he ran up the steps and bumped into, of all people, Natasha Tucker. This time, though, Natasha didn't seem upset about banging into someone. Instead she let out a torrent of girlish laughter as Dan said something to her, and then she placed her hand softly on top of his as they chatted.

Seeing them together like that made Issie feel sick to her stomach. She'd never actually thought about Dan as a boyfriend or anything before, but now that she saw him smiling and laughing with Natasha, she realised she was more than a little jealous.

"God, she is such a flirt!" Issie muttered under her breath.

"What's that?" asked Ben, who was busily tucking into his third piece of bacon and egg pie.

"Uhh, nothing," Issie pulled herself together, "I was just wondering what we'll be doing first after lunch."

"They're setting up the games now so I suppose it will be bending and flag races," Ben said, sounding a little disappointed. "It's a shame really. I had been hoping to get in some jumping training."

"As if you need it!" Issie laughed. "I'm the one who needs the jumping training. I'm entering the one-day event."

"On Blaze?" Ben was shocked. "Well, you're right. You do need to train more than I do. Dan and I are already having lessons on Wednesday and Thursday with Tom. Why don't you join us? We meet here at the club grounds at four."

"That sounds great!" Issie agreed. This would give her a chance to prepare Blaze for the one-day event – and hang out with Dan at the same time. Life was definitely starting to improve, she decided as she took another egg sandwich and lay back on the grass with her eyes shut and the sun on her face.

CHAPTER 11

"Working Trot at K, proceed around the arena to H..." Tom Avery was reading instructions out loud from a piece of paper as Issie trotted Blaze around the dressage arena. There were just two weeks to go until the one-day event, and Avery was taking his squad one by one through a practice run of their dressage tests. For the big day the riders would have to know all the movements off by heart, but today he was reading the test out for them as they rode.

The dressage arena had been marked out with white boards, each one painted with a large capital letter. The letters were set up at various points around the ring and Issie had to make sure Blaze did exactly as she asked when she reached the right marker.

"At C, canter on in a twenty metre circle..." Avery's voice boomed across the ring.

Issie held Blaze lightly with her hands and asked her gently with seat and legs to move into a canter. The pretty chestnut needed only the subtlest of commands, she was so responsive. As she flew around the ring in a graceful canter, Issie could almost imagine she was competing at some huge event like the Badminton Horse Trials. She pictured Blaze with her blonde mane and tail perfectly plaited up, with tight white bandages over her white socks. And there she was on her back in tails and a top hat, entering the ring, saluting the judge...

"No, no, no! Wake up, Issie, you're not paying attention! You should be changing the rein at B across the arena!" Avery barked at her. "Change the rein, change the rein! Then turn up the middle at A, halt at X and leave the arena on a loose rein."

Issie woke up with a jolt and got back on track, trotting up the centre line beautifully to halt and salute with Blaze standing perfectly square and calm.

"If I keep daydreaming like this," Issie muttered to Blaze as they left the arena, "we'll never make it to the Chevalier Point one-day event, let alone Badminton."

Avery smiled at Issie as she pulled the chestnut mare up beside the other riders. "Well, apart from having a dilly dream for a rider, Blaze is doing pretty well," Avery said. "Seriously though," he continued, "all your hard work is beginning to pay off." Avery ran his hand across Blaze's shoulder. "Look how much her muscle tone has improved. And look at the shine on her coat. She's a different horse from the sad, skittish thing I dropped off here a few months back. You've done a fantastic job."

Issie blushed. She wasn't used to such praise from Avery. He was usually so tough on his riders that it meant a lot to her. But before she had time to feel too proud he was off again. "Still an hour left, people. Let's get them over some cross-country jumps. All right then, who's first? How about you, Ben?"

"Oh, no," Ben groaned. "Why do I have to go first? Max is totally hopeless today." He trotted off to warm up over a practice fence, while Dan trotted over to sit next to Issie and wait for his turn.

"Avery is right, you know," Dan said. "You and Blaze have come a long way."

"Thanks." Issie felt her cheeks flush pink for the second time.

"I suppose you're too busy training for the one-day event to take time out and go to Summer in the Park this weekend?" Dan asked.

Issie's heartbeat quickened. Was Dan asking her out on a date?

Summer in the Park was a series of gigs that local bands put on every year at Chevalier Point Park. Her mum had always said she was too young to go, but this year maybe she'd be allowed...

"Because if you are going," Dan continued, "we could always meet you there. Natasha and me are getting a whole group together. You should come along."

Natasha? Issie couldn't believe it. Suddenly Dan's invitation sounded less like a date and more like her tagging along while he hung out with Natasha.

"I didn't know you knew Natasha..." Issie was trying to sound casual, trying to keep the hurt out of her voice.

"She's in my class at school," Dan said, "and my mum knows her mum so we kind of made friends."

Dan was a year ahead of Issie, and didn't go to Chevalier Point High. He went to Kingswood, a school on the other side of town.

"We met at pony club the other day," Dan continued. "She told me she liked Smoothy, this really cool band who are playing this Sunday, so I said I'd take her along."

Issie couldn't believe it. How could Dan like Natasha? OK, she was sort of pretty in a boring girly blonde sort of way, but she was also stuck up and rude and mean-tempered. She couldn't believe Dan would fall for all that flirting Natasha did. It was so shallow and obvious.

"Typical! Boys are so, so… stupid!" Issie huffed under her breath.

"What's that?" Dan said.

"Umm, I said, I don't think I can make it. Sorry. I'm going to be really busy with Blaze this weekend. We still have a lot of work to do."

"Your turn Dan!" Avery shouted out. Ben had just completed his round and it must have gone well because he looked pleased with himself, riding back towards them wearing a grin from ear to ear.

"Dan, come on!" Avery yelled again.

"Ohmygod!" Dan groaned. "I was so busy talking, I haven't even warmed Kismit up yet."

He gathered up the reins and trotted off towards Avery, leaving Issie sitting by herself in the worst mood she had been in for weeks.

Issie was still in a sulk two days later, when she met up with Kate and Stella down at the River Paddock: "So then he tells me that he's going to Summer In The Park with Natasha!" Issie whined. "I don't know why he even asked me to come along at all!"

Kate and Stella both shook their heads in amazement as they listened to Issie's story of the whole stupid misunderstanding and how she thought Dan was asking her out when in fact he was going to the gig with Natasha.

"I can't believe he really likes her," Stella said. "That Natasha is just so pushy. I bet she's behind this."

"Well, it doesn't matter anyway," Issie said icily. "I've got too much to do getting Blaze ready for the one-day event to worry about a dumb concert."

Stella gave Kate a knowing glance. The two friends could tell Issie was really upset about Dan and Natasha, but she obviously didn't want to talk about it. The best thing to do was go for a good gallop and let the wind whip through her hair and blow the whole thing away.

For the past six weeks the girls had been riding to a strict training schedule that Avery had prepared for them in preparation for the one-day event. On Mondays and Wednesdays they practised their dressage tests. On Thursday and Sunday they practised jumps – showjumping and cross-country. And on Tuesdays, Fridays and Saturdays they did "interval training", trotting and cantering back and forth around the paddock until they were exhausted and the horses were wet with sweat. It was dull work and hard on a rider's bottom too. But today, instead of riding endlessly around the paddock, the three girls were taking the horses out for some road work, riding all the way to Winterflood Farm.

Winterflood Farm sat on a jut of green land right at the edge of Chevalier Point where the river met the sea. It wasn't a big farm, just ten acres divided into neat square paddocks fenced with posts and rails. A slender, tree-lined driveway ran down the middle of the fields leading to a gravel courtyard, which joined a stable complex to a small wooden cottage. The stables had been deserted for years until Tom Avery took over the farm. Now he kept his three young sport horses that he was training in the stables – although most of the time they grazed outdoors in the paddocks that surrounded the farm.

The girls would be able to ride across pasture land most of the way – the hunt club had a special route to Winterflood Farm that was open to all local riders.

"But we'll have to stick to a trot along the grass verges on the roadside until we get down to the bend in the river," Stella explained. "Then we'll be able to go cross-country so that we can get some good galloping practice in."

Issie felt a tingle of nerves. She had never galloped Blaze in the open countryside before, and after that ride in The Pines she was a little nervous about the hotheaded Arab bolting again.

"Are we ready to go?" Kate was dead keen to get Toby out on the open roads and start riding. So keen that the pair of them were pacing impatiently at the gate.

"Let's do it!" Issie clucked Blaze into a trot, but instead of rising up and down in her stirrups she stood up in them and practised her two-point cross-country position, balancing easily in midair with space to spare between her and the saddle.

Blaze jogged along, letting out snuffly snorts of excitement as if she knew they were leaving the paddock and going somewhere new.

"Remember to keep to single file near the roads," Stella shouted out. "I'll go up front with Coco since she's not likely to charge off. Issie, you can go in the middle with Blaze and Toby can bring up the rear."

The three of them set off at a brisk trot. A bit too brisk for Issie's liking – Blaze's trot was still bouncy enough to throw her about in the saddle, and she couldn't wait to reach open land so they could canter.

By the time they'd reached the open fields of the hunt-club land, the horses were in a sweat from the trot work. Tiny Coco was flecked with white froth on her neck and had green foam oozing out of her mouth from working the bit.

"Everyone ready to canter?" Stella yelled back over her shoulder. Issie and Kate both gave a silent nod and the three of them loosened the reins and let Coco, Toby and Blaze have their heads.

Issie looked down at the ground and watched as it became a blur of green and brown as Blaze cantered on. The chestnut mare was fast, Issie knew that much already. But it seemed that with each week, as her fitness improved, her speed increased.

"Steady, girl, easy now," Issie breathed to her horse, but the wind pushed her words back down her throat. Blaze had opened up and had started to gallop. She was wild with the thrill of running, and even with a firm hand on the reins Issie knew it would be hard to stop her now.

This time, though, instead of trying to hold the mare back, she gave Blaze her head and sat high in the saddle. *Let her run*, Issie thought. *Let's see what this horse can do.*

To the left of her, Kate was on Toby, urging the

long-limbed Thoroughbred on. Toby was an ex-racehorse, and yet, even at full gallop, Blaze could match him stride for stride. As the two horses ran on, Blaze's stride lengthened until she began to edge ahead of the big bay. By the time they reached the road leading to Winterflood Farm Blaze was ahead by a length. The mare's chestnut neck glistened with sweat and her breath was coming hard and raspy with the effort of the run.

"Easy, girl, slow down now." Issie tightened her grip on the reins and Blaze responded to the pressure, slowing her pace. Kate pulled Toby up next to her and the two girls and their horses came to a stop next to the farm gate to catch their breath.

"That was amazing!" Kate panted. "Toby was really stretching out back there and Blaze still beat him! I had no idea she was so fast!"

"Neither did I!" Issie said. She reached down and gave the mare a solid pat on her sweaty neck.

The sound of pounding hooves behind them made the two girls turn around. Stella and Coco were bearing down on them as fast as they could canter.

"Thank God I've finally caught up with you two!"

Stella pulled Coco up to a halt. "I've been trying to get your attention ever since we started cantering." Stella looked concerned.

"Have you noticed it? Over there. That white van? Careful, don't let them see you looking!" Stella tried to gesture over her shoulder without actually turning around. Behind her a white van was parked on the grass verge that led to the hunt-club fields.

"Yeah, what about it?" Kate snapped. She was distracted, still having trouble hanging on to Toby as the Thoroughbred stomped about, all overexcited from his run.

"I'm sure it's the same one we saw the other day at the River Paddock," Stella whispered. "I know it sounds stupid, but I think it's following us."

"You know, they're parked miles away, Stella, they can't hear you, you don't need to whisper," Kate groaned.

"Look, I'm serious!" Stella insisted. "They've been driving along watching us. I'm sure of it. It's really creeping me out. I think we should turn around and go home."

"Nonsense!" Kate was in no mood for this now.

"You and your stories, Stella! I'm going over there to ask them what they want."

Without any more discussion on the matter she wheeled Toby around and cantered the big bay off towards the parked van.

In the distance the figures of two men suddenly sprang into motion. The driver, a short stocky type with a thick black bushy beard, jumped behind the wheel of the van while the other man, much skinnier and taller than the driver, ran around the van, quickly leaping into the passenger seat. The engine revved and, by the time Kate reached the grass verge, the van was gone.

"You were right," Kate had to admit as she trotted back to join the group. "They must have been watching us. At least they tore off in an awful hurry for some reason. This is creepy."

"I'll tell you what else is weird," Stella said. "You know how the spare paddock keys went missing the other day? Well I found them again! They were back on the hook in the shed as if they were there all along!" Stella narrowed her eyes. "I bet it's got something to do with those guys in the van."

Kate shook her head and sighed at Stella's latest revelation. "Oh, for heaven's sake, Stella, now you've got me falling for your crazy mystery stories! Those keys probably just got lost under that big mess of horse blankets you were chucking around."

"No, they didn't!" Stella was red-faced. "I looked everywhere for them! Someone took them and then they must have put them back again!"

"Anyway," Kate wheeled her horse around impatiently, "let's head for home." She looked across at Issie. "But no galloping this time, eh? I'm too exhausted. Let's just trot the rest of the way."

Issie nodded in agreement. But she wasn't really listening to Kate. She was looking up the road where the white van had disappeared. Stella was right. It was the same van they had seen parked down by the paddock the other day. And now the question was beginning to puzzle her. Just who were they following? And why?

CHAPTER 12

The dream started as it always did – with the sound of hoofbeats. Issie stared into the pitch-blackness, the thunder of hooves seemed to be surrounding her. This time, though, the grey horse didn't appear from the dark. Instead, the hoofbeats stopped and she could hear a soft whinny, calling to her, calling her out of sleep.

Issie woke with a start. Her dreams about Mystic had always seemed vivid, but never as real as this. She could have sworn she heard the neigh of a horse outside her bedroom window. She held her breath – there it was again! Only she was awake now, and still she heard it!

Issie crept up to the window as if she were stepping on broken glass, slowly, carefully. Through the lace of the curtain she could make out a shape moving on the lawn. She pulled the curtain back and peered out into the dark. It looked like a horse all right, but it was impossible to see properly. She would have to get dressed and go outside.

Quickly pulling on an old pair of jeans, a polar fleece and boots she ran for the back door that led to the lawn. Her mind was racing. How could a horse end up in her garden? She had an idea, but it was silly, impossible. She opened the back door and stepped out into the yard.

At first, she thought the horse must have vanished. In the dark it seemed like the green expanse of the lawn was empty. But then, in the corner of the garden underneath some tall birch trees she saw him. A dapple-grey, she could tell that much, even at this distance. But she needed to get closer. Silently she took one step, then another and then another, edging her way towards the horse. When she was a few metres away the little grey let out a low nicker, and stepped forward out from under the trees to meet her.

Tears filled Issie's eyes as she buried her head in the grey mane. It was Mystic. And he felt real and warm to her touch, not like a ghost horse, but like her own pony. She could even smell his sweet horsy smell as she kept her head pressed hard against his neck and tried to stop the tears from coming.

"Easy, boy, easy, Mystic," Issie cooed gently to him.

But Mystic would not stand still. He pulled away from her, shaking his head to free her hands from the tangle of his mane, and began to paw the ground in a frantic state. Then he let out a wild snort and wheeled about, racing all the way to the far end of the garden where the gate led to the street, then galloping back to stand in front of Issie. Again and again he repeated his frenzied run, charging up and down the lawn.

As Issie watched him gallop once more for the gate, she finally realised what Mystic was trying to tell her. He wanted her to ride him. Each time he ran down to the far end of the garden, Mystic came to a halt right in front of the five-barred gate that led to the street. Now Issie could see that the gate was the perfect height for her to climb up and mount the grey horse.

As he headed back down the lawn for the fourth

time, Issie ran after him. This time, when Mystic reached the gate he paused and waited for her to catch up to him. Then he stood still, snorting and quivering with anticipation as she clambered quickly up the gate rails and, hesitating just for a moment, threw herself lightly on to his back.

If this is a dream, Issie decided, *I must surely wake up now*. Instead she felt the sleek coat of her horse warm underneath her, and the ropey fibres of horsehair between her fingers as she buried her hands in Mystic's mane. The little grey leapt forward as he felt her weight on his back but Issie quickly calmed him, making him stand still so she could lean over to unlock the latch on the gate.

There was a slice of moon in the sky that provided just enough light so that Issie could make out the blurry outline of a horse beneath her. In the moonlight, Mystic's dappled coat seemed to melt into the night. It was almost as if she was riding a vapour, a wisp of grey smoke.

For a moment she wondered again whether she was dreaming. Then the clatter of hooves on tarmac jarred her back to reality as Mystic stepped through the gate and out on to the road. Now the streetlights were there to illuminate their path and Issie could clearly see her horse's grey ears pricked forward in front of her, swivelling occasionally to listen to the sound of her voice.

Issie clucked Mystic gently on, and without a bridle to steer with, she used her legs to guide the horse to the grass verge on the side of the road. With the soft grass underfoot she let the little grey break into a canter and felt a thrill tingle through her. She had forgotten how wonderful it was to ride this horse. The weeks of riding Blaze without a saddle had paid off, and Mystic's paces were so smooth and gentle, Issie felt as if she were riding a rocking horse. The summer breeze whipped her hair across her face. Blinded for a moment, she let her hands slip through Mystic's mane and had to scramble to grab another handful of horse hair.

"Even if this is a dream, I'd better hang on," she reminded herself. She realised now that there was no use steering. Mystic seemed to know where he was going. Instead of trying to guide the grey pony, Issie let him take her along for the ride.

The cold nip of the evening air made her eyes stream

tears, and the chill of the wind in her face froze a rosy pink glow on her cheeks. "Just hold tight," she told herself out loud. And at that moment she realised just what a strange picture the pair of them must make. A young girl, her black hair caught in the wind, her pyjamas sticking out from underneath the polar fleece jumper, riding bareback without a bridle in the middle of the night on a grey ghost, a horse whose dappled coat was hardly visible against the trees in the moonlight. No one would believe this. She didn't know whether to believe it herself. All she could do was hang on.

Away from the streetlights now, in the darkness, it was impossible to tell where they were. Now and then she would pass a house with the porch lights on and she'd be able to make out a familiar shadow or a street sign, but she was far too busy trying to stay on Mystic's back to look too hard at anything else around her. So at first, when Mystic came to a halt, she felt completely confused, directionless. Then she heard the sound of the river flowing fast and strong beside them and could make out the shapes of horses grazing in the field in front of them.

Of course! They were here, at the River Paddock.

But why? Why had Mystic brought her here tonight?

She was about to dismount and stretch her legs, try to figure out what was going on, when she heard the sound of a car engine cruising up the street behind her. Car headlights caught her in their beam, momentarily blinding her.

The drivers of the car couldn't have seen her because they kept driving straight past her towards the paddock gate. As they drove past, Issie's eyes adjusted back to the darkness. And then she saw who it was. Not a car at all, but a white van. The white van. The same one that had been parked outside the paddock watching them. The same one that had followed them on the ride to Winterflood Farm. The bearded man and the skinny one were sitting in the van just like before. But this time they were towing a red horse float behind them.

The van stopped and one of the men jumped out to open the gate to the horse paddock. Issie's mind was racing now. What were these men doing here? None of the horses that grazed at the River Paddock belonged to them. Besides, why would they come here in the middle of the night? What did they want?

On the other side of the van the door opened and a man stepped out. Then Issie saw he was holding a halter in his hand and she realised: they were here to steal a horse.

All this time, Mystic had been quiet underneath Issie, his dapple-grey coat was the perfect camouflage in this darkness amongst the willow trees by the river. There was no way the men could see them. But they might hear them. In the still of the night, Mystic gave a gentle nicker and the sound carried across the paddocks.

"What was that?" the big, bearded one barked out.

"What?" the other shouted back.

"That noise. It sounded like a horse."

"Well, of course it did, you idiot. We're at a horse paddock, aren't we? It's full of horses. Now stop mucking about, throw over those keys to the gate and then give me a hand. Remember, we're looking for a chestnut with four white socks. She shouldn't be hard to find – she's the only chestnut in the herd."

Issie felt her heart stop. A chestnut with four white socks? They could only mean Blaze. They were here to steal her horse! This was a nightmare. She had to do something. But what? She could try to get to Blaze before they did, but in the dark there was no guarantee that she would find her horse first. And even if she caught Blaze, what then? There were two of them and their van was blocking the only exit in the paddock, making escape impossible. No, she had to stop these men. And for that she would need some help.

"Come on, boy, we've got to go," she spoke gently under her breath to Mystic, turning the little grey away from the paddock and back towards the Point. Winterflood Farm was ten minutes away at a fast gallop. If she could just find it in the darkness. And if she could only make it in time. She had to make it in time.

For the first minute, Issie had to force herself to keep calm and walk on. She was dying to get moving but she didn't want the men to hear the sound of Mystic's hooves pounding on the soft grass.

As soon as she knew she was safely out of range, Issie urged Mystic on into a canter, then a gallop. In the dark she knew it was risky. Mystic's night vision couldn't be much better than her own. There was always the chance that the grey pony might lose his footing or injure himself by getting a leg caught in a rabbit hole. But she had ridden this way before, just the other day on Blaze, and she knew it well enough.

Then there was the chance that at full gallop she might lose her balance, fall to the ground. Riding at this speed bareback was foolhardy at best. Issie knew that. But she also knew she had no choice.

If the wind had whipped her hair before, now it lashed it across her face with the sting of a birch branch. But she couldn't free her hands to wipe the strands away, she was too busy hanging on, clenching with her fingers so that Mystic's mane cut into the flesh of her hands. Her legs gripped firmly around the horse's belly, and she could feel herself sliding on Mystic's back as the grey pony became slick with sweat.

When she had ridden this same path on Blaze it had been daylight and she had the luxury of a saddle. Now, in the pitch black with nothing but her skill to keep her on Mystic's back, she was riding as if her life depended on it. *Now I know*, Issie realised. *Now I know what it's like to really ride a spirited horse.*

Despite the speed of Mystic's gallop, the ride from the River Paddock to Avery's house seemed to Issie like it took an entire lifetime. Then finally she heard the clatter of gravel under Mystic's hooves and they rode into the driveway of Winterflood farm.

Mystic pulled to a halt, but before he even had a chance to stop, Issie was vaulting lightly to the ground and running on her own. Running for Avery's front door.

She pressed the buzzer. Nothing. She pressed it again, hammering on the door too this time until her fists were sore. A light went on and then another, and then the door opened and the bleary-eyed face of Avery was staring at her full of amazement.

Ohmygod! Issie suddenly thought. *What if he sees Mystic?* But when she glanced back over her shoulder at the gravel courtyard the little grey was nowhere to be seen.

"Issie! It's three in the morning, girl! What the hell are you doing here?"

A thousand explanations seemed to choke themselves up in Issie's throat. She realised she had no time for words.

"Please, Tom, please. No time for that. Grab your coat and your car keys and let's go. Blaze is in danger."

CHAPTER 13

Avery drove the Range Rover at top speed back towards the River Paddock while Issie peered out into the darkness that surrounded them, keeping an eye out in case the white van was already making its getaway with the stolen horse onboard.

"We're almost there, Issie," Avery said, his eyes focused straight ahead, concentrating on the road in front of them. "So you'd better start explaining yourself now. What on earth is going on here?"

Issie quickly unfolded as much of the story as she could. She told Avery about the two men in the white van that had been following them, and how she arrived at the paddock tonight to find the same two men looking for Blaze and overheard their plans to steal her horse.

"When I left to find you they had grabbed a halter and a torch out of the van and they were hunting for her," she explained. "A chestnut with four white socks they said, and Blaze is the only chestnut that grazes at the River Paddock…"

"Wait a minute. What were you doing down at the paddock in the middle of the night all by yourself?" Avery asked.

"Ummm…" Issie faltered, "I was worried about Blaze, I guess. You know, because she's been so sick and with the event coming up. The weather had got so cold and I'd forgotten to put her cover on. I rode down to check on her on my bike and that's when I saw them."

Thankfully, it seemed that Avery was satisfied with this explanation.

He nodded his head thoughtfully, his mouth set in a grim line. Then he spoke.

"The question is, Issie, what are we going to do when we get there? There's just two of us, so I don't know how much use we'll be against two burly chaps.

Listen, you'd better hunt around in my glovebox there for my mobile. When we get to the paddock I'll go off and see if I can find these men and make sure they haven't hurt Blaze. Meanwhile you stay back at the car, and if you haven't heard back from me in about five minutes, give the police a call. Tell them what's going on as best you can and tell them to get down here straight away, that there's a theft in progress. Can you do that?"

Issie nodded. But she was worried. "Can't I come with you, Tom? There are two of them after all. You're going to need my help."

"It's too dangerous, Issie. You did the right thing coming to get me. Now do what I tell you and stay in the car."

They weren't far away from the paddock when Avery turned off the headlights on the Range Rover. "If they don't see us coming it will give us the element of surprise," he explained to Issie.

"That is if they're still there…" Avery squinted into the dark. "…I don't see anything in the paddock. Maybe they've already got Blaze loaded on and taken off…"

Issie's stomach churned as she peered desperately out into the gloom. There it was! The glow of the tail lights of a horse float. They hadn't gone. They were still there!

"Tom, over there!" she whispered.

"I see it," Avery confirmed. And with that, he switched off the Range Rover engine and let the car coast down the hill towards the paddock.

"Element of surprise again." He smiled at Issie. "We don't want them to hear us coming either, do we?"

The Range Rover coasted silently to the side of the road and Avery quietly unlatched his door and jumped out. "Change of plan," he said. "Call the police now, Issie. There's a chance we can catch these guys in the act. I'm going to take a snoop around and see what's going on. Now, remember, after you call the cops, you stay here in the car. I don't want you getting yourself into trouble." Avery gave her a reassuring smile and closed the car door.

Under the shadows of the willow trees Issie could just make him out now, hunched low to the ground, running towards the back of the tack room.

Issie picked up Avery's mobile and dialled the

police. Her heart was racing as she heard the dialling tone on the phone. The phone rang once, rang twice, rang a third time... and then stopped.

"Hello? Hello?" Issie's voice was wobbly with nerves. Why had the phone stopped ringing? Why wasn't anyone answering? She lifted the mobile up so she could see its digital face more closely. There in the right-hand corner a red light was flashing steadily on and off. She knew what it meant. Dead battery.

"Not now! It can't be!" Issie stared at the red light in disbelief. The mobile let out a low beep, a sign that the battery was about to die completely. *About to die*, Issie thought. *But it's not dead just yet. Maybe it still has enough power left to make one last call. Even if I don't get through to the police maybe somehow they can trace my signal or something.*

Issie didn't know much about how mobile phones worked. All she knew was that she had to try something. She dialled the police number again and hung on as the phone rang once, rang twice.

"Hello?" said a voice at the other end of the line. "Which service do you require – police, ambulance or fire?"

"Listen," Issie hissed, "I don't have much time. My phone is going dead. I need the police. This is Issie Brown. I'm down at the River Paddock near Waterstone Street and we need help…"

There was a dull buzz in her ear as once again the line cut out. Issie looked at the blinking red light. It was still flashing, so there must still be some juice left in the phone. Should she try again? She dialled the number once more. This time there was a dialling tone, the sound of a phone ringing and then nothing. Even the red light had stopped flashing now. There was nothing more that she could do. The battery was well and truly dead. Had the police got her message? There was no way of knowing.

Out there in the darkness, Avery was expecting help to arrive at any moment. He didn't know that the police might not be coming at all. She had to do something.

In the quiet night air the sound of the Range Rover door creaking open was almost deafening to her. She left the door hanging open, too afraid of the noise that shutting it might make, and crept forward from the car, staying low to the ground, sticking to the belt of trees that provided shadow cover.

Instead of climbing over the gate to get into the paddock, she slunk around behind the tack room and carefully, slowly, climbed over the wire paddock fence, using the wooden fence batons to balance herself. She landed lightly on the other side of the fence and there was a twang as a wire snapped back after being stretched by her foot during the climb.

"What was that?" she heard a voice say in the darkness, not more than ten metres away from her.

"What was what?" Another voice was talking now. "Probably just a possum. Don't worry about that, come over here. I finally caught that damn horse. Let's get her on to the float."

The field was suddenly lit up as the headlights of the white van were turned on, and Issie could see the two men clearly. One of them, the one with the beard, was leading a horse. Her horse!

Into the shining white beams of the headlights now stepped Blaze. Even from this far away Issie could see the whites of her eyes showing with fear. Her ears, normally pricked forward with excitement, were flat back against her head. As the man led her up to the ramp of the horse float she jerked back violently on the lead rope, trying desperately to back away.

"Stand still, you pig!" The man yanked the rope furiously, startling Blaze even further. "Stand still or I'll take the stick to you!"

He bent down to the side of the horse float, and when he stood up again Issie could see that he held a length of thick black rubber pipe in his hand. As he turned Blaze around to face the ramp of the float once more he lifted the rubber pipe in the air and brought it down hard and fast on the mare's flank.

Blaze let out a frightened squeal and jumped forward, not up the ramp of the horse float as the man had hoped, but out to the side of it. As she landed, her right hind leg caught on the edge of the ramp, grazing against it, and when she turned to face the ramp again Issie could see that she was bleeding. A steady trickle of dark red ran down her white hind sock.

"Give us a hand with this beast!" the fat, bearded

man yelled to his mate who was sitting in the front cab of the white van waiting to drive off.

"Can't you sort it out yourself?" the skinny one whined as he came around the back of the horse float to help.

"Stand there!" the bearded man instructed, pointing to the side of the horse-float ramp. "That way, she won't be able to escape to one side; she'll have no choice but to go on the float."

He turned Blaze again. This time as he went to lead her back towards the float, the chestnut mare reared up, pulling the lead rope almost out of his grip.

"That's it!" the man screamed with fury. "You're going on this float right now, or you're going to get the beating you deserve." He circled Blaze one more time, then, driving her towards the float, he lifted up the black length of pipe and brought it crashing down on her rump.

The final blow was too much for Issie to bear. She started to run forward, opened her mouth to shout out at the two men, to scream at them and make them stop hurting her horse. But before she could get a word out a hand covered her face from behind, and she felt the crushing weight of someone on top of her tackling her to the ground.

Issie tried to scream, but no sound could come out: her voice was stifled by the hand across her face.

"Shhh, shhh. It's OK. It's me," Avery growled in her ear. "Listen. I know you want to help Blaze, but this isn't the way. Stay where you are, stay quiet and trust me. Can you do that?"

Issie nodded mutely and Avery slowly removed his hand from her mouth. Together, the pair of them stayed on their bellies, lying flat on the ground and watched as Blaze, finally tired of the fight, placed one hoof after the other on to the ramp of the horse float and walked on board.

"Got her!" the bearded one said gleefully as he lifted up the tailgate behind her and closed the ramp, bolting Blaze in.

"Let's roll," he said to his friend, and the two men clambered back into the cab of the white van, ready to set off with their prize.

"Avery! We can't let them get away with this. We've got to stop them now!" Issie was almost in tears. The police hadn't arrived and these men had all but got away. They had to do something. She looked across at Avery who, strangely, had a sly smile on his face.

"Don't worry," he said, "they're not going far."

A minute passed, then another and another and still the two men in the white van didn't move. Then a door opened and Issie could hear the bearded man shouting, "The keys! The keys! How could you lose our keys? Well, come on, they've got to be here somewhere. Start looking!"

Issie looked at Avery in disbelief. "Tom, you didn't…"

Avery grinned and produced a set of shining silver car keys from his pocket. "I nicked them out of the ignition while the thin chap was helping to load Blaze into the float," he smirked. "They won't be getting far without these. Now all we have to do is wait for the police to turn up and…"

"Oh, Tom," Issie sighed, "that's the problem. I'm not sure that…"

Issie was about to explain the mobile drama when there was a sudden blare of a siren behind them and a flash of blue and red light. Two police cars had pulled up, blocking the exit at the paddock gate.

"The police!" Issie yelled. "They did get my message. They've come." Before Avery could say anything she was up off the ground and sprinting towards the police car.

With a sense of total relief, Issie watched as the rear door of the police car opened. She was about to blurt out the whole situation, explain to the police that they had to arrest these horse thieves who were trying to take her Blaze away. But as the figure emerged from the car, she found herself lost for words.

The person that stepped out of the police car wasn't a uniformed officer at all. It was her mother.

CHAPTER 14

It was five a.m. by the time they all arrived back at Avery's farm house. Mrs Brown headed straight for the kitchen. "I think we could all do with a nice hot mug of tea," she said, "and once I've sorted that out, Isadora, you've got some explaining to do."

Issie sighed and collapsed on to Avery's living room sofa. At first, when she had seen her mother emerge from the police car she had been relieved. But relief had quickly turned to terror when she realised that she still hadn't told her about Blaze. Her mum was right. She did have some explaining to do.

Mrs Brown reappeared from the kitchen now, with

three great steaming mugs of tea and some shortbread biscuits. "Is Tom back yet?" she asked her daughter.

"He shouldn't be much longer," Issie said. "He just had to give the police a few more details and then he was allowed to leave."

It already seemed as if they had been at the River Paddock for ever that evening. Once the police had arrived and the horse thieves had been taken away, Issie and Avery had been left with a young constable to answer some questions. Then they had been able to unlatch the horse float and let Blaze back out again.

The chestnut mare was naturally a little upset after her ordeal. Issie had taken her for a walk to calm her down and it was during the walk that she noticed Blaze was lame. She was favouring her right hind leg, the one that had been injured on the horse-float ramp. Issie had put an antiseptic on the cut, and wrapped the wound in a soft bandage to keep it clean. Then she had put antiseptic cream on the two deep gashes on Blaze's rump caused by the blows with the black rubber pipe. Finally, she had mixed Blaze up a special late-night supper – a mix of oats, hard feed and pony pellets with a wedge of hay on the side – and put her in the pen near the tack room so she couldn't do her leg any more damage overnight.

All of this time her mother had sat quietly in Avery's Range Rover waiting for her. But Issie knew that eventually her mum's patience would run out and it would be time to answer a few questions.

"Ah, excellent! Tea!" Avery stepped through the door, shedding his heavy jacket and boots in the corner of the kitchen. "Well done, Mrs B."

"I don't mind making the tea, Tom," Mrs Brown said, "as long as you don't mind explaining what you and my daughter were doing at that horse paddock in the middle of the night."

"Well," Avery began, "I've been talking to the police and it turns out that those two chaps they've caught are in fact Blaze's owners. That is, the ones that were mistreating her when the horse protection society found her. They must have seen Issie out riding on her and realised it was their horse and tried to steal her back again. Of course they've got no legal right to her. A complaint has already been lodged against them for what they did to Blaze and by rights they'll never be allowed to own any horse ever again. Although I'm still not completely convinced that they ever really owned one in the first place," he added.

"Blaze's bloodlines seem to be Anglo-Arab and I wouldn't be surprised if she's worth a lot of money..." Avery mused "...a lot of money. In fact, she's such a valuable mare, I suspect those men had already stolen her from someone else before we found her and saved her. I got the police to check their records to see if there had been a report of a horse theft that fits Blaze's description, but there was nothing on file.

"Naturally I told the officer that we'll be pressing charges over this whole matter. Horse thieves are bad enough, but people who abuse their horses are even worse," Avery growled.

"I'm sorry," Mrs Brown looked puzzled, "I still don't understand. What does all this have to do with Isadora?"

"Well," Avery said, failing to notice Issie making frantic gestures at him, "Blaze is her horse of course! She's done a fantastic job nursing her back to health after we recovered her from those criminals."

"Is that true, Isadora?" Mrs Brown looked at her daughter.

"I was going to tell you, Mum, honest," Issie pleaded, "only you were still angry at me for getting my belly button pierced. And then after that the time never seemed quite right. And then after I'd left it for a while, I didn't know how to bring it up. I mean, what could I say? I've owned a horse for three months now without mentioning it to you?"

"What?" Avery sputtered. "You mean you never told your mother about Blaze? Mrs B! I'm so sorry. I never bothered to tell you myself because I assumed that Issie had asked you and it was all OK..."

"Of course you did, Tom. Don't worry. It's not your fault. You, on the other hand," she exclaimed, turning to Issie, "I can't believe you! What if something had happened to you while you were out riding? Horses are dangerous, Isadora. You don't just charge off by yourself to go riding without telling me!

"And speaking of charging off..." Mrs Brown looked suspicious. "How did you get here in the middle of the night anyway? And how did you know those men would choose tonight to try to steal the horse?"

A chill passed over Issie. Mystic! Where was he? She

had left him outside in the driveway just next to the stables when she came to find Avery. The horse must have trotted off across the courtyard into the shadows by the stable block as Issie ran for the front door. And she hadn't seen him since. Now, sitting here in a brightly-lit living room, sipping tea and talking to her mum, she knew how ridiculous it would sound if she told the truth. The truth. That her horse, the horse that was supposed to be dead, had come to her bedroom window and warned her of danger. That she had ridden him bareback in pitch blackness halfway across town to catch the thieves, and that she now had no idea where he was, that he had disappeared.

"I rode, umm... I rode my bike here," Issie replied weakly, looking down into her tea cup.

"In the middle of the night? All the way across town? Issie, you could have been hit by a car!" Mrs Brown let out an exasperated gasp. "Look, I'm too tired to even begin discussing this here and now. We'll get to the bottom of it all tomorrow. Right now I think we should be getting home to try and get some sleep before it starts getting light." She stood up and passed her half-finished tea back to Avery.

"Thanks for the tea, Tom. We'll come back in the morning to pick up Isadora's bike, and I'll talk to you then about what is to be done with this horse that you've given my daughter." She paused. "Not too early in the morning, though; I imagine we'll all want a bit of a sleep-in after this. It isn't every night I get a wake-up call from the police dragging me out of bed at three a.m. and hopefully," she turned and frowned at Isadora, "I won't be getting any more calls in future."

Thankfully, Mrs Brown seemed content to let the whole Blaze affair drop during the car ride home. And after the evening's excitement Issie was grateful to slink off to her bedroom. She found herself falling asleep the moment her head hit the pillow. But instead of sleeping in, she was up again just a couple of hours later as soon as the dawn light came flooding in her window. In the dark last night it had been hard to tell just how serious Blaze's injuries really were. And with the one-day event now just a few days away she had to find out whether her horse was still fit enough to compete.

Of course there was another reason for getting up early. Last night Issie had lied to her mum, telling her that she rode her bike around to Avery's house. She could hardly tell her mother the truth, that she had galloped there bareback on a ghost horse in the middle of the night. In fact, she didn't even know if she believed the truth herself.

No, in this case it was definitely better to tell a white lie. The problem was, Mrs Brown was expecting to go around to Avery's later this morning and pick up the bike. The very same bike that was already parked exactly where it had been all along – right here at home in the corner of the garage.

The solution, Issie decided, was to leave her mum a note saying that she was walking over to Avery's to pick the bike up by herself. Then, instead of going to Winterflood Farm, she would cycle straight down to the horse paddock, check on Blaze and cycle home again.

Issie was feeling smug about her plan as she walked down the stairs to the front door. Until she saw her mother nursing a cup of coffee and flicking through the paper at the kitchen table.

"Up already?" Mrs Brown spotted her daughter heading for the door. "I'll put on some toast for you and make you a cup of tea and then we can go and pick up your bike."

"Ummm, thanks, Mum." Issie sat down reluctantly. Her plan was already falling apart and she hadn't even left the house yet!

"Isadora," her mother began, "I know I should be mad at you for what happened last night. God knows I should be furious that you've been riding this horse all this time and not telling me about it! But..." she paused to pour hot water into the teapot, "I guess in a way I can understand it. After the way I reacted to your belly-button thingamy-gig it's no wonder you were too scared to tell me about Blaze."

She sat down now and faced her daughter.

"I'm not saying that you were right to tear off and get your body pierced without telling me. Or worse yet, get a horse and fail to mention it for months! But maybe if I hadn't overreacted about that ring in your tummy. Or maybe if your father was still here..." Mrs Brown took her daughter's hand. "Issie, I know that since your dad left things have been tough, but we're getting on OK, aren't we? I'm on your side, remember that. I want you to feel that you can tell me anything, honey, OK?"

Issie nodded. Anything. Yeah right. She was sure "anything" didn't include going for midnight gallops on ghost horses. Still, her mother had a point.

"I do, Mum. And I'm sorry." Issie held her breath. *Might as well ask now*, she thought. "If you're not mad at me does that mean I can keep Blaze?"

"Well, if you've really managed to do such great things with her the way Tom says you have, I don't see how we have any choice." Mrs Brown smiled. "She must be a beautiful horse if those men wanted her so badly they were willing to steal her."

"She's perfect!" Issie glowed. And she started to tell her mother about how difficult Blaze had been to begin with, and how she had won her trust, and how the pair of them had been training for the one-day event.

"It's this weekend, so I hope Blaze's leg will heal in time. That's why I want to go down to the horse paddock this morning and check on her," Issie explained.

"What about your bike?" Mrs Brown said. "We can pick it up from Tom's on the way to the paddock."

"No!" Issie squawked. "I mean, if you drop me at the paddock I'll walk up to Winterflood Farm after I'm finished with Blaze and then I can ride the bike home."

"Well, OK. If that's what you'd prefer," Mrs Brown agreed.

And so, that afternoon Issie found herself walking the long roads back home from the horse paddock to her house, pretending to return a bike that was already safely locked up where it had always been, in the garage at her house.

At least, she thought to herself as she trudged along, *at least Blaze's wound seems to be healing well.* In fact when she had checked on the chestnut mare she seemed to be in fine spirits and was hardly favouring her injured leg at all. The chances were she would be well enough to compete at the one-day event. But with just days left, and lameness ruining their chances of fitting in any more training sessions, the question remained – was Blaze ready to go out there and win?

CHAPTER 15

In front of the green canvas marquee a crowd was beginning to gather. The judges had posted the dressage scores on a large whiteboard on the side of the tent and the riders were jostling about, trying to see over one another's heads, to check out how well they had done.

Stella, who had already pushed her way to the front of the crowd, peered hard at the board. "Let's see," she said, "novice dressage tests, group three... now where are we..." Her eyes scanned the board and then suddenly she let out a whoop of delight. "Issie, Issie," she yelled, racing across the field towards the area where the horse trucks were parked.

Issie was busily bandaging Blaze's tendons in preparation for the cross-country when she heard Stella hollering out her name.

"Issie! You'll never believe it," Stella panted with exhaustion as she reached her friend. "I'm coming fourth out of the whole novice class. Fourth place in dressage – can you believe it?"

Before Issie had a chance to answer Stella was off again, "And that's not all. Guess what? You're coming second! Isn't that cool?"

"I don't believe it!" Issie was stunned. "Do you hear that, girl?" she said to Blaze, who was busy making short work of her breakfast hay net. "We're in second place."

After all they had been through in the past week, Issie was amazed to be here at all. Yesterday the vet had arrived at the River Paddock, given Blaze's hind leg a final checkup and pronounced her perfectly sound. And today, here they were – riding at their first one-day event.

This morning in the dressage ring Blaze and Issie had managed to put the past week behind them and performed a perfect test. Even so, Issie could scarcely have hoped for such a result. After all, there were nearly sixty riders here today competing in her class.

"Did you see who's coming first?" Issie asked the overexcited Stella.

"You're not going to believe this one either," Stella groaned. "It's Natasha. She's in first place on fifty-nine points. You're right behind her on sixty-one."

Issie was puzzled. "How come I'm behind her if I've got more points?"

"Man, you really are green at this game, aren't you?" Stella giggled. "The winning dressage rider is the one with the *lowest* score. You take each dressage score and you add the faults that the rider gets in the cross-country and then the faults from the showjumping, and the one with the lowest score at the end of it all is the winner.

"The dressage score is important," Stella continued, "but it's the cross-country that is crucial. You get twenty faults for every refusal and sixty faults if you fall off. It doesn't matter how good your dressage score is if you have to add sixty faults to it! The showjumping isn't so tough – it's just five faults for every rail.

"So," Stella grinned at her friend, "all you've got to do now is go clear on the cross-country and the showjumping and you're in the running for a ribbon."

"Yeah, right," Issie joked, "two clear rounds? That sounds really easy – not!"

"We'll see about that." Avery's voice behind her caught her off-guard. "Come on, girls. Tie your horses up and let's get a move on and walk the course."

Walking the cross-country course was a crucial part of the one-day event, and earlier that day Avery had offered to take Issie and Stella around the fences on foot, pointing out the different angles and approaches for the fences and the best way to handle each obstacle. However, she hadn't counted on the fact that Dan and Ben would be coming with them as well.

As Avery's students set off towards the first fence of the course, Dan slowed down so that he and Issie were walking together at the back of the group.

"Hey, Issie!" Dan seemed excited to see her. "I heard all about what happened with you and Blaze. Pretty freaky stuff, huh? It sounds like you and Avery were real heroes, catching those guys like that."

"Mmmm…" Issie tried to act casual. Inside, she

was dying to tell Dan all about how they saved Blaze from the horse thieves. But she was still in a huff with Dan over the whole Natasha thing so she felt obliged to give him the silent treatment instead.

"Are you OK, Issie?" Dan's cheery tone was beginning to slip a little. "I mean, I know you must have been pretty busy over the past week or so but I was kind of hoping you would come along to Summer in the Park with me."

"With you and Natasha, you mean!" Issie snapped and then realised what she had done. *Ohmygod*, she thought. *Now Dan will realise that I'm jealous of him and Natasha. This is so embarrassing...*

"Gather round, everyone, let's check out jump number one." Avery interrupted her thoughts as he drew their attention to the first fence, a rustic wooden rail that stood around eighty centimetres high and was strung with old car tyres.

"This is a simple fence, with a clean take-off and landing point," Avery briefed them. "What I want you to concentrate on here is getting a smooth stride happening. Your horse should already be in a steady cross-country gallop. I want you to check them a few strides out and bring them back to a strong canter, then pop over it and pick up the pace again. It shouldn't give you any trouble."

"Issie," Dan whispered in her ear as Avery kept talking, "Issie, I think you have the wrong idea about Natasha and me."

No use trying to act cool about this now, Issie thought to herself; Dan knew what she was thinking. "Well, if you mean that Natasha is your girlfriend, I think I've got the right idea," Issie muttered back.

"Girlfriend!" Dan squeaked. "No way! Issie, I only took Natasha to Summer in the Park because her mum asked my mum if I would take her along. I mean, they've only just moved to Chevalier Point and, well, I know Natasha can come across as really snobby, but I think maybe that's just because she's got no friends here and she's afraid of us because we're all so close and we all get on so well… Well," he added glumly, "at least I thought we did, but lately I'm not so sure. You won't even talk to me."

"Jump number two, quite a wide ditch, this one," Avery explained. "Your horse is likely to take off too soon and bunny hop across, so keep your legs on…"

But Issie wasn't listening. Her head was buzzing now. So Dan wasn't interested in Natasha after all!

"I'm sorry if I haven't been myself lately." Issie smiled at Dan, taking in his thick waves of blond hair and soft blue eyes. "I guess I've just been really worried about things – you know with Blaze nearly being stolen and everything. But yes, of course we're friends. And maybe you're right about Natasha," she added, "but I'm still not so sure. She seems pretty stuck-up to me."

With the misunderstanding cleared up, Issie and Dan walked the rest of the course in silence, concentrating on Avery's advice.

"Now this is truly a natural obstacle." Avery grinned as they neared the end of the course. Issie found herself standing at the edge of a deep gully with steep banks on either side. To enter the gully, riders had to jump over a large fallen tree, and then immediately after the tree the ground fell away steeply so that the horses literally slid down a muddy slope until they reached the bottom of the gulch, where another fence was constructed out of oil drums. The horses would have to leap over the drums before cantering back up the other side of the mud bank, taking the post-and-rails fence that sat at the top of the ridge.

"I'd like you to slow down to a trot coming into this one," Avery said. "The fallen tree is a quite a big spread, but the horses should be able to jump it at a trot, and approaching at a slow pace will give them enough time to realise that there's a steep bank behind the fence – so they don't spook at the last minute. Then, once you're over the tree, all you really need to do is hang on. The horses will be moving pretty fast down the muddy bank and they'll have no trouble with the oil drums. Then they'll power back up the other side and take the post and rails. They'll really be flying by them, so hang on."

It made Issie nervous to see that the ambulance van, which was always present at events like this one, had parked itself at the top of the gully next to the fallen tree. "They must be expecting some crashes here." She nudged Dan and pointed towards the white van. He nodded in agreement.

"After the hollow, the trick will be calming them down again and getting them back into stride to take the next fence," Avery explained as he approached the cotton reels.

The cotton reels were a row of huge wooden spools that looked like they might once have been part of a giant's sewing kit. Issie didn't know what they had really been used for, but she guessed they were from a construction yard or something. They were big – she knew that much. And the horses would have to jump clean over them.

"Finally, we have the bank," Avery said, turning his attention to the last fence, a high grassy mound that the horses had to jump up on to, then canter along for two strides before jumping a fence that dropped away dramatically to ground level.

"By now your horses will be dead tired," Avery continued, "so don't thrash them by racing for the finish flags. By all means, keep your speed up to try and avoid time faults, but don't exhaust your mounts. Remember, there's still the showjumping to come after this."

Back at the horse truck Issie took out Avery's prized flat-seat saddle and began to tack Blaze up in preparation for the cross-country. The mare knew that today was special somehow. The sight of the horse floats and trucks and the noise of the loud speaker had her keyed up and she danced as Issie tried to do up her girth.

"Easy, girl, you'll get the chance to show them how good you are any minute now," Issie whispered to her horse.

She swung herself into the saddle and was adjusting the competition number attached to her back protector when Stella rode over to see her.

"I was just down at the judges tent and it looks like Natasha has gone clear on the cross-country. No faults! Can you believe it? You'll have to get a clear round now if you want to keep up."

"Thanks heaps," Issie groaned, "that's just what I need, Stella – more pressure. I'm nervous enough as it is."

"Competitor number thirty-eight please, number thirty-eight." Issie looked down at the number on her chest. "That's me. Wish me luck," Issie said. But she was too nervous to hear Stella's reply.

"Are you ready? Lining up now… five, four, three, two, one… go!" The starter's gun sounded and Issie felt the chestnut mare leap out from underneath her and instantly break into a gallop, her long stride devouring the ground. She let Blaze run on until the first fence was in sight, then she eased her back, collecting her into a canter. Blaze gave an indignant snort and popped over the tyres as if they were barely there, moving swiftly back into a gallop again.

Riding crouched over her neck, Issie felt the rush of speed, the power of the horse beneath her. At the ditch, Issie was cautious again and slowed Blaze down, but the mare popped over it with ease.

The next fence was a three-barred gate stuffed with dried brush. Issie heard the thick rasp of the branches scraping against Blaze's bell boots as they breezed over it. She gave the mare her head and let her gallop on to the next part of the course.

As they tackled fence after fence without missing a stride Issie's confidence grew. Not only was Blaze's leg completely healed, the horse seemed to thrill at the chance to run. So much so that it was tempting to let her have her head as they approached the gully. Still, Issie remembered Avery's advice and pulled hard on the reins, easing Blaze back to a steady trot so that she had time to get a good look at the fence.

They were still a good few strides out from the jump when Blaze spooked. Issie lost a stirrup and was nearly thrown out of the saddle as her horse lurched suddenly to the left.

"Come on, girl, what's wrong?" Issie kicked her on, hauling on the right rein at the same time to get Blaze back on track. But it was no use. Blaze was in a state, highly-strung and confused, not listening to Issie's aids. The mare trotted up skittishly towards the jump, then spooked again at the last minute and came to a dead stop.

Issie couldn't believe it. A refusal would cost them twenty faults! Not only that, but now Blaze was standing there in front of the jump all wild-eyed and trembling with fear. What on earth was wrong with her?

As she tried to calm her horse, Issie's mind began to

race. Why was Blaze so terrified? It wasn't the fence, she was sure of that. Blaze had taken jumps just like this one before without any trouble. No, she decided. Something else had scared her horse – and it was still spooking her now. And if Issie didn't figure it out quickly her chances of winning the one-day event were doomed.

CHAPTER 16

As Blaze stood trembling in front of the fence, Issie looked up at the white ambulance van parked at the top of the ditch and suddenly everything clicked into place.

It was a white van. A van just like the one the men had used when they had tried to steal Blaze. Of course! It wasn't the fence that had spooked the horse but her fear of the white van that had made her refuse the jump.

Issie circled her horse away from the fallen tree now, talking softly to her, "It's OK, Blaze, no one's going to hurt you." She spoke calmly and gently.

Issie knew that normally when a horse is afraid of something the best thing to do is confront their fear. If she gave Blaze the chance to check the van out thoroughly, eventually she would no longer be afraid of it. But right now there was no time for that solution.

Instead, Issie turned to take the fence again, this time aiming her horse at a sharp angle, so that she was facing away from the van.

Approaching the jump on the diagonal wasn't easy, and it also meant taking Blaze down the slipperiest part of the slope, but Issie knew it was the only way.

With the white ambulance out of her line of sight, Blaze was a different horse. She leapt easily over the fallen tree and powered down the hill, over the oil drums and up and out the other side over the post and rails. "Good girl." Issie gave her a firm slap on her sweaty neck.

Blaze was back in good spirits, all memories of the white van were put behind her. Now there were only two fences to go.

At the cotton reels, she flew over the jump with almost half a metre to spare and it was all that Issie could do to slow her down in time to take the grassy bank.

Riding up the bank, Issie tried to remember to sit well back in the saddle, then lean back as Blaze leapt off into midair to land on the ground below.

And then they were racing, Issie leaning low over Blaze's neck and pushing her home through the finish flags.

"Oh, well done, girl, well done!" Issie was thrilled. Blaze's fright at the sight of the white van had cost them dearly. Twenty faults for a refusal. But they had been going so fast around the course they had no time penalties in spite of their delay at the gully. And with the showjumping still to come, maybe they stood a chance of a ribbon – if they could make it a clear round.

As the totals went up on the scoreboard for the cross-country Issie was amazed. It looked like hardly any of the other riders had managed a clear round either. Even with twenty faults, her chances of a ribbon looked good. In fact she was still in second place – only Natasha had gone clear on the cross-country to stay ahead of her. Poor Stella had had three refusals at the cotton reels and had retired on Coco. She was too depressed to come with Issie to check out the scores and was back at the horse truck giving Coco a good brush down before rugging her up. Her disastrous cross-country meant that she wouldn't be riding in the showjumping.

The first competitors for the showjumping phase were beginning to warm up now, and it wouldn't be long until they entered the ring. Issie looked across at the showjumps and saw Natasha leaning up against the rails, waiting to see how the other competitors tackled the course before she too began to warm up.

The sight of Natasha filled Issie with dread. She wanted to hide – to duck out of sight behind the horse floats and avoid her. But then she remembered what Dan had said about Natasha not being mean really, just lonely. So she decided to do the grown-up thing and go over and say hi.

"Hey there, Natasha." Issie smiled. "It looks like

you and Goldrush have been having a good day; you've got the top score so far."

Natasha turned around and gave Issie a snooty look. "I'm sorry? Do I know you?" she said vaguely, acting like she had never met Issie before. Her lips curled up in a wicked smile. "Oh yeeesss," she purred, giving Issie the once-over as if she were being asked to give her points out of ten for her appearance. "You're that girl from the pony club, aren't you? The one with the scruffy chestnut. What are you doing here?"

Issie couldn't believe it. Why was she even bothering with this snob? *Keep calm*, she told herself. *Remember, she's only trying to be mean because she feels insecure. Remember she's new in town and she has no friends.*

"I'm riding actually," Issie said, trying to keep her smile fixed to her face. "In fact, I'm coming second to you. We had a little problem on the cross-country. Blaze got spooked at the top of the gully and we had a refusal and got twenty faults."

"Mmmm?" said Natasha. She clearly couldn't be bothered talking to Issie at all and was looking away now to watch the next competitor enter the ring.

"Well, sounds like you need to get a decent horse, don't you? Or maybe some riding lessons."

And with that, she turned back to watch the showjumping, leaving Issie standing with her mouth hanging wide open.

"I mean, just because her mother buys her some flash horse doesn't make her such a great rider!" Issie fumed to Stella. The pair of them were back at the horse truck now and Issie was tacking up for the showjumping.

"A decent horse? And she called Blaze scruffy. Scruffy! She's got such a nerve! I should have told her that Blaze was actually part Arab and she's probably worth more than she paid for silly old Goldrush anyway. Oh, who cares! She doesn't even really like horses, you know. And no wonder she doesn't have any friends. I should never have listened to Dan. I don't know how he can even put up with her for a minute!"

"Issie, Issie calm down." Stella laughed. "It's nearly your turn for the showjumping. Shouldn't you be taking Blaze over a few practice jumps instead of worrying about Stuck-up Tucker?" Stella glanced across at the show ring. "Hey," she said to Issie, "wait a minute. It's Natasha's turn now."

"She hasn't knocked down four rails, has she?" Issie was sulking, refusing to look. "Because that's how many points she needs to lose before I'll beat her."

"Umm, no... but..." Stella said. "Oh, oh wait a minute. Ohmygod!"

"What? What is it? What's happening?" Issie had completely forgotten about her sulk and stopped what she was doing to join Stella.

In the showjumping ring, Natasha was far from her usual smug self. Goldrush had refused at the green gate twice now, and as she turned her a third time to face the fence, giving her a thwack across the rump with her crop, the palomino reared up, promptly dumping Natasha on the ground.

"You brute!" Natasha screamed, still hanging on to the reins with one hand and making a lunge across the ground to pick up the riding crop with the other.

Goldrush backed away from her, snorting with fear, but Natasha hung on to her and, with the crop in her fist, she raised her hand high above Goldrush's head and prepared to bring the whip down. "That's the last time you do that to me, you useless animal!" Natasha cried as she brought the whip down hard.

But before the riding crop could connect with its target, a large hand was wrapped around Natasha's arm, holding her back. "And that's the last time you hit a horse, young lady. You're disqualified," Tom Avery said. "Now come with me to the judges' tent. I'm sure they'd like to discuss this bad-tempered performance with you in person."

"Competitor number thirty-eight into the ring please," the announcer's voice came over the loud speaker. At the far end of the practice paddock Issie popped Blaze one last time over the practice jump and then cantered towards the gate.

With Natasha out of the competition, Issie was in the lead, but there was no room for even a single mistake. Knocking down just one rail would lose her five points and drop her back all the way to third place. Two rails would cost her ten points and she'd lose out on a ribbon entirely. No, it had to be a clear round or nothing.

At fence one it looked like it was going to be nothing! Forgetting Avery's constant advice to remember to ride at the first fence seriously, she approached the jump far too slow, not really concentrating on it, and Blaze almost baulked. Luckily the fence wasn't huge and the chestnut mare was so honest she took the jump anyway, leaping like a jack rabbit almost from a standstill, flinging Issie back in the saddle.

The fright at fence one woke Issie's ideas up. She collected Blaze up into a bouncy canter and rode hard at the second fence, clearing it perfectly. Then came a double with a bounce stride, and Issie had to check Blaze hard to slow her down so she wouldn't rush the fences.

With a clear round so far and only two fences to go, Issie was sick with nerves as they approached the green gate where Goldrush had been eliminated. The gate was the biggest fence on the course. There were two slender potted conifers standing on either side of it and the jump was so tall it was almost as big as the trees themselves. It had to be nearly one metre twenty, Issie decided. It was almost the biggest fence she had ever faced.

"Still not as high as that gate between the River Paddocks though, eh, girl?" Issie murmured to Blaze. She tightened her grip on the reins, sat back hard in the saddle and pushed the chestnut mare on. Blaze flew over the jump, flicking her heels up beautifully so that she didn't even touch the poles. Then over the last fence and through the finish flags. A clear round.

"Oh, Issie, you did it!" Stella came racing up as Issie emerged from the ring. "Wasn't Blaze fantastic? Just the best!" Stella was bubbling with excitement. She took Blaze by the reins and led the mare back towards the truck as Issie walked alongside them, still feeling a little stunned by her own success.

"Well, well. Who would have thought that my groom would be such a star?" Issie turned around to see Dan smiling at her. "Seriously, Issie, congratulations. It was a brilliant bit of riding..." he said. He was about to say something more when Issie heard her name being shouted out across the field.

"Isadora! Isadora!" Issie's mum had her hands full

with a tea thermos, an umbrella and a blanket, most of which got dropped on the grass as she ran up to her daughter.

"Oh, well done, sweetheart!" she said, letting everything in her arms tumble to the ground now as she embraced Issie in a huge bear hug.

"And well done, Blaze!" Mrs Brown said, and she reached out a careful hand to give the mare a tender pat on the nose.

"Mum!" Issie was shocked. "I thought you didn't like horses?"

Mrs Brown looked her daughter in the eyes. "Oh, Issie, I still don't like horses. When I think of all the danger that you've been through over the past few months…" she sighed. "But I know that you love them," she turned to the little chestnut, "so I guess that means Blaze and I are going to have to be friends, aren't we, girl?"

She stepped forward to give the horse another nervous pat and Blaze, eagerly anticipating that she might be in for a treat, gave Mrs Brown a vigorous, snuffly nudge with her nose. Issie's mum jumped back with a shriek and everyone else burst out laughing.

"She just wants a carrot, Mrs B – I think she likes you!" Dan was smirking.

"Well," said Mrs Brown, smiling back now, "I guess after today's performance she deserves one. Now hurry up and get back on," she told her daughter. "You don't want to be late for the prize-giving, do you?"

Blaze was still wearing her winner's ribbon when Issie unloaded her from the horse truck back at the River Paddock later that evening. The deep red satin sash was knotted around her neck, with its gold fringing dangling down.

"You look like a proper Arab now, all dressed up with gold fringes," Issie teased the mare. But there was some truth in what she said. Blaze didn't even resemble the sickly pony that Issie had adopted three months ago. This was a horse in her prime and her fine bloodlines were finally in full evidence, from the high arch of her graceful neck to the soft dish of her face with its pure white blaze.

"You're so beautiful, I can hardly believe you're

mine," Issie whispered into Blaze's neck as she gave her a hug, undoing the sash at the same time and shoving it into the pocket of her riding jacket.

"Pretty exciting, eh? Winning your first one-day event?" Avery's voice behind her startled her.

"I guess so," Issie said, "but after all we've been through in the past few weeks I think I've had enough excitement. Mostly I'm just glad that Blaze is OK."

Avery ran his hand down the mare's hind leg. "That wound seems to be completely healed. You probably won't even be able to see the scar, Issie."

He looked back up at his star pupil.

"That night of the horse thieves, there's something I'm still puzzled about," Avery said. "I know you told your mother that you had cycled to my house. But I'm sure I didn't see your bike in my driveway. Besides, how did you know they were going to try to steal Blaze in the first place? Issie, do you want to explain to me what really happened that night?"

Issie smiled. "I've been going over and over it in my mind, and no, I can't explain it. At least not yet. I'm not even really sure I understand it myself."

Avery nodded, "Well, if you ever want someone

to talk to, give me a try. I bet you'll find me more understanding than you think."

After Avery had loaded off the other horses, he backed the truck out the gate and left Issie alone in the paddock with Blaze.

Even though she ached all over and was dying for a hot bath, Issie knew she had to take care of her horse before she could finally go home. In the tack room she scooped out four big handfuls of pony pellets and mixed in some oats and a little chaff. Then she grabbed Blaze's cover off a hook on the wall.

As the chestnut mare ate her dinner, Issie did up the cover straps and unbandaged Blaze's legs. Then when she'd finished the last of her food, Issie slipped the halter off her slender head and let her loose.

"Typical!" Issie grinned as Blaze trotted off, her nose trailing the ground, heading straight to the dustiest patch in the paddock to have a good roll. Dropping to her knees, Blaze gave a satisfied grunt, then a series of ecstatic groans as she rolled from one side to the other, getting herself covered in thick dirt in the process.

Standing up again, the mare shook herself and a cloud of dust rose off her cover. There were clumps of grass stuck in her mane.

"Oh, Blaze," Issie sighed, "it'll take me hours to groom that out!"

But Blaze wasn't listening. She had headed off down the paddock in a high-stepping trot, her head held erect. Issie watched as the mare let out a shrill whinny, looking for paddock mates. She was surprised when she heard another whinny in reply.

The whinny rang out across the paddock and then, at the far end of the field, down by the river, Issie saw him. A grey horse. Not a big horse, no more than fourteen hands probably. Light grey, with his dapples faded from old age. As he whinnied again, Blaze lifted her head and broke into a canter, running to him.

Issie watched in silence as the two horses began to run together. Over the past few weeks she had begun to think that maybe Mystic was her guardian angel. Now, as she saw her two horses together, Issie wondered: was it really her that Mystic had been looking after? After all, it was Blaze's life that he had saved. Was it possible that horses could have guardian angels of their own?

"Don't worry, Mystic," Issie called out to him, "I'll take good care of her."

She turned her back on the horses and threw Blaze's halter over the handlebars of her bicycle. It was getting dark and it was a long ride home.

PONY 🐎 CLUB SECRETS

Blaze and the Dark Rider

For Michael

CHAPTER 1

The lights had gone out. In the gloom of the circus tent Issie looked around frantically for Stella and Kate. She edged forward in the blackness, feeling her way. "Ow! Watch where you're going!" a man snapped.

"Excuse me!" Issie winced – she had just stood on his foot.

What a nightmare! Trying to find your seat while keeping three ice-cream cones balanced in one hand was hard enough, and now it was too dark to see.

"Issie! Over here! Hurry up, the show is about to start!"

Issie looked ahead of her. Thank goodness! There

they were. She could just make out Stella's bright red curly hair. Stella and Kate were both waving excitedly at her. Issie waved back with her free hand then wriggled past another row, trying not to stand on any more toes.

"Excuse me! Excuse me!" She threw herself down into the empty seat next to Stella, Kate and her mum. Her friends quickly made a grab for their ice-cream cones before they fell out of Issie's hands.

"Oh, this is going to be great!" Stella whispered loudly. "Thanks for bringing us, Mrs Brown." She took a big lick of her ice cream and peered into the darkness, trying to see if anything was happening in the arena down below them.

"Mmmm, yup, thanks, Mrs Brown," said Kate, who was concentrating on eating and not getting her ice cream stuck in her long blonde hair.

"Yeah, Mum! This is the best birthday ever!" Issie beamed.

"Good grief! I've never seen you girls so worked up." Mrs Brown laughed. "I knew this would be a good surprise."

It was Issie's thirteenth birthday tomorrow. So she

wasn't at all suspicious when her mum suggested that they celebrate a day early by taking her best friends Stella and Kate to the movies. Then, in the car, Mrs Brown had produced tickets to El Caballo Danza Magnifico – the Magnificent Dancing Horses. The girls had screamed so loud that Mrs Brown threatened to pull the car over to the side of the road so that she could cover her ears. They hadn't calmed down since.

"Look!" Kate squeaked out. "I can see something happening down there. Here they come!"

Suddenly, there was a blinding glare as spotlights cast perfect circles on the sawdust floor of the arena below. Then the silence was broken by the clack-clack-clack of castanets, and the strumming of flamenco guitars over the loudspeakers. The twelve spotlights were circling now like searchlights. The guitars were getting louder.

The spotlights froze on the entrance to the arena and out came two rows of perfect white horses. Their manes, which were so long they hung down well below their necks, flowed like silk. Their tails trailed behind them like a bride's wedding train, snowy white and almost touching the ground. The twelve horses moved gracefully in pairs down the centre of the ring, trotting in perfect time to the clack-clacking of the castanets. Then they fanned out and moved to the side of the arena, each of them drawing to a halt, illuminated by their own spotlight.

In the full beam of the lights the horses were so white that they glowed like marble statues. Issie admired the high arch of their necks, and the classical shape of their head. These horses were Lipizzaners – the famed white horses used in the Spanish Riding School in Vienna, bred from the ancient bloodlines of six great sires.

The horses held themselves so proudly, they reminded Issie of those paintings of horses on the sides of Roman urns. Their riders, were dressed in classical military uniforms. On their heads the men wore curved black and gold hats with a bright red feather plume which stuck out the top.

The first rider took off his plumed hat now and bent his head to bow. As he did so, his horse dropped to one knee beneath him and bowed too. The girls clapped with glee as, all the way along both sides of the arena, each horse and rider bowed in turn until all twelve horses were down on one knee. Then, with a flourish of their hats, the riders pulled their horses up to a perfect square halt, wheeled them about on their hocks, and began to canter in formation around the ring.

"Oh! I like that one!" Stella whispered to Issie, pointing to the horses.

"Which one?" Mrs Brown laughed. "Stella, how can you even tell them apart? They all look the same to me."

"No, they don't!" Stella insisted. "The one on the end over there has a pretty face and the best mane."

"Are they girls or boys?" Mrs Brown asked.

"Mum, they're stallions. It says so in the programme," Issie groaned. Her mum knew nothing about horses.

Issie read aloud from the El Caballo Danza Magnifico programme on her lap. "The dancing stallions have all been trained in the classical art of *haute école* dressage. *Haute école* is an ancient form of horsemanship that was once used to train horses for battle. The horses of El Caballo Danza Magnifico have spent many years perfecting the Airs above Ground – movements that were used in warfare. They include the Courbette, the Levade and the Capriole…"

The horses in the ring fanned out once again and came to a halt in two precise rows down either side of the arena. The spotlights dimmed and then a single light was trained on the centre of the ring, where a horse now emerged riderless, accompanied by a trainer on the ground with a long whip.

Unlike the other horses, which were pure icy white, this stallion was a dapple-grey, with a long, thick grey mane, dark points on his legs, and dark smudgy circles around his eyes and his nose.

He looks a bit like Mystic, Issie thought to herself, and her smile suddenly faltered.

Mystic had been Issie's first pony and she had loved him more than anything in the world. She felt a special bond with the little grey gelding, more powerful than anything she had ever experienced before.

And then suddenly, tragically, Mystic had been killed. It was an accident. She knew that. They were trying to save three other horses – and they had saved them too – when Mystic had been hit by the truck that took his life. She also knew that if it weren't for Mystic's courage, she might easily have been killed.

Losing Mystic had been unbearable. Issie had

missed him so desperately. Since then, though, strange and exciting things had happened. Mystic had come back to her – not like a ghost, but like a real horse. He returned to help her save Blaze's life. And Issie knew that Mystic was still there, somehow. He was watching over Issie and her chestnut mare. Waiting, in case they needed him again.

Issie's mother looked across at her now and, seeing the look on her daughter's face, she reached over and took Issie's hand and gave it a gentle squeeze, as if to say, "Is something wrong?"

Issie smiled back and shook her head, banishing her gloomy thoughts. Now was not the time. This was her birthday. She was determined to have fun.

Down below them in the arena, the trainer positioned the grey horse in the centre of the ring and prepared him. He stood behind the horse's hindquarters, restraining him with a pair of long black leather reins which he held in his white gloved hands.

The music changed now from the brisk clacking of Spanish castanets to the dramatic strains of a classical orchestra. The horses on either side of the arena who had been standing perfectly still all this time suddenly wheeled on their hindquarters and cantered out of the arena leaving just the grey stallion and his handler standing there alone.

"This stallion you see before you is the purebred Lipizzaner Marius, with his trainer Wolfgang Herzog," the announcer's voice boomed over the loudspeaker. Wolfgang bowed low to the audience, and Marius let out a long, low snort as if he knew the announcer was talking about him.

"Marius and Wolfgang will now attempt the Courbette, the most difficult of all the High School Airs above Ground," the announcer continued. "The Courbette was used in warfare to protect the rider as the horse moved through enemy infantry. The horse must stand up and hop on his hind legs to protect his rider."

With that, Wolfgang spoke a single word to his horse and gripped the reins firmly as the stallion began to trot on the spot. The trainer spoke again now: short, sharp words in a foreign language that Issie didn't understand. But his horse clearly understood him. He snorted and gathered himself, moving forward across the ring in a series of elegant bunny hops, before rising up on his hind legs. Still rearing, he leapt forward now on his hind legs, springing across the arena like a bunny rabbit, his long grey tail thrashing the ground behind him as he leapt.

Issie, Stella and Kate clapped and cheered. The trainer took a low bow and then turned his horse once more to face the crowd.

"And now – the Capriole!" the announcer's voice had a dramatic boom. "This movement takes many years to perfect. Once again it was used in battle. The horse must leap in the air and kick out its hind legs to attack any enemies who might be approaching from behind."

Wolfgang steadied the stallion and spoke once more to him. Then he urged the grey horse forward on the long reins, halting him again suddenly and touching his hindquarters at the same time with the long whip. Marius jumped into the air like a ballerina and flung his hind legs out behind him. Issie gasped. It was as if the stallion was flying! He was suspended in mid air for a moment and Issie held her breath. Then the stallion landed down with a snort and turned to face the audience once more as Wolfgang took a long, low bow.

Issie, Stella and Kate whooped with delight.

"That was amazing!" Stella said as Marius and Wolfgang left the arena.

Issie opened her programme again. "The Dance of the Seven Veils is next," she told the others. "It says here that the riders perform the dance on Anglo-Arab mares…"

Snake charmer music started up and six spotlights shone on the arena as the dancing horses entered down the centre of the ring, following each other nose to tail and then pivoting on their hind legs and facing the audience. The riders were women this time, all dressed like belly dancers in Arabian Nights costumes made out of flowing chiffon. The girls wore harem pants instead of jodhpurs and veils covered their faces. Each of them wore a different colour and their throats and wrists sparkled with jewels that matched the colours of their outfits – emeralds, rubies, sapphires, aquamarines, gold and silver.

While the riders all looked different, their six horses matched so exactly you could have sworn they were clones of each other. They were all the same height, around fourteen-two, with deep liver chestnut coats, white socks and flaxen manes and tails. Their legs were as finely turned as ballet dancers, and their delicate Arab blood showed through in their arched necks and dished noses.

"Ohmygod!" Issie gasped. She stared at the horses, too shocked to speak. Then she turned to Stella. "Is it just me or do you see it too?"

Stella nodded, "Totally!"

"Issie," Kate said, "those horses... they all look just like Blaze!"

It was almost midnight by the time the audience had finally filed out of the pavilion after the show.

"Where is she?" Stella whined. She was standing by the doorway of the main tent with Kate and Mrs Brown. They were waiting for Issie, who, supposedly, had just popped off to the toilet, but was taking ages.

"Sorry I took so long!" Issie yelled out to them. She came running now, not from the direction of the toilets after all, but from the other side of the arena. A dark-haired woman in fawn jodhpurs and a pink cashmere jersey, her hair tied back in a smart chignon, was striding across the sawdust behind her.

"Mum, Kate, Stella, this is Francoise D'arth." Isadora introduced the woman with the dark hair.

"*Bonjour*," Francoise said in a syrupy French accent. She smiled coolly as she shook hands with each of them. "I hope you did enjoy the show?"

"Francoise was one of the riders with the Arabian mares," Issie explained to the others. "She trained at the Cadre Noir de Saumur in France."

"*Oui*," Francoise smiled. "But that was a long time ago, Isadora. I have been now with El Caballo Danza Magnifico for many, many years. I train all the horses at their riding school back in Spain, and when the school goes on tour I come along too and I ride in the shows."

She smiled at Mrs Brown. "Your daughter, Isadora... such a pretty name. She tells me that her horse, Blaze, is very much like my own dancing horses? Is this so?"

"I expect it is," Mrs Brown nodded, "but I'm hardly the one to ask. I can hardly tell one end of a horse from the other. It's the girls that you should be talking to."

"Blaze is exactly the same as them!" Stella blurted out uncontrollably. "She is the same size and the same colour and she's totally beautiful just like them. Honestly! You should see her!"

"Perhaps I will," mused Francoise. "Why not? We

are in town for several weeks putting on the show. It is not far from the city here to Chevalier Point, is it? I will be able to come one day to see you, no?"

"No – I mean yes!" Issie laughed. "Yes please, Francoise. I would love it if you came to the pony club to meet Blaze."

"Then it is a date." Francoise smiled. "*À bientôt!* I must go now and help my girls to groom the mares and put them to bed. It can be very tiring when you are doing two shows a day! See you soon."

Francoise waved goodbye and headed back towards the stables.

"Come on, girls, we need to get you home. Look at the time!" Mrs Brown said, holding out her watch. It was five minutes past twelve.

"Hey, Issie! It's after midnight. That means it's your birthday!" Stella laughed.

"So it is!" Mrs Brown smiled. "OK, let's go home, birthday girl."

Issie paused and stood there for a moment, watching the dark-haired Frenchwoman as she disappeared through the vast stable doors on the other side of the arena. Then she turned and ran to catch up to her mother and her friends. She couldn't believe she was actually thirteen. It felt different somehow. Something told her this was going to be a very big year.

CHAPTER 2

The first rally of the new pony-club season had finally arrived and Stella was fizzing with excitement. "It's so great to be back!" she grinned as she tied Coco up next to Blaze underneath the big plane tree at the far end of the Chevalier Point grounds.

"Coco is totally psyched to be here, aren't you, girl?" Stella giggled and gave her chocolate mare a slappy pat on the neck.

Coco, who never got excited about anything ever, looked at Stella with a sleepy expression and immediately shut her eyes and began to doze away in the shade, her tail lazily flicking away the odd fly that happened to buzz by.

"Yeah, Stella, she's thrilled," Issie laughed.

Even if Coco wasn't excited by the prospect of the new pony-club season, the girls certainly were. This summer the club schedule was jam-packed and the most important event on the competition calendar was the Interclub Gold Shield.

The Interclub was a huge event involving all the clubs in the Chevalier district, from Chevalier Point in the north to Garnet Ridge in the south. Teams trained for the competition throughout the season and then the six district clubs competed in the grand event to see who would take away the trophy.

"St Johns, Mornington, Marsh Fields, Westhaven and Garnet Ridge!" Stella rattled the names of their rivals off by heart.

"Have you seen the Gold Shield? I've seen it. Whoever wins gets all their names engraved on it!" Stella was raving to Issie. "It's not actually a big gold shield at all – well, it is big, but it's made of wood and then it has all these little gold shields all over it and each shield has the names of that year's winners engraved on it. It's like, centuries old. OK, maybe not centuries, but really, really old. Even Avery has his name on it! He was in the team way back in, like, the seventies or something—"

"It was 1985 actually, Stella, thanks for making me feel even older than I usually do," Tom Avery said stiffly.

"Oh no," Stella groaned. She hadn't noticed their riding instructor standing right behind her.

"Hi, Tom!" Issie grinned. Most of the riders at Chevalier Point were scared of Avery. He had a brisk, authoritative manner. But Issie knew that a lot of his strict attitude was just an act he put on for show.

Avery loved horses with a real passion. He worked part-time for the ILPH – the International League for the Protection of Horses. It was Tom who had brought Blaze to Issie so that she could be her guardian. She still remembered that day when he turned up at the River Paddock with the sickly, half-starved chestnut mare that he had rescued. Even though Issie was still hurting after losing Mystic she knew immediately that it was her job to nurse this mare back to health. And she had done just that. Blaze was now a beautiful, incredible horse.

Today, as usual, Avery carried a tan leather riding crop, which he now struck vigorously against his right boot with a loud thwack to get the girls' attention. "Right. Got yourselves sorted for the first event this morning, I hope? We'll be fielding a team of six riders at the Interclub, which I will be choosing today…"

Avery paused for a moment as he noticed Coco dozing next to him. He shook his head, tut-tutted and made an adjustment on the throat lash on the mare's bridle, tightening it by three holes. "Two fingers," he told Stella, placing his own two fingers in the gap between the throat lash and the horse's windpipe to illustrate his point. "Leave no more than a two finger gap on the throat lash…" he trailed off again.

"Anyway, yes, as I was saying – at the last two Interclubs we have been pipped at the post each time by our archrivals at Marsh Fields. But not this time. This time I mean to choose a team that will win us back that shield and do us proud."

He looked Stella in the eyes. "Selection day is serious. I am not in the mood for hijinks today. Are you in the mood for hijinks, Stella?"

For once the bubbly, freckly redhead seemed to have nothing to say for herself. "Ummm, no?" Stella offered eventually.

"Excellent, excellent!" Avery smiled at her. "Off we go then. Mount up and round up the rest of your mob. Your groups are all listed up on the walls of the clubhouse so head over there to see who you're teamed up with. Right? Excellent." Avery gave the side of his boot one more thwack with the whip for emphasis and then spun about and set off.

He was only just out of earshot when Stella whacked her leg with her crop just as Avery had done, imitating his gruff voice and barking at Issie, "Are you in the mood for hijinks, Isadora?"

Issie fell about laughing.

"What's so funny?" Kate asked as she trotted Toby over, pulling up to a halt next to Blaze and Coco.

"Avery," said Issie. "He's not in the mood for 'hijinks'. He's determined to win the Interclub Shield back again."

"Well, I can't say I blame him," Kate said. "Marsh Fields have really rubbed it in ever since they won it for the second time in a row."

"So Avery is choosing six of us out of the whole pony club?" Issie asked. She felt a sudden tingle of excitement as she realised how much this mattered to her.

"Eight, actually," Kate told her. "Six riders plus two team reserves."

"Dan and Ben are both bound to get in," Stella groaned, "so that's two places gone already!"

Dan and Ben were the girls' closest friends at the club – and they were both really good riders. Dan had blond curly hair, startling blue eyes and rode a leggy, flea-bitten grey called Kismit. Ben was dark-haired, always teasing the girls, and had a sullen bay Welsh pony called Max.

Stella turned to her little chocolate mare. "You'd better wake up, Coco! We're going to have to do our best to make the team."

Coco reluctantly raised her head to see what all the fuss was about, and looked up at the girls now with her big brown eyes, then shut them again and dozed some more.

Kate and Issie were laughing, but Stella frowned as she reached for her hard hat and began to tighten her girth. "Sometimes, Coco, I think you aren't taking this seriously enough."

"How many events do we have to do for the selection?" Issie leaned over Kate's shoulder to look at the schedule that she had written down.

"Five," said Kate. "Rider on the flat, rider over hurdles and a showjumping course against the clock, and then there's the team events – the flag-race relay and the bending relay.

"I hope Toby and I do well in the jumping," Kate sighed. "We'll never get picked for the team when it comes to the games. Toby is useless at bending. He's far too big and his stride is too long to wind through the poles."

Kate was only thirteen and in the same year at Chevalier Point High School as Issie and Stella. But she was tall for her age with lean, long legs, and her parents, who didn't want to buy a pony only to have Kate outgrow it, had thought it sensible to progress her straight on to a horse. Kate's horse Toby was a rangy bay Thoroughbred, standing a massive sixteen-two hands, which came in useful for Kate in the showjumping ring. But he was not so good at games like bending and flag racing where the poles were set up at the right distance for the short strides of little ponies, not the huge, ground-swallowing strides of an ex-racehorse.

The bending poles had already been set up for the

games. The poles were about two metres high, stuck upright in the ground and evenly spaced with about three horse lengths between each pole. To win the race, riders needed to serpentine their way as fast as they could down through the poles, turning tightly around the last pole at the end, and slaloming back through again as fast as they could to cross the finish line.

For flag races, the same poles were used, but this time a flag was secured with a rubber band near the top of each pole. The riders had to race their horses to each pole in turn, pluck off the flag, then race back and drop the flag precisely into a small wooden box on top of an oil drum. If they missed the box, they had to dismount, pick up the flag, put it in the box and mount up again before they could continue the race.

"At least Toby is a star when it comes to jumping against the clock. You're bound to win selection points in the jumping," Issie consoled Kate. "Come on. Let's finish tacking up and go."

Issie ran her stirrups down the leathers, gave Blaze's girth a final check and popped her foot in the stirrup iron, bouncing herself up lightly on to Blaze's back.

"Here we go again, eh, girl?" Issie said, leaning in

low by Blaze's neck to whisper in her ear. The mare danced and fidgeted anxiously beneath her as they waited for Kate and Stella to get ready. Then the three girls set off at a trot towards the bending poles and their first event of the day.

At the clubroom, five other riders were already waiting on their mounts. All of them were wearing the navy jersey and red tie which were the Chevalier Point Pony Club colours.

One of the girls, a blonde with two perfectly straight plaits, starchy white jodhpurs and a sour expression, sat astride a glossy, golden palomino. She saw Issie, Stella and Kate heading towards her and gave them a haughty smirk.

"Oh no, not Stuck-up Tucker!" Stella muttered under her breath. "Why does she have to be in our group? I wish I was doing jumping first like Dan and Ben."

"Be nice," Issie warned Stella. Issie knew that being nice to Natasha Tucker wasn't easy, in fact she was gritting her teeth too in anticipation. The last time Issie had crossed paths with her had been in the jump-off at the one-day event, when Natasha had been eliminated for hitting Goldrush with her whip and Issie had gone on to win.

Needless to say, Natasha wasn't pleased to see Issie again. "We've been waiting for you lot for absolutely ages! I hope you're not planning to make us late all day," Natasha said as the girls trotted up to join them. This clearly wasn't true as the clock on the wall of the clubroom said nine exactly, which was when the rally was due to start.

"Hi, Natasha," Issie said, deciding it was best to simply ignore her sniffy comment.

"Hi, Issie. Don't worry about it, we only just got here too," said a cheerful girl on a dinky twelve-two grey pony. The girl was Pip Miller and her horse was called Mitzy. Next to Pip was her little sister Catherine who rode an even smaller twelve-hand grey called Nemo. The girl beside them was Annabel Willets, who was in the year above Issie at school. Annabel's horse, Eddie, was a pretty palomino gelding with a wall eye.

The fifth rider, who was hanging back on the edge of the group, was a girl that Issie had never seen before.

She had long dark hair just like Issie, but her skin was pale to the point of being ghostly. Her club jersey and tie were clearly brand new. She had a navy gilet over the top of her jersey and a shiny white helmet. Her pony, who was jet black, was pretty and dainty and about the same height as Blaze.

"Who is she?" Kate wondered out loud.

"Hmmphh?" Natasha Tucker overheard her. "Oh her? That's Morgan. She's just started going to my school."

Natasha didn't go to Chevalier Point High with Issie and the others. She went to Kingswood, a private school on the other side of town.

"Her mummy used to be frightfully famous in horse circles, apparently – she was a really good rider back in the day. Now what's their name again?" Natasha paused. "Oh yes, Chatswood-Smith. Morgan Chatswood-Smith. Her mum's name is—"

"Araminta Chatswood-Smith!" Issie squeaked. "I know her! She was a totally amazing showjumper. I have all of her books."

"Ah, all here then?" Avery said as he emerged out of the clubroom and bounded down the stairs. "Have you all introduced yourself to our new girl Morgan?"

He walked over to the girl on the jet black pony and gave the pony a firm pat on his glossy neck.

"Morgan's mother and I used to be great rivals when we were riding." He smiled at her. "Welcome to Chevalier Point Pony Club, Morgan. I'm sure talent runs in the family."

Morgan sat looking at Avery blankly. Eventually she managed to give him a weak smile in return.

"Good, good," Avery said, turning to the rest of the riders. "Let's get on with it then, shall we?"

Avery had set up four rows of poles for the bending so the riders were divided into two heats. After all the riders had been given a quick practice run through the poles, Stella, Kate, Pip and Catherine were the first ones to line up at the start line. "On your marks... get set... go!!" Avery shouted.

The horses leapt forward on Avery's word and began to weave in a slalom through the four rows of bending poles. Stella was bent low over Coco's neck as the chocolate mare zipped through her poles at a swift canter. She turned the last pole well ahead of the rest of the riders and breezed home easily in the lead across the finish line.

Kate was not so lucky with Toby who reached the last pole and, instead of turning, kept right on cantering. "Toby!" Kate hauled on his left rein to try and get him to circle. By the time she had got the big bay's attention and manoeuvred him around, even Catherine on little Nemo had beaten her and was trotting gaily through the last pole and over the finish line.

"Next riders up!" Avery called. Issie, Morgan, Annabel and Natasha lined up at their poles.

"On your marks…" Avery began his countdown. But Issie was still trying to calm Blaze down. The mare was so excited, she couldn't stay still. She snorted and fretted and Issie was forced to keep turning her in tight circles to stop her bolting over the line and being disqualified.

"Get set…" Avery continued.

"Wait!" Issie squawked. She wasn't "set" at all– her reins were in a tangle and her arms hurt from holding Blaze back.

She needed to turn the chestnut mare back in time to face the starting line but Avery hadn't noticed that she was struggling. "Go!" he shouted.

Blaze leapt forward – in completely the wrong direction!

By the time Issie had turned Blaze around, the other riders were halfway down the row of bending poles. Issie tried to steer her through the poles but Blaze kept yanking the reins out of Issie's fingers; she was far too excited to pay attention. Blaze had missed two poles before Issie had the chance to haul her up and go back again. By the time Issie finally got her under control the others had already crossed the finish line. She was dead last.

The only thing that cheered Issie up was the fact that Natasha hadn't won either – Annabel had taken out the heat on Eddie.

Of course that didn't stop Natasha being a know-it-all. "Hey, Isadora, I think you're going in the wrong direction. The bending poles are that way!" she needled Issie as she rode Goldrush past.

Issie watched as Natasha pulled up next to Morgan. Natasha leant over and whispered something to Morgan and then began to giggle.

"Oh no. I think the new girl is friends with Natasha!" Issie groaned to Stella.

"It's not her fault. She's new. Wait until she gets to know her!" Stella rolled her eyes and giggled.

The flag races went a little better than the bending. Stella won her heat again, this time narrowly beating Morgan, who rode like a daredevil but still couldn't catch up with Coco, who was brilliant at stopping dead at each pole and then breaking into a gallop to deliver the flags back to the box.

Issie and Blaze managed their heat well too – no starting hiccups this time. And when Natasha dropped a flag, Issie raced into the lead and this time she beat her across the line.

"Lunch break!" Avery boomed at them all. "Go and tie your horses up – you've got an hour off and then you're doing rider on the flat and jumping this afternoon!"

Issie's Mum and Dan's mother, Mrs Halliday, were arranging the lunch on tartan picnic rugs as the riders pulled up their mounts.

"I am totally starving!" Stella said, casting her eyes

over the spread. She could see asparagus rolls, little miniature meat pies, club sandwiches, jam roll, chocolate cake and strawberry tarts, all lined up in Tupperware containers on the rug, with a big thermos of tea for the parents and apple juice for the riders.

"You boys! Put that down and wait until the girls have tied their horses up too," Mrs Halliday said firmly to Dan and Ben, who had already thrown themselves down on the picnic rug and had their hands on the meat pies.

Dan gave his Mum a big grin and bit into the pie. "Too late!" he said with his mouth full. "Better tell them to hurry up!" The food was gone in no time flat.

"Can we get ice creams, Mum? It's so hot today," Issie begged.

"Yes! Ice creams!" the others agreed, leaping up off the rug and heading for the clubroom.

"I wonder if they'll have this morning's results posted up yet?" Dan said. He and Ben were both feeling confident that their skill in the showjumping ring would earn them both a place in the Chevalier Point team.

"Kismit is jumping brilliantly at the moment." Dan grinned.

Ben nodded in agreement. "We've both been having

extra lessons lately with Iggy Dalrymple. He's really helped my technique."

They stepped up to the door of the clubrooms now, and heard a woman's voice inside. She sounded upset. "What went wrong?" she was saying. "These results are dreadful!"

"I don't know, Mum. I had a bad start in the bending and then Jack was nappy in the flag race, I guess…" a girl's voice responded.

"Well, now you'll have to make up lost ground this afternoon," the woman said briskly. "Come on, saddle up. We'll pop Black Jack over some practice fences and I'll look at your position before they get back underway."

The woman and the girl headed for the door of the clubroom and Issie, Stella, Kate, Ben and Dan all scattered to the sides of the steps to let them through.

Morgan came out first. She looked much slighter than she did on her horse. She was sparrow-like, with skinny arms and legs and that long, dark hair and pale skin. She gave Issie a wan smile as she walked past.

Behind her, a woman stepped from the dark of the clubhouse to the bright light outside. She too had jet black hair and pale skin. She was tall and very glamorous in violet Hunter wellingtons, sky blue jodhpurs and a dark navy shirt, with a violet Hermes scarf tied around her hair and big, black sunglasses.

Like Avery, she carried a riding crop in her hand which she tapped lightly against her boot as she looked down now at the five riders on the clubroom steps below her.

Issie held her breath. She knew this woman. She recognised her at once because she had a picture of her on her bedroom wall. It was Araminta Chatswood-Smith.

CHAPTER 3

Most thirteen-year-old girls have pictures of pop bands and Jake Gyllenhaal on their walls. But Isadora Brown was a horsy girl. In her bedroom, horses – bays, chestnuts, greys, Appaloosas, paints and palominos – covered every square inch of wallpaper.

Issie had cut pictures out of magazines of her favourite horses and riders. There was Pippa Funnell at Burghley on her big bay Supreme Rock. Next to that was a big poster of Zara Philips taking a water jump on Toytown. And on the back of her bedroom door there was Araminta Chatswood-Smith, jumping an enormous brick wall on her horse Wilful Lad in the showjumping at the World Equestrian Games.

Issie had spent a long time staring at that picture of Araminta and "Willy" on her door. Now, she was staring at the real rider herself.

Araminta cast a brief look down at Issie and her friends, gave them a stiff smile, and slid her dark glasses down from her scarf where they were perched so that they shielded her eyes.

"Minty!" Avery's voice boomed across the paddock as he came striding towards them. Araminta's smile grew wide as she saw him approaching.

"Tom! How glorious!" she said, trotting down the stairs with her arms outstretched. She gave him a firm embrace and pushed her sunglasses back up again, looking at Tom with warm, hazel brown eyes.

"It's been years!" Araminta said. "Are you still competing?"

"No." Avery shook his head. "After that bad fall at Badminton they told me I shouldn't really ride again. So now I teach here and, of course, I'm still working for the ILPH."

"That's where I got Blaze from!" Issie blurted out.

Araminta and Tom turned around to see Isadora,

Stella, Kate, Dan and Ben all standing there on the clubroom steps, clearly making no bones about snooping in on their conversation.

"Araminta, have you met my star riders?" Avery grinned at them. And he did introductions, naming each of them in turn and telling Araminta a little about the young riders and their ponies.

"...and finally, this is Isadora," Tom said. "Issie's a terrific rider. She's been looking after Blaze, an Anglo-Arab mare that the horse protection league found. Totally nursed her back to health and then won the Chevalier Point ODE on her last season."

"So you own the mare now?" Araminta asked Issie.

"Umm, no," Issie said, "I'm just her guardian. Blaze still belongs to the ILPH."

"Well, it sounds like you're quite the horsewoman. I respect your dedication," Araminta said. She checked her watch. "I'm sorry, Tom, we'll catch up another time. I have to go and help Morgan get some last-minute practice in for this afternoon."

"If she's anything like you were in your day, Minty, she won't need any practice," Tom said.

Araminta sighed and shook her head. "Tom, I was

only good because I used to practise so hard. Morgan needs to realise that she could be great too if she worked at winning. I need to push her all the time. She's got to be committed to be a star. That's what I keep telling her—" She stopped suddenly and gave Avery a smile again. "Anyway, I need to go and help her warm up now. It was lovely to see you, Tom. And to meet you." She smiled at Issie and her gang. "See you soon."

Araminta strode off to the practice jumps on the far side of the paddock where Morgan was warming up her black gelding.

"Come on," Dan said, charging up the clubroom stairs now that Araminta was gone, "are we getting ice creams or not?"

The Chevalier Point clubroom looked like an old shearing shed, which was exactly what it had once been. It was raised up on poles allowing storage space under the floor at one end for hay bales during the winter months. Underneath the other end was a locked-up space for equipment like bending poles, hard feed for the horses, saddle horses and racks for tack which the riders stored here when they were grazing their ponies at the club grounds.

Upstairs, the clubroom itself was warm and dry, with a musty smell of hay and the sweet warm hint of pony sweat.

At the far end of this big barn-like space was the area that everyone called the "Riders Lounge". The lounge was made up of five old worn-out armchairs, all of them with the stuffing coming out of the arms and fabric worn threadbare so that the springs showed. A large, very worn Persian rug covered the floor and there was a long, low coffee table with old copies of *PONY Magazine* stacked on it.

At the front end, near the clubroom door, was the kitchenette, with a freezer and an honesty box for ice creams and a cold drinks machine. Coffee mugs hung on a wooden tree next to the sink and there was a big handwritten notice that said, PLEASE DO YOUR OWN DISHES – THE PONIES CAN'T CLEAN UP BY THEMSELVES!

Opposite the kitchenette on the main wall was the noticeboard and it was here that Avery had posted up the results.

"Yikes!" Stella squealed. She had been examining the pieces of paper on the corkboard and adding up who had the most points. "Look at this! I'm winning!

I've got the highest score so far!" It was true. Stella was the only one who had won her heats in both the bending and the flag races that morning.

Issie searched frantically for her name on the corkboard. Her eyes scanned the column. There she was – Isadora Brown. She had three points so far for winning her heat of the flag race. Stella had six points and so did Dan and Ben. Issie knew she would have to ride really well this afternoon if she wanted to win enough points to make the team. She suddenly felt her tummy churn with nerves, almost putting her off her ice cream. "Come on," she said to Stella, "let's go get saddled up."

That afternoon seemed to fly by as the days always do at pony club. By the time they reached the last event of the day, Issie and Kate had both ridden well in the rider on the flat and over hurdles and both girls had added to their points tally. Each of them had six points now just like Stella. There was only the showjumping against the clock to come.

"There are ten fences in the course. You'll be jumping this same height at the Interclub on Shield Day when the fences will all be between eighty centimetres and one metre," Avery explained. "It's the same system today as the Interclub. You will receive four faults for every rail you knock down. The rider who completes a clear round with the best time on the clock will win."

As Stella and Kate rode off to warm up over the practice jumps, Issie sat by the ring to watch the first rider and see how they handled the course.

As she was watching the horse take the first fence she looked across and saw Morgan. The girl was sitting all by herself on her black gelding, looking extremely bored.

It must be awful, Issie thought, *being the new girl and not knowing anyone – even if you are the daughter of a famous rider like Araminta Chatswood-Smith.*

"What do you think, Blaze? Shall we make friends?" Issie murmured to her horse.

She picked up the reins and trotted Blaze over to the shade of the large plane tree where Morgan and her pony were standing alone.

"Hi," Issie smiled brightly at Morgan, "I'm Issie,

well, Isadora really, but everyone calls me Issie." Issie patted her liver chestnut mare, who gave her head a shake and jangled her bit as if to suggest that the introductions weren't quite finished yet.

"And this is Blaze!" Issie laughed. "I think she wants to meet your horse. What's his name?" she asked, gesturing towards the black gelding.

"Black Jack," Morgan replied in a quiet voice, "but I just call him Jack. We were—"

"There you are, Morgan!" The sharp voice of Natasha Tucker trilled out, interrupting them. Natasha pulled her horse up between Black Jack and Blaze and cast a snooty look at Isadora. "It's so nice to have you here, Morgan," Natasha purred. "So nice to have a proper rider at this club with me finally. And with a proper horse too," Natasha added, looking at Black Jack. "I can tell that he's a purebred. Goldrush is too, you know. Bloodlines are so important, don't you think? It's a shame they let all sorts of mongrel ponies join the club these days. I think you'll find that some people at this pony club have horses that are simply out-classed by horses like ours. They can't afford well-bred mounts like we can," she said. She gave Morgan a sly smirk. "You're new here, but you'll learn. I'm sure I can fill you in on who's worth bothering with."

"What-ever, Natasha," Morgan replied dryly. "I think I can figure out good breeding all by myself. And I know exactly who is worth bothering with – and who is not!"

And with that she leaned over in front of Natasha and smiled broadly at Issie. "Your horse is beautiful. I love chestnuts with blonde manes." She looked admiringly at Blaze's flaxen mane, which was pale honey blonde, long and silky. "Is she an Arab?"

"I think so." Issie smiled back. "Avery says Anglo-Arab, but I got her from the ILPH so I don't really know for sure."

As the two girls nattered happily away, Natasha's face darkened. She gave a haughty sniff, pretended she had somewhere better to be and rode off in a sulk.

"I'm so glad she's gone!" Morgan pulled a face as she watched Natasha ride off.

"I thought you were friends?" Issie was confused.

"No way!" Morgan was shocked. "She is horrible to me at school. Natasha and her friends are all in the 'popular' group and they won't even speak to me. Now suddenly she turns up at pony club and discovers who my mum is and wants to be my best friend!"

Issie nodded. "That sounds like Natasha all right."

Morgan sighed. "It happened at my last pony club too. All these girls who just wanted to hang out with me because of my mum…"

"It must be amazing." Issie grinned. "I mean, having a mother who is a really great rider. My Mum can't stand horses."

"Yeah, it's OK," Morgan said without much enthusiasm. She looked at Issie. "It's just that everyone expects me to be this fantastic rider just because Mum is. And everyone is always asking me about her."

Issie felt herself blush. "I'm sorry, I didn't mean to… I just thought it would be so great to grow up in a horsy family. How old were you when you first learned to ride?"

"I was three. Mum took me out hunting before I had even turned six." Morgan rolled her eyes dramatically. "Mum thinks I should be the youngest ever rider to win Badminton. She says she expects me to do it by the time I am eighteen years and 246 days old – since Richard Walker was eighteen years and 247 days old when he won it on Pasha in 1969!"

Issie sighed. "Oh, I wish Araminta Chatswood-Smith was my mother! My mum thinks Badminton is a game you play with a shuttlecock and a racket."

Morgan laughed at this.

"Do you want to come and meet Kate and Stella?" Issie offered.

Morgan nodded and the two girls were about to leave when another voice called Morgan's name. "There you are! What are you doing? Why aren't you warming up?" Araminta Chatswood-Smith demanded as she strode purposefully towards them.

"There are only three more riders before it's your turn," Araminta said. "You should be at the practice fence giving Black Jack a bit of last-minute schooling."

"Sorry, Mum," Morgan sighed.

"Well, let's go then," Araminta said, turning on her heels and marching off towards the jumps. She looked back over her shoulder. "I mean now, Morgan!"

Morgan shrugged, waved goodbye to Issie and gave her a smile as she trotted off after her mother.

Issie watched as Araminta schooled her daughter over the two low practice fences, back and forth again and again. She looked very serious as she called Morgan to her, making gestures and gripping Morgan's hands in her own to adjust their position on Black Jack's reins. Issie could hear her saying, "Half-halt... then leg on... try to keep your head in the game this time, Morgan!"

By the time it was Morgan's turn to ride the showjumping course she looked tense in the saddle. Her face looked even paler than usual as she entered the ring.

At the first jump, Morgan rode hard at the fence. "Get up!" she shouted in a frightened voice at Jack as they approached for the final stride. But the little black gelding stopped dead in his tracks, and Morgan flew forward out of the saddle and on to his neck. She scrabbled back down and got her seat back, turning Black Jack and riding at the first fence again. This time she shouted more firmly, and he leapt with a snort and cleared it easily. She finished the round with four jumping faults and a very slow time.

It was enough to put her well out of the running. By the time the riders had all been through the course, there would be eleven clear rounds in total that day. With so many clear rounds, only the riders with the best times on the clock stood a chance of receiving points.

"Well, that rules me out!" Kate said grumpily. She was still grouchy with Toby, who had got a bee in his bonnet about something at the third fence and refused twice.

It was no surprise to anyone when Dan, Ben and Stella managed to come out on top as the three fastest riders on the day.

"I told you we'd been having extra practice." Ben grinned as he and Max scooped up two more points.

"It's all right for you," Stella groaned at him, "you came second. Now you're bound to have made the team."

"Oh, Stella! You'll get in. You got third and you did brilliantly at the games," Kate tried to reassure her.

But Stella shook her head. "Don't! I don't want to jinx it. Avery said he would be posting the final team lineup at the end of the day. Let's not talk about it until then!"

"Stella's right. There's nothing we can do now so

let's go and have afternoon tea," Issie suggested. "Meet you back at the picnic blanket?"

The girls all agreed that this was a good idea and they decided to ask Morgan too – after Issie told them the story of what happened with Natasha.

But when Issie rode over to ask Morgan to come and join them, Araminta couldn't have been less enthusiastic. "I hope you don't mind, Isadora, but I'd prefer to give Morgan a bit of extra schooling after Black Jack's performance in the ring today," she replied coolly.

"Oh, Mum, we're all done for the day! Can't I just go and unsaddle and get a drink and hang out with Issie and her friends?" Morgan pleaded.

Araminta fixed her with a steely glare. "I think you need to work on your position, Morgan. There was no excuse for that refusal." She turned to look at Issie and her frown unfurrowed a little. "I'm sorry, Isadora," she said, "Morgan is busy for the rest of the day. That is final."

"Wow. It sounds like Araminta is pretty tough on Morgan," Stella said as Issie told her what had happened. They were lying on the tartan rug and munching the bacon and egg pie and some more sponge cake that clever Mrs Brown had kept back from lunch.

"Araminta is super-competitive. I guess she really wants Morgan to win." Issie shrugged.

Still, Issie knew what Stella meant. Poor Morgan had looked so desperate to go and hang out with Issie and her friends instead of training for a change.

While Issie and Stella had been lying on the picnic blanket finishing off the bacon and egg pie, Kate had been in the clubroom. She emerged, running towards them with a piece of paper gripped tightly in her right hand.

"Ohmygod!" she said. "You are not going to believe it." Her face was stiff and miserable.

"What?" Issie and Stella cried out together.

"I've got the team list results," Kate said. She looked deadly serious now. "And, well… they're terrible. None of us have made the team."

CHAPTER 4

Stella's horror at being left out of the team quickly turned to anger. "What? I can't believe it!" she squawked. "I have ridden better today than I ever did in my life! I won all the games! I have loads of points!" Her cheeks flushed hot pink against her red curls. "Issie? I can't believe it! Issie?"

She looked at Issie, who had a smirk on her face, and then back at Kate, who, incredibly, was also smiling.

"I can't believe you fell for it!" Kate laughed. "Of course you made the team, Stella! We all made it!"

Stella gaped open-mouthed like a goldfish at her friends and her eyes grew wide with disbelief as it dawned on her that the whole thing had been a trick. Then she sputtered and gasped and finally broke out into a huge grin too, and the girls all hugged and squealed, falling down finally on to the picnic blanket with a case of hysterical giggles. Kate opened up the team list and they all sat there and looked at it for ages just to make sure that it was really true. There it was in black and white. They had made the team.

There were eight names on the list. It read in alphabetical order, which meant, Issie noted proudly, that her name came first.

Chevalier Point Interclub Gold Shield Team:

Isadora Brown

Dan Halliday

Kate Knight

Ben MacIntosh

Stella Tarrant

Annabel Willets

Reserves:

Morgan Chatswood-Smith

Natasha Tucker

"Do Dan and Ben know that they've made the team too?" Stella said.

She heard a loud whoop behind her and saw the two boys running across the paddock towards them. "I think that's a yes!" Kate laughed.

That afternoon, Avery gathered his new team together in the clubroom. "Well done, all of you!" he said. "But I hope you realise that making the team means hard work. I'm going to be scheduling in extra training sessions each week from now until the Interclub."

He turned to Morgan and Natasha. "I expect to see both of the team reserves at training too. If, for any reason, one of our team can't compete, then I'll be calling on you to ride in their place. You need to be ready."

Natasha rolled her eyes and leaned over to whisper dramatically to Morgan, "I don't see why we should turn up if we don't actually get to ride at the competition."

Issie overheard her say, "Especially when some people only make the team because they are Avery's special pet!" Then she turned to Issie and gave her a smirk. "Isn't that right, Isadora?"

"Don't worry about Stuck-up Tucker," Stella said to Issie afterwards. "She's just got it in for you because she didn't make the team."

Kate agreed, "Natasha spent a fortune on her pony. It's, like, just because she's rich she thinks she should automatically be chosen."

"But why is it always me she picks on?" Issie sighed.

"Are you kidding?" Stella grinned. "It's so obvious that she is jealous of you, Issie. She's never recovered from the time you beat her at the one-day event."

Even Natasha's cattiness couldn't crush Issie's good mood. She had made the team. That night, as a celebration, Mrs Brown made Issie's favourite dinner – cottage pie with minted peas and chocolate ice cream for dessert.

Afterwards, Issie lay on her bed, still in her jodhpurs, feeling too tired and stiff to take them off and change into her pyjamas. She was just thinking that this was possibly one of the best days she had ever had when the phone rang.

"Mum! Can you get it? I can't stand up because my legs have fallen off!" Issie yelled out.

She heard her mother yell something back, but then she heard her get up from the kitchen table and walk towards the phone. Her legs-falling-off excuse must have worked. She could hear her mum talking in her proper phone voice that she reserved for people she didn't know very well, and then she called out, "Isadora, it's for you."

"Who is it?" Issie asked as she took the receiver. Her mother just smiled and handed her the phone.

The voice on the other end of the line was syrupy and warm, with a strong French accent. "*Bonjour*, Isadora," said Francoise D'arth. "*Ça va?* How are you? I am calling as you suggested to ask if you are free tomorrow? I would love to come and meet your pony."

As she cycled towards the pony club the next morning Issie felt sick with nerves. She had never dreamt that the glamorous Francoise D'arth would really be interested in Blaze. To Issie, Blaze was the most beautiful horse in the world – but what would an expert horsewoman like Francoise think? Francoise would probably be disappointed when she came all the way to the pony club to meet her and saw that Blaze was just an ordinary pony, not anything special at all.

It was eight a.m. and the morning air still had a slight spring chill in it, despite the fact that summer was almost here. Issie wished she'd worn her jacket. By the time she reached the pony-club gates, though, the bike ride had warmed her up and her cheeks were flushed from the fresh air. Next to the gates was a black car, and out of it stepped Francoise, who had been waiting for her.

"*Bonjour*, Isadora," she said. "Thank you very much for meeting with me. Now, where is this pony of yours that looks so much like my dancing horses?"

Issie grabbed Blaze's halter out of the tack room, and she and Francoise set out together across the paddocks.

"I usually graze her at the River Paddock," Issie explained, "but we had a pony-club rally yesterday and I kept her here. Avery says we can graze them at the pony club for as long as we like now that we're in the team."

The pony club was divided into three fields. You came off the main road down a long gravel driveway, lined with giant magnolia trees. The first gate opened into the paddock where the cars and horse floats usually parked on rally days. There were large plane trees running like a leafy spine through the paddocks, providing extra shade for the horses and riders on hot days, and the clubroom which straddled the fence line between paddocks one and two. Paddock three was the furthest away. The jumping arena had been erected there, and the perimeter of this paddock was bordered by a thick privet hedge. Issie looked out to the far paddock where she could see the outline of three horses grazing – Blaze, Coco and Toby.

"There she is," Issie pointed. "She's the one standing by the stack of cavaletti."

Issie and Francoise climbed over the turnstile in the fence and began to walk through the lush, spring grass towards the far paddock.

As they got closer, Issie made a clucking noise with her tongue and Blaze raised her head from the rich, green spring grass to look up at her. She gave a soft nicker.

"She usually comes if I call her," Issie said proudly. She made the clucking noise again and Blaze gave another little whinny now and broke into a high-stepping trot. When she reached the fence line that separated her from Issie she looked for a moment as if she were considering jumping the fence, but instead she came reluctantly to a stop. Snorting and shaking out her mane with frustration, Blaze trotted up and down along the fence line impatiently.

Issie watched her horse in motion, her flaxen mane and tail flowing freely and her dark liver chestnut coat glinting in the morning sun. Blaze's paces were so light she seemed to be floating above the ground. Her neck was arched and her ears were pricked forward. Issie smiled at how beautiful her horse was when she moved – surely Francoise would be impressed by how gorgeous the chestnut mare looked.

She turned expectantly to look at the dark-haired Frenchwoman next to her. But Francoise was not smiling. Far from it. She was standing perfectly still, and the look on her face was one of shock. It was almost as if she had seen a ghost.

Issie noticed that her hands were trembling. Francoise seemed to realise this too because she now entwined her hands together to steady herself, clasping them under her chin as if she were praying.

Francoise stood perfectly still in this way for a long time. Issie heard her muttering something under her breath in French. Then Francoise raised her hands to her face, cupping them around her mouth. She pouted her lips and blew a shrill high whistle.

Blaze, who had been trotting back and forth anxiously along the fence line in front of them, came to a sudden halt.

Francoise whistled again. It was a different whistle this time: sharper and shriller than the first, in three repeated short bursts, like a bird call.

The mare's ears pricked forward and her nostrils flared wide. She let out a low, deep snort. Then, with a defiant shake of her head, she threw herself back and reared up on her hind legs so that her hooves thrashed wildly at the air in front of her.

"Blaze!" Issie cried, rushing forward.

Too late. Blaze spun around on her hind legs and hit

the ground at a gallop. With a rush of speed she charged around the paddock at full speed, her head held high, her legs flashing over the ground beneath her.

"Blaze, stop! You'll hurt yourself!" Issie felt her chest tighten in fear. What was wrong with her? Why was Blaze behaving like this? She looked back at Francoise, whose face was aghast as she watched the mare.

"Come on," Francoise said to Issie, breaking into a run, "she will stick a hoof in a rabbit hole and hurt herself if we do not calm her down."

The two of them both broke into a run, heading for the paddock gate. When they reached it, Issie climbed the turnstile, but Francoise simply vaulted lightly over the gate like a gymnast, hitting the ground running on the other side. By the time Issie was on her feet again and running after her, Francoise already had her hands held wide to stop Blaze as she circled around again at a frantic gallop.

This time, when Blaze rounded the perimeter of the paddock, Francoise stood in her path. As Blaze charged down at her, Francoise, still with her arms outstretched, let out a long, low whistle, a single note. Blaze's pace abruptly slowed to a canter and then a trot, and finally, she calmed right down to a walk.

By the time Issie reached them, Francoise had grasped Blaze around the neck and was holding on to her mane, waiting for Issie to arrive with her halter.

Isadora slipped the halter quickly over Blaze's head and did up the buckle. She let out a sigh of relief, and ran her hand down her horse's neck. Blaze was damp with sweat and her flanks were heaving after her mad gallop.

"Here!" Francoise offered Issie. "I will hold her while you check her legs to make sure that she is OK." She put out a hand to take the lead rope which Issie reluctantly handed over to her. She was confused. It seemed like Francoise had deliberately frightened Blaze when she whistled at her, but now she seemed so helpful and so genuinely concerned.

"Shhhh," Francoise soothed as she ran her hand down the mare's crest, stroking her gently. She murmured to Blaze, French words that Issie did not understand, although she noticed that the mare was calmed by her voice.

Issie ran her hands down Blaze's legs. They seemed fine; there were no scratches or marks on her.

"Watch her as I lead her forward and we will check

if she is lame," Francoise said. She clucked gently to Blaze and the mare stepped forward in an easy walk and then a fluid, high trot as Francoise jogged her down the paddock and back to Issie again.

"No, she's fine. I don't think she's sore at all," Issie said. Francoise looked relieved.

"I am sorry, Isadora, for startling her," Francoise said. Her eyes were still glued to Blaze, taking in the scoop of her beautiful dished nose with the white blaze tapering down to her muzzle.

"Do you think she looks like your dancing mares, Francoise?" Issie asked.

Francoise turned, her face serious once more. "*Oui*, Isadora. Very much so. She is a mare of great beauty. How did you say you came to own her again?"

And so Issie told Francoise the whole story. How Tom Avery had found Blaze half-starved and terrified and had rescued her.

Avery had appointed Issie as Blaze's guardian, but at first things hadn't been easy. Blaze had been treated so badly that she didn't trust anyone. Issie, who had sworn she would never ride again after that awful day when Mystic had been killed, was scared too. How could she ever love another horse as much as she had loved Mystic? It took Issie a long time to win the trust of the beautiful chestnut and nurse her back to health.

"And then," Issie told Francoise, "there were the horse thieves who came to steal her!"

"Horse thieves?" Francoise was shocked.

"Yes! They tried to steal her from the River Paddock but Tom and I stopped them and the police came just in time."

"And you never found Blaze's real owners?" Francoise asked.

Issie shook her head. "We don't know where she came from."

"But does that mean that you have no papers for her? You do not know the origins of her bloodlines?"

Issie shook her head again.

Francoise looked at Blaze. "Such a pity," she said quietly.

She ran her hands down the fine cannon bones of the mare's legs, stroked the outline of her withers through to her hind quarters and then stood back to admire her once more.

"The Anglo-Arab is not only the most beautiful of

all horses," Francoise said, "she is also the smartest, the most trainable. In our school the stallions are all full-blooded Lipizzaners, bred for the *haute école*. But our mares are Anglo-Arabs, delicate, graceful and clever. They are so divine, they seem to almost dance underneath their riders. In Arabia their bloodlines are valued above all else and they are the most cherished and valuable possessions, worth more than rubies or gold…"

Francoise hesitated. She looked as if she were about to say something more, and then suddenly she changed her mind and was silent for a moment.

"Come on!" She smiled at Issie. "She must be nicely warmed up from that gallop. Shall we get her saddled up? I want to see you ride!"

CHAPTER 5

It took Issie for ever to get to sleep that night. She spent ages lying there and thinking about Blaze. What had made her act so strangely?

Issie had been so deep in thought about her mare that at first when the shrill neigh pierced the stillness of the night air, it was hard to tell if she was asleep or awake. Was she dreaming or did she really hear a horse? And then – there it was again! Unmistakeable this time, the sharp whinny that a pony makes when it is calling for its paddock-mate. Issie's heart raced. Mystic?

She threw back the duvet and flung herself at the

window in one swift, fluid movement. It took a moment to get the window open and then she was craning her neck to see out into the back garden, blinking and squinting as she tried to make her eyes adjust. She was desperately looking for a horse-sized shape, but it was no use, she couldn't see a thing. The only thing to do was go outside. If Mystic was there, she figured, he would be where she had found him last time he came to her, underneath the big tree at the far end of the lawn near the gate that led to the street.

As she pulled on her jeans and boots and shoved a thick jumper over her pyjama top, Issie prepared herself for disappointment. She had been so desperate for Mystic to come to her, she was sure she was dreaming all of this. "You are probably asleep right now," she told herself firmly.

Still, despite her efforts to be sensible, she could feel her heart soaring. Mystic was back! She knew he hadn't really left her.

Then a grim thought struck her. If Mystic was here, then that must mean that something was terribly wrong. The grey gelding had only turned up last time because there was trouble brewing.

She looked at the clock by her bedside table. It was three a.m. If her mum woke up and caught her sneaking around outside now, she'd be in big trouble. She had to be quiet. She had been about to pull on her clompy jodhpur boots, but now she stopped and changed her mind, carrying them instead as she tiptoed down the carpeted stairs in her sock feet and ducked out the back door and into the garden.

Across the cool concrete paving stones she scuttled in her socks, stopping on the edge of the damp lawn briefly to pull her boots on before she stepped on to the grass.

It was dark in the garden tonight. The moon was not much bigger than a fingernail in the sky. The last time she had taken a midnight ride on her ghost pony there had been almost a full moon and Issie had been able to see quite clearly. Tonight, she could only just make out the shadows and the shapes of trees.

At the far end of the garden, though, there was a golden halo cast by the street light that stood on the other side of the garden gate and it was towards this light that Issie now found herself moving.

Still aware that she mustn't wake her mum, but

unable to resist calling for her horse, she whispered softly, "Mystic?" Issie called the gelding's name then clucked her tongue gently, encouraging the pony to come to her.

In the still night air, Issie held her breath and listened for her horse. At first she couldn't hear a sound, and there was a sickening moment when she realised that maybe she really had been imagining the whole thing.

She was halfway across the lawn before she heard it again. From the inky darkness underneath the boughs of the big beech tree came the unmistakeable sound of a horse, his soft nicker returning her calls.

Issie began to run. Her heart was racing and she could feel a tight knot in her throat. "Mystic!" she hissed, trying hard to keep her voice at a whisper.

As she reached the trees, the horse nickered again and stepped out of the shadows and on to the lawn in front of her.

And there he was. Just as she remembered him. A soft, faded dapple-grey pony, not much more than fourteen hands high, stocky and swaybacked, his black eyes surrounded by dark coal smudges poking out from beneath a thick forelock of silvery hair.

Now, here in the still of the night, those dark eyes focused intently on Isadora. The gelding took a step forward towards his owner and nickered softly once more, as if to say, "Yes, it's really me. I'm home."

Issie raised a hand carefully, afraid that if she moved too quickly, Mystic might simply fade like a wisp of grey smoke, and her hand would be left clutching at thin air. But no, there he was. She felt her fingers wrap around the coarse, ropey strands of his silver-grey mane, and before she could stop to think about it she was hugging him, her face buried deep into Mystic's neck, choking back her tears and inhaling deeply, breathing in his wonderful horsy smell.

Everything about Mystic felt real and warm. It was as if the accident had never happened and her pony was still alive after all.

Issie knew now that she wasn't dreaming. And she also knew that if Mystic was here then it meant just one thing – Blaze was in danger. This time, she needed no encouragement from Mystic – she knew exactly what she had to do.

"Come on, boy," she said, "you want to go for a ride again, don't you?" And she walked with the grey gelding by her side towards the backyard gate, where she climbed up the rails and vaulted lightly on to Mystic's bare back.

"Steady," she breathed to the pony as she eased him forward a couple of steps to unlatch the gate hook. And then they were trotting out together, Mystic's hooves clack-clacking briefly as they crossed the tarmac of the street behind Issie's house, down on to the grass verge by the side of the road and out into the blackness of the night.

Once they reached the grass, Mystic broke into a canter, and Issie wound her hands tight into a hank of his mane and wrapped her legs firmly against the barrel of his belly to keep from sliding off.

Riding bareback didn't scare her. When she had first been given Blaze she didn't have a saddle for the mare and so she had learnt to ride well without one. Besides, Mystic's canter had always been so smooth to ride. Tom Avery had always laughed and said it was like riding a rocking horse instead of a real pony.

Even now, with no bridle or anything else to grip on to, Issie felt secure on Mystic's back. She buried her hands further into the thick mane and bent down low over the pony's neck as his rocking-horse canter turned into a gallop. The road in front of her was barely lit by the moon and she couldn't see where she was going, but Mystic knew where to go. Issie felt certain that he was taking her to the pony club to see Blaze.

Road lights lit their way clearly now as they left the backstreets and struck out along the main road that led to the pony club. In broad daylight this road was nerve-wracking to ride alongside because of the traffic. But now, at three in the morning, there were hardly any cars at all. The rhythmic pounding of Mystic's hooves striking against the soft grass of the verge was the only sound in the quiet of the night, and Issie found herself almost hypnotised by the steady stride of the horse beneath her.

As they turned off into the side road that led to the pony club, Issie felt her heart pounding. She and Mystic hadn't been here together since the accident. This time, though, it was Blaze that was in danger. Issie was sure of it now.

But what kind of danger? The paddocks looked quiet and empty, and Issie's eyes, which were well-adjusted to the dark now, couldn't make out anything unusual.

She clucked Mystic forward and leaned down to unlatch the gate to the first paddock. Her hands slid over the hard metal of a large padlock. Of course! The pony-club gates were always padlocked shut. She didn't have the keys with her but she knew that there was a spare set in the tack room underneath the clubroom.

"Wait here, boy," she said to Mystic, and she slid down lightly from the grey gelding's sleek back, landing like a cat on the ground beside him.

Issie tried her best to be quiet but the gate creaked a little as she climbed the metal rungs and jumped down on the other side. Silhouetted against the paddock, she could clearly see the clubroom, and she headed quickly towards it now, her eyes scanning the far paddock horizon to see if she could make out the shape of Blaze grazing there. She wanted to run straight to her to see if she was OK, but first she needed to look for those keys so she could let Mystic in through the gates.

Instead of going up the front steps to the clubroom door, Issie crept around the side of the building to the door underneath that led to the downstairs tack room. The tack room was bound to be locked too, but the riders kept a spare key on a hook hidden behind the hay bales. She was about to search for the key, but first Issie put her hand on the door handle and gave it a turn just in case. She was surprised when the door sprang open easily in her hand.

If her eyes had adjusted to the night sky, they were not prepared for the darkness of the tack room, which was pitch black. Issie stepped forward with her arms outstretched, as if she were blind. *To the right-hand side of the doorway there should be a light switch*, she thought, and she moved that way now with both hands still raised in front of her, feeling her way to the wall and the light switch.

A shuffling noise made her instinctively look up, even though she couldn't see anything in the pitch black. She was shocked by the sudden impact of a body ramming up against her, shouldering her down to the floor. For a moment she struggled against the weight pressing down on her. Terrified in the dark, she fought her way free. Then she felt someone pushing past her and out the door of the tack room, and she heard the sound of footsteps. Whoever had knocked her down had gone, making a run for it across the paddock.

Breathing hard with shock, she leapt up, groping at

the walls in the darkness, looking for the light switch. Her fingers found it and she was suddenly illuminated in the golden glow of the room. The bare bulb cast enough light for Issie to just make out a figure in the distance, a woman she was pretty sure, with long dark hair, running back towards the main road.

Issie began to chase after her, but within a few strides she realised she was too far behind to catch up. The figure vaulted easily over the paddock fence and the next thing Issie knew there was the sound of a car engine starting up and the squeal of tires. And then there was silence.

Issie stood shaking and bewildered in the darkness. What was going on here? An hour ago she had been tucked up in bed, dreaming about horses, and now here she was again, knee-deep in trouble with a mystery on her hands.

She heard a nicker behind her and realised that Mystic was still at the paddock gate. "I'm OK, boy!" she yelled back to him. Then she added quietly to herself, "Oh, Mystic! What on earth have you dragged me into this time?"

CHAPTER 6

School was a nightmare the next day. Issie was exhausted after spending half the night sneaking about at the pony club.

After her tussle with the stranger in the tack room Issie had gone back and found the keys to let Mystic through the gate. Then, with Mystic's help, she had eventually found Blaze in the far paddock where, to Issie's great relief, the mare appeared to be safe and sound.

As the dawn haze was just beginning to creep up the horizon, she had ridden home on Mystic, making it back in time to slip into her room and back into bed before her mother noticed she was missing.

It seemed to Issie that her head had only just hit the pillow when her alarm went off again and she had to get up and pull on her school uniform. She had to get to school early to find Stella and Kate before class and tell them about what had happened.

By the time she reached school it was too late, the bell had gone. Luckily, their first class that Monday was P.E. with Miss Burgess, which meant that Issie could fill her friends in on everything while they got changed into their gym gear.

Well, not everything, exactly. She skipped the bit about Mystic of course. Sometimes she longed to tell her best friends about the grey ghost horse, but she knew instinctively that Mystic was meant to be her secret. And so she told them that she had woken up from a dream, a premonition that Blaze was in danger, and biked up to the club grounds instead.

"Issie! How dangerous!" Kate said when she told her about the stranger who had knocked her down.

"Did you get a good look at her?" Stella asked.

"No, not really." Issie shook her head. "It was dark in the tack room and by the time I switched the light on she had gone. I'm pretty sure it was a woman, and she had long, dark hair. And, well, Francoise had just been to see Blaze that morning and Blaze had acted so strangely!"

"Do you think it might have been Francoise? Maybe Blaze is connected somehow to the El Caballo mares?" Stella's eyes were shining with excitement now. "I mean, if she has no papers, but she really is an Anglo-Arab and she's the same colour as them then maybe they're from the same bloodline?"

"Oh, don't be silly, Stella! There are loads of horses who are the same colour and it doesn't mean they're related or anything!" Kate said sensibly.

"But, I mean, they even have the same colour manes and white socks as Blaze. Deep liver chestnut with flaxen mane and tail? It's not a boring, common colour like bay..."

Kate glared at her. Stella realised what she had said. "I don't mean that Toby is common and boring. I just meant... Anyway," Stella continued, ignoring the fact that Kate was now in a sulk, "if Blaze isn't related to the El Caballo mares then why was Francoise sneaking around like that? What does she want?"

Issie looked serious. "Stella, we don't know that it

was Francoise. She seemed really worried about Blaze when she bolted in the paddock."

"Why did Blaze bolt?" Stella was puzzled.

"It was weird," Issie said. "Francoise did this whistle with her hands and then Blaze just went crazy. I don't know why, but that's how it seemed anyway. I mean, why would someone whistling make her act so strangely. I've never seen her rear up like that before and it took ages to calm her down."

"Is Francoise coming back again to see Blaze?" Kate asked.

"No, but she said if we wanted to, we could go to the show again. She's going to leave us tickets on the door and we can go backstage afterwards and meet the horses," Issie said.

"We should definitely go!" Stella said. "Issie, we need to find out more about Francoise and why she was at the paddock in the middle of the night. And besides," she added, "I want to learn how they teach those horses to bow – then I can teach Coco to do it!"

"Oh, Stella!" Kate rolled her eyes. But she agreed that they should all go and see the El Caballo Danza Magnifico horses again.

The girls didn't see each other again at school that day until lunchtime. They were sitting in the sun on the sports field eating lunch – or rather Kate and Stella were eating their lunch, and Issie was poking suspiciously at a lettuce and tomato sandwich that her mother had packed for her – when Annabel Willets came over to say hi.

Annabel was a year older than Issie, Kate and Stella, and she was in year nine this year, so they hardly ever saw her at school. But now that they were all in the same team for the Gold Shield, Annabel was much more chatty.

"Avery suggested that we should get together tonight to do some practice for the relay races," Annabel told them.

"Good idea," Kate agreed. "We need to tell Dan and Ben to be there too. Issie, why don't you phone Dan to check that he knows about the practice tonight?"

"Why me?" Issie squeaked. She felt a bit embarrassed around Dan these days. Ever since he asked her to go and see the bands play at Summer in the Park and she had got angry with him because she thought he was going out with Natasha Tucker… well, everything had got so confused. She knew now that Dan was never dating Natasha. He had only asked her along because his mum made him. Dan did seem to really like Issie. You could tell because he always, always smiled at her and kind of teased her. But she had hardly seen him all winter. They went to different schools, after all, and it had only been at the pony-club rally last weekend that they had really started hanging out together again.

Issie felt weird about phoning up Dan. But she realised that if she told Kate and Stella that, they would know that she really did like him. She faltered for a moment, "I mean, I don't think it would be a good idea for me to call him. It's Avery's job to organise team training. It would be a better idea if we got him to call Dan and Ben, and he'll probably want to get Natasha and Morgan along too because they're the reserves."

To Issie's relief everyone agreed that this was the best plan. Avery would call the others and they could all meet that afternoon at the pony club for the first team practice session.

It was already getting late in the afternoon when the girls arrived at the paddock to bring their horses in to prep for the training session. Issie's mum had given them a lift so they wouldn't have to ride their bikes along the dangerous main road at dusk.

"If Mum only knew that I rode here in the middle of the night on Mystic to see you," Issie whispered quietly to Blaze as she brushed the mare. Blaze nickered back to her, and Issie giggled. Last night's drama in the tack room seemed so distant now that Issie began to wonder if she had imagined the whole thing.

She had gone into the tack room as soon as she arrived with Stella and Kate, and all three of them had taken a good look around. They had all left their tack there overnight – and so had Annabel Willets – and nothing seemed to be missing.

"It can't have been thieves," Stella pointed out, "because nothing was stolen. It must have been Francoise. Who else would have a reason for being here in the middle of the night?"

Annabel had walked into the tack room at that point to grab Eddie's halter, so the girls had stopped talking about Francoise and gone to catch their ponies and saddle up too.

By the time they had brushed out their manes and tails, everyone had arrived.

As they saddled up, Avery rallied the parents together, "Come on Mrs B and Mrs H," he said to Issie and Dan's mums. "Let's get the games sorted, shall we, while the kids tack up?"

While the team got ready the mums helped Avery prod the bending poles into the ground in two neat rows. "We're going to practise relay races," Avery explained, "so we'll only need the two rows of poles – one for each team."

Avery split the riders into two teams. Natasha, Morgan, Dan and Ben were on one team. Issie, Kate, Stella and Annabel were on the other. The riders stood there, lined up in front of Avery in their two teams, and he explained what they were about to do.

"You've all done bending races before and you're all very quick through the poles," Avery said, "but as I've said before, the Gold Shield is all about teamwork and you'll need to play to your strengths if you're going to make a good time in the relay event.

"There will be six of you in the relay race team at the real event, but today for training purposes I've split you into two teams of four," Avery continued.

"The idea is to pass the baton from one rider to the next. You cannot cross the line and start the race until the baton has been passed to you."

"We need to find the fastest riders to go first and last. One of you will hopefully set the pace and get us an early lead. The other rider brings up the rear in the running order so that if we are losing in the final stages then we still have a chance to make up lost time and win. The rest of you will make up the middle order, and the main thing to remember is do not, no matter what, drop that baton."

Avery looked serious. Issie remembered what Kate had said about Marsh Fields rubbing it in the last time they won. She also remembered Avery's own name on that Gold Shield when his team had won it back in 1985. *This must mean a lot to him*, Issie thought. Avery clearly meant for his team to win this time.

"Now," he eyed up the eight riders, "do any of you

have horses who don't get along with each other? I want to make sure there's no trouble while the horses are lining up to race and the last thing we need is a grumpy mare taking a swipe at the horse next to her."

Stella raised her hand. "Coco can get a bit stroppy sometimes and she doesn't like standing next to Max," she admitted.

"Good. Thanks for that, Stella. Let's make sure Coco and Max are separated in the running order. Anyone else with problems?" Avery looked around the group. "No? Excellent. Let's begin then, shall we?"

Avery passed a baton each to Issie and Natasha, who were both first to ride in their groups. The two girls lined up at the starting line and the other riders lined up in two rows behind them.

"Now, as you race for the finish line at the end you need to pass the baton right hand to right hand," Avery pointed out to them. "So you must all take the right hand side of the very first pole. Otherwise you'll be on the wrong side and you'll get yourself in an enormous tangle." He looked at them with a considered gaze.

"Get it? Good. Let's give this a practice run without a stopwatch just to see how you go," he said.

"On your marks…" his voice was deep and serious, "get set… GO!"

Issie and Natasha both shot forward at the same time and began to weave their way furiously at a fast canter through the bending poles. By the time they reached the last pole at the end of the course, Issie was just slightly in the lead. Then Blaze made a tight, hard turn at the last pole that put her almost a length ahead on the way home.

"Go, Issie! Go!" Stella and Annabel were screaming her on as Issie slalomed through the very last pole with her arm outstretched, the baton in her hand. On the other side of the start line Kate clucked Toby on so that he was already in a canter as he crossed the line and Issie smoothly passed Kate the baton.

"Go, Kate!" the others on the team shouted. But Toby was slow and lumbering through the bending poles. They lost their lead to Dan who was over a length ahead and already passing his baton to Ben.

As Kate finally weaved her way to the finish line she got the baton tangled in her reins and fumbled it as she charged past Stella. Toby kept right on cantering and Kate still hadn't handed Stella the baton.

"Stop him, Kate!" Stella screamed at her as she turned Coco around and cantered frantically after the big bay who was still heading off towards the clubroom.

Kate finally managed to pull Toby to a halt and pass the baton to Stella, who wheeled Coco around again and took off hell for leather towards the bending poles, but by then the girls had well and truly lost their lead. The other team were ahead by over three lengths.

"It's up to you, Annabel, you'll have to make up the lost time," Issie told her as Annabel lined Eddie up at the start line.

"I'll try," Annabel said, trying to keep Eddie steady as he danced nervously waiting for their turn to race.

Stella had made up almost a length in her race against Ben and now she handed the baton smoothly to Annabel.

"Get up!" Annabel shouted to Eddie as she charged forward at a belting canter towards the first pole. She was standing up in her stirrups in two-point position, leaning over Eddie's neck as she urged the pony on, trying to make up the last two lengths distance that now separated her from Morgan, who was racing against her.

"Go, Annabel! Go, Eddie!" Issie, Kate and Stella yelled at the top of their lungs, urging her on.

As Annabel took the last pole, she turned Eddie hard. The stocky palomino gelding responded brilliantly, pivoting hard on his hindquarters to twist around and come back again.

But as he turned there was a sickening lurch. Eddie snorted with surprise and leapt suddenly to one side and Annabel, who had been low over his neck, twisted around and fell underneath him, narrowly avoiding his hooves. She hit the ground hard and lay very still, and the next thing Issie saw was Avery and Mr Willets running. Mr Willets had a terrified expression on his face.

"I'll get the first-aid kit," Mrs Brown shouted after them, and she turned and ran into the clubhouse.

Avery made a grab for Eddie's reins. The gelding was panicked but seemed fine. Annabel, meanwhile, had regained consciousness, but was crying in pain.

"I think she's got a broken leg," Mr Willets called out to Tom. "She can't move it."

"What happened?" Stella was watching open-mouthed. "She just seemed to go flying when they took the last pole."

"I think this answers the question," Avery said to the girls as he led Eddie back over towards them. In his left hand he held up a stirrup leather.

Issie looked at it and realised that the leathers had broken clean in two. "It must have been loose stitching."

Avery shook his head as he examined the leathers. "But these leathers are brand new! And they're good ones, too. It looks like the leather was cut. I don't understand it!"

Issie looked at Stella and Kate. "I think I understand it," she muttered to them. "The tack room. Last night, remember? Annabel's gear has been sabotaged! Maybe the intruder wasn't trying to get to Blaze after all..."

CHAPTER 7

That Wednesday night, in the Riders Lounge at the Chevalier Point Pony Club, a secret meeting took place. The big, tattered armchairs were arranged in a tight circle around the coffee table, and in the chairs sat Kate, Stella, Isadora and Ben. The sound of the front door opening suddenly made all four of them jump in their seats, and then collectively breathe a sigh of relief as Dan walked in through the clubroom door.

"Good! We're all here, then, we can get started at last," Stella said. She popped up from her chair as Dan sat down in his and paced the floor around the wooden coffee table, looking serious.

"Get started on what, Stella?" Dan smiled. "What on earth is all this about? Mum had to drop me off here and I had to tell her it was a team tactics meeting for the Interclub Shield. Now, what's going on?"

Stella scanned the room as if she was checking to make sure no one else was here to snoop on their conversation, then she paused again, clearly enjoying the dramatic moment, before she finally spoke: "We're here to solve the mystery, of course. We're here to figure out who sabotaged Annabel's stirrup leather." She paused again then added, "The five of us must solve the crime or who knows who might be next!"

There was a muffled laugh from Ben, who had to stick his hand over his face at this point, and then Kate, who was trying to suppress a case of the giggles, completely lost it and doubled over with laughter.

"Kate, this is serious!" Stella looked darkly at her.

"Oh, for goodness sake, Stella. We're not the Famous Five!" Kate blurted out before succumbing with the others, who were rolling about in fits of giggles.

"Ohh! It's like *Scooby Doo*!" Ben wheezed, his hand on his chest as he tried to pull himself together and breathe between giggle attacks.

Stella glared at them, her hands on her hips. "Come on! Issie, you tell them. You heard what Avery said – that stirrup leather was no accident. And you said yourself that you thought other riders could be in danger. I don't think there's anything funny about us trying to find out who did it."

"No, Stella is right," Issie agreed. "This is real. Someone cut that stirrup leather. Annabel said afterwards that she had just bought new ones last month, so there is no way that the leather snapped by itself."

"Has anyone seen Annabel? Is she OK?" Ben asked.

"The three of us went to visit her in hospital yesterday," Issie said. "They've put her leg in a big long cast that goes all the way to her hip. The doctor said she won't be able to ride again for at least six weeks."

"Poor Annabel," Kate sighed. "And Eddie was going so beautifully lately. His dressage was really coming along…"

"I think we're getting a little off the point here," Stella snapped. She was still pacing around the coffee table, her hands clasped behind her back as if she were Sherlock Holmes addressing the crowd as he summed up a case.

She stopped now in front of them, raising one finger aloft as if she were making a very crucial point. "Who would have a reason to want to hurt Annabel?" Stella asked.

"Oh, Stella, this really is too silly." Kate was grouchy now. "No one had any reason to hurt Annabel. It was just an accident, obviously."

"Or maybe," Stella continued, "maybe they just got the wrong girl!" Stella turned to Issie. "Isadora, you said you saw Francoise coming out of the tack room in the middle of the night. Couldn't she have done this? I mean, couldn't she be the one who cut Annabel's stirrup leather? She must have mistaken Annabel's saddle for yours and sabotaged her leathers instead!"

"What? What are you talking about?" Dan broke in. "Who is this Francoise and why would she be in the tack room in the middle of the night? Issie? What is this all about?"

And so Issie and Stella and Kate all started talking at once over the top of each other. They told Dan and Ben all about El Caballo Danza Magnifico and the horses that looked just like Blaze, and how Francoise had come to visit that day.

When they had finished their story, Dan and Ben both sat gobsmacked in their armchairs. "Well, Issie," Dan shook his head in disbelief, "you are most definitely the most interesting girl I have ever met!"

Issie blushed at this, and then Dan, realising what he had said, blushed too and added hurriedly, "I mean, I think Stella is right, maybe this Francoise does have something to do with Annabel's accident. I think we should investigate further."

"Ohhh, you should come with us!" Stella suggested. "To El Caballo Danza, I mean. Kate and Issie and I are going to go along on Sunday. Francoise said she would give us free tickets to the show, and we're going to go backstage afterwards and meet all the horses. I'm sure she won't mind if you and Ben come too."

Everyone agreed that Ben and Dan should come with them that weekend to the show.

"Meanwhile," Stella instructed, "I think all of us should keep our eyes open during the next practice session on Saturday, just in case any other gear gets tampered with."

The five of them took a vote that night on whether to tell the other riders about this. "After all, Natasha and Morgan are in the team too," Ben and Dan had argued. It was harder for them to keep it a secret, Issie realised, because Dan and Ben both went to Kingswood, the same school as Natasha and Morgan.

"No," Issie had said, "we don't know that it was Francoise who did this. And if there is someone else out there who is sabotaging the Interclub team, then the less people that know about it the better. We need to keep this to ourselves until we have more proof."

Besides, she thought to herself, *Natasha would only laugh at them if they tried to warn her.*

"Well, if we don't tell them that they're in danger then I think we should at least try to keep an eye on them too, and check that their gear is safe," Stella suggested. The five of them agreed that this was a good idea. Issie would somehow get close enough to Natasha to check on Goldrush, while Stella would keep an eye on Morgan.

When they all left the clubroom that night, they carefully checked the tack room downstairs – Ben tried to make ghost noises in the dark to scare the girls. Then they made double-sure that the door really was locked before they went home.

The next Saturday morning, when they were saddling up at the club, all the riders made sure to check their stirrup leathers and girths extra carefully just in case. Stella took her sleuthing duties very seriously and when Morgan and Araminta arrived at the club with Jack in the horse truck, she shot off instantly in their direction.

Kate shook her head as she watched Stella racing off towards the truck. "What's she going to say to them?" Kate wondered. "How do you casually ask someone if you can check their horse to see if they've been sabotaged?"

A few minutes later Stella was running back across towards them with a huge smile on her face. "Did it!" she beamed proudly. "I told Morgan that Avery was getting me to do a routine gear check on all the riders after the accident. Well, Morgan looked a bit spooked at first but she let me check over her saddle and bridle, and I got Araminta's autograph at the same time," she said, pulling a piece of paper out of her jodhpur pocket.

"It's not for me, it's for my little sister," she added hastily.

"Well, then, I guess it's your turn, Issie," Kate said. "What excuse could you possibly have that Natasha will believe?"

Issie looked over at the silver Mercedes SUV and silver horse float where Goldrush was tied up. Natasha appeared to be lying down on the back seat of the car looking bored, while her mother tacked up her pony for her.

"I'll think of something," Issie said hopefully as she set off reluctantly in their direction.

Luckily, it looked like she wouldn't even need an excuse. She watched as Mrs Tucker and Natasha walked away from the float and headed off for the clubroom. Now was her chance!

When Issie reached the horse float, she slipped between Goldrush and the float where she couldn't been seen. Then she examined the saddle, checking on the stirrup leathers, which showed no signs of being tampered with. She checked the girth too, flipping back the top flap of the saddle to examine the straps. They seemed fine.

Issie slipped under Goldrush's neck and back through to the other side to do the check on that side of the saddle too. Unfortunately, just as she bobbed up from under Goldrush's neck she saw Natasha walking back towards her from the clubroom with her mum.

Frozen with panic, Issie considered running away. But it was too late. Natasha had definitely seen her. No, she had to come up with something else. She gave a smile and a wave and Natasha, after checking over her shoulders to see who Issie could possibly be waving at, gave her a reluctant wave in return.

"Hi, Natasha, hi, Mrs Tucker!" Issie smiled. Her brain was racing now. What on earth was her excuse?

"Oh, it's Isabella, isn't it?" Natasha said frostily. She had met Issie a million times but seemed to delight in never knowing who she was.

"Isadora," Issie said, trying desperately to keep the smile plastered on her face.

"How is that scruffy old charity pony that you got given?" Natasha smirked at her.

"Blaze is great, thanks," Issie said. "Umm, in fact that's why I came over here. A whole bunch of us are going along to El Caballo Danza Magnifico – you know, the show with the dancing horses? Well, the mares look just like Blaze and I know the woman who runs it and we've got free tickets for tomorrow to see the show…" Issie gulped, she had no choice, it was her only solution "…and I was wondering if you'd like to come with us."

Please say no. Please say no, Issie wished as soon as the words were out of her mouth.

Natasha gave a sneer of disinterest and Issie's heart soared. Then she sighed with boredom and finally spoke, "OK, why not?" She turned to her mother. "I can go, can't I, Mum?"

Mrs Tucker nodded. "Yes, of course. Thanks very much, Isadora, Natasha would love to come with you. Is your mum taking you? I'll drop her off at your house tomorrow. What time is it?"

"Umm, we're leaving at midday," Issie said.

Mrs Tucker smiled. "Lovely, see you then." And she walked off, leaving Natasha and Issie still standing there.

"I can't wait to see the show," Natasha said to Issie. And then she added, "because I bet those dancing mares don't look anything like your scruffy mutt of a pony. There's no way she's a purebred Anglo-Arab.

A horse like that costs a fortune, just like Goldrush here. She has impeccable English riding-pony bloodlines. I won't even tell you how much she cost, but it was more than Mum's Mercedes."

Natasha eyed Issie up and down. "Your charity pony isn't a purebred. You don't get given horses like that, Isadora. And," she added, "in your case you most certainly could never afford one."

"How did it go?" Stella was bright-eyed with excitement as Issie came back over the paddock towards her.

"Great, Stella. Just great," Issie replied. "Thanks to your brilliant plan I had to ask Natasha Tucker to come to El Caballo Danza with us!"

The news that Natasha was going to be joining them tomorrow didn't go down too well with Kate either. "Couldn't you think of any other excuse?" Kate sighed.

Issie shook her head. "I know; it was a bit dim of me. But anyway, it probably won't be that bad."

Kate and Stella looked at her as if to say that in fact

it would probably be even worse than bad, but no one said anything – it was clear that Issie felt bad enough about the whole thing.

Apart from the Natasha Tucker incident, the training session went well that day. Issie and the gang were on the look out for anything suspicious, but nothing strange happened at all. The riders all swooped gracefully between the bending poles, practising their relays and their baton passes, and Avery kept checking his stopwatch and nodding with a look of quiet satisfaction on his face.

In the afternoon they did practice sessions for rider on the flat. Avery stood in the middle of the arena as judge, and all the riders walked, trotted and cantered around him in a twenty-metre circle, concentrating on keeping in the very best possible position to impress the judge.

"Heels down, hands still, eyes up!" Issie chanted to herself in her head as she trotted.

"Canter on!" Avery called to the riders, and he watched them now as they rode, calling out advice to each of them in turn. "Stella, you're gripping up with your knees. Relax your knee and keep your heels down... Ben, you're dropping your shoulder in... Morgan, keep Jack on the bit, don't let go of the contact... Good, Issie, very good. A bit more impulsion at the canter, yes, that's it... lovely stuff!"

Issie focused hard on keeping her position perfect and keeping Blaze at a balanced, steady canter. The mare was going so beautifully and Issie was thrilled that the rearing incident didn't seem to have affected her. Blaze was her old self again.

"Excellent effort today!" Avery said as he walked down the row in front of them all at the end of the practice session. "I know that some of you have been to visit Annabel in hospital." Avery smiled at Stella, Kate and Issie. "And the news is good – she will be fine. But there's no way that leg of hers will heal in time for her to ride at the Interclub."

He turned now to his two reserves. "Natasha, I've decided that with Annabel out for the competition, you will be our new team member. Morgan will remain as our reserve. Right? Excellent!"

And with that, Avery strode off towards the horse

floats. The team, including a rather smug Natasha, turned and began to head in the same direction to unsaddle and go home.

Issie was about to ride after the others when she noticed Morgan hadn't moved. She was sitting quite still on Jack and she was trying desperately not to look upset, but failing utterly.

"Are you OK?" Issie asked her.

"Uh-huh," Morgan nodded, although she was clearly trying not to cry. "I just thought... I thought that with Annabel gone Avery would put me in the team. I never thought that it would be Natasha."

Morgan sighed, "Mum will kill me when she finds out."

"Why?" Issie was puzzled.

A single tear trickled down Morgan's left cheek. "Oh, you know, she really, *really* wants me to make the team," Morgan said. "She wants me to ride for Chevalier Point in the Gold Shield like she did when she was my age."

"I'm sure Avery just chose Natasha because she's been at pony club for longer than you have," Issie offered hopefully.

Morgan looked at her darkly. "I didn't expect you to understand. The Gold Shield means everything to Mum. I need to get my name on it, just like she did," she said. There was a chill in her voice now as she turned to Issie and wiped away the tear. "Anyway, you'd better catch up with the others. You don't want to let your team down," and she spun Jack around and kicked him on into a canter, leaving Issie standing alone and wondering what she had done wrong.

CHAPTER 8

True to her word, Francoise had left the girls' tickets at the door for the matinee session of El Caballo Danza Magnifico.

"Wow!" Stella was impressed. "These must be the best seats in the house. We're so close to the arena we could almost touch the horses as they go past."

"Maybe we will actually get to touch them," Issie said. "Francoise is going to show us around backstage after the show and she said she would introduce us to the horses and riders."

"I doubt it," Natasha sniffed. "They don't just let the public go backstage, you know. These are very valuable animals." She turned to Issie. "When are we going to see the dancing mares that look so much like your mongrel pony?"

"They don't come on until later. It's the stallions first," Issie replied.

The matinee show was very much like the performance the girls had seen when they came for Issie's birthday. But none of them minded watching it a second time. When the white stallions came out doing a Spanish Walk, with their legs lifting out into the air in an exaggerated flamenco prance, the girls clapped and cheered louder than anyone. They held their breath when Marius strutted into the arena, kicking his hindquarters elegantly back in a Capriole. They were sitting so close they could smell the horse sweat keenly in their nostrils and hear the grunts and snorts as Marius performed the most spectacular *haute école* movements.

As Marius left the ring, Issie looked at the programme that each of them had been given with their tickets. "The Arabian mares are next," she said excitedly. "They're going to do the Dance of the Seven Veils. Listen to this..." Issie began to read out loud from the programme.

"The Dance of the Seven Veils is performed by the school's six prized Anglo-Arab mares, all of whom share the same ancient Arabian bloodlines. These horses have been trained in the movements of the *haute école* like prima ballerinas, schooled by the famous Francoise D'arth, senior rider at El Caballo Danza Magnifico, formerly the head trainer at the Cadre Noir de Saumur in France. The Dance of the Seven Veils is an ancient tale. It was famously performed for the wicked King Herod by the beautiful Salome."

Suddenly there was a hush throughout the arena as the lights went out and the spotlights were trained once more on the sawdust floor of the ring. There was the faint tinkle of saddle bells and strains of exotic music, then the audience started clapping as the dancing Arabians cantered gracefully into the arena.

Blaze could be an Anglo-Arab just like these mares, Issie thought. If that were true then, like Natasha said, she must be worth a fortune. The Arabians were all a deep, burnished liver chestnut with pale creamy flaxen manes and tails. Today their manes had been plaited up and the horses each wore scarves of silk chiffon knotted into their braided manes to match the veils worn by their riders.

Issie spotted Francoise D'arth immediately. She was leading at the front of the ride, wearing a veil and harem pants in deep midnight blue covered with tiny clusters of diamond stars. As she rode past Issie she raised one hand to give her a wave, and Issie caught Natasha Tucker giving her a look of astonishment. Even snooty Natasha would have to believe that this famous rider was Issie's friend now.

Was Francoise really her friend though? Issie had waved back as the rider went past, but she didn't return her smile. Issie's instincts told her to trust Francoise. And yet, the more that she thought about it, the more certain Issie was that she was the mystery woman in the tack room that night. Why would the French trainer be prowling about the pony club in the middle of the night? Had she meant to cut Issie's stirrup leathers and got mixed up and injured poor Annabel instead?

At the end of the show, instead of following the crowds out into the main foyer, Issie and the others all walked across the sawdust of the main arena towards the doors that led out to the stables. When they reached the vast arched doorway that the horses came through to enter the ring, a big burly security guard emerged from behind the pillar to block their path. "Sorry, kids. Riders only. No entry for tourists here," he said sternly.

"It's OK, Rene, these are the young riders I was telling you about. They're with me," a voice behind the guard instructed. Francoise D'arth stepped forward out of the darkness and stood in front of them, smiling warmly. She had changed out of her costume and was wearing a pair of dark navy jodhpurs and a crisp white shirt with the sleeves rolled up.

"*Bonjour*, Isadora!" she said, greeting Issie and looking along the row of faces beside her. "I know Kate and Stella, but you three I do not know." She smiled at Dan, Ben and Natasha.

"Oh, sorry," Issie said, "this is Dan and Ben, and this is Natasha. We all go to pony club together."

"I hope you all enjoyed the show?" Francoise asked.

"Yes, thanks. Thanks for giving us the tickets," Ben and Dan said together.

"Yes, it was a fabulous show," said Natasha. "Your horses must be very expensive."

Francoise laughed at this, "Well, yes, I suppose they are," she replied. "All of our horses are bred from very select bloodlines that have been refined over centuries. The mares and stallions are chosen for their looks and temperament, and from the moment they are born, they are raised to be part of the riding school, to perform *haute école* movements and to dance for the crowds who come to see them—"

Natasha interrupted, "Yes, yes, but how much would my mum need to pay to buy me one of these horses?"

Francoise raised one eyebrow and smiled at her. "Oh, but I am afraid they are not for sale at any price. Besides, I am not sure that you could ride them. These horses are very finely trained in the ways of dressage and they all know a trick or two." She turned and smiled at Isadora. "It takes a very special rider to handle an El Caballo horse. "Now," Francoise said, "who would like to meet my horses?"

The stables for the El Caballo Danza Magnifico were divided into two separate wings. "One for the stallions," Francoise explained, "and one for the mares. When we are touring like this we do not spend much more than a month in each place," Francoise continued, "and during that time we must always find suitable accommodation for our stars."

They were standing now in a long avenue of stables, with a broad concrete floor bordered by stalls on each side. Francoise walked up to the first stall and unbolted the top half of the Dutch door, swinging it open so that Issie and the others could look inside.

As the young riders moved closer to look Francoise gave a sharp whistle and there was a nicker in reply from the rear of the stall. There was the sound of hooves on straw and then an elegant chestnut mare popped her head out over the bottom half of the door. Issie was struck immediately by how much she looked like Blaze. She had the same delicate dished nose, but instead of a blaze, she had a perfect diamond-shaped star on her forehead.

Francoise murmured something to the mare in French and the horse lowered her head so that

Francoise could give her a scratch underneath her forelock. The mare grunted with pleasure at this. "This is Jetaime, one of my six dancing mares," Francoise said. "She is just finishing her hard feed now and I was about to give her a hay net."

"Are all the mares in the show sisters?" Stella asked. "They all look so alike." Stella cast Issie a meaningful look.

"No," Francoise said. "They are not all sisters, although they do look alike, don't they? Many of them do have the same sire. Some do not. We choose them to match each other, and many of our troupe are handpicked before they are even a year old."

"What about the stallions?" Kate asked.

"The white ones are Lipizzaners, all bred from the ancient bloodlines of six great sires. There is some Arab blood in there, Andalusian, too, from Spain, and also from the sturdy white Karsk horses of Eastern Europe. Today we keep our herd on a farm in Spain, where we train the horses at our own stables and choose the best stallions to perform in our shows," Francoise said.

"What sort of a horse is Marius?" Kate asked.

"He isn't white like the rest of them."

Francoise smiled. "Marius, the grey horse which you saw performing alone, is a Lipizzaner too, but he is younger than the rest. Lipizzaners only become white when they reach a certain age. Marius is still young – he is only eight. When he was born he was almost black, but now as he grows up his coat is dappled. Perhaps when he is ten, his grey will have faded completely and he, too, will be as white as the others."

"Can we meet Marius?" Issie asked.

"Of course! He is in the round pen now with Wolfgang. They usually spend a little time together after each performance. Now, who would like to give Jetaime her hay net before we go? Stella, why don't you help me?"

After Stella, who was quite overcome with excitement at being chosen for the task, had fed Jetaime, the others took it in turns to give the mare a brush with a body brush while Francoise undid her plaits and combed out her mane.

Then Francoise closed the stable door and led them down the concrete corridors and through another door to a new row of stables. "This is where we keep the stallions," Francoise said. "Although occasionally if the weather is nice, we graze all the horses outside – keeping the mares and stallions in separate fields, of course."

Francoise walked briskly down the concrete corridor towards wide wooden double doors at the end of the hall. "This is the round pen. I think Marius is in here still," she called back over her shoulder.

Francoise swung open the doors and they found themselves in a round wooden room with a high ceiling. It was a bit like the bullfighters' rings that Issie had seen on TV. They were standing up high now behind a railing, and in front of them the space dropped away so they were looking down on a round arena sunken into the floor below them. The arena, which was about twenty metres wide, was bordered all around by three metre high wooden walls, and the floor was covered in sawdust. In the middle of the ring stood a tall man with short blond hair. He was holding a long, black lunging whip which he now lifted up above his head. As he waved the whip he gave a whistle.

In front of him, the dapple-grey stallion shifted his hooves uneasily and backed up, reversing so that he was almost sitting on his hocks. The horse gave a low snort and Wolfgang began to circle the whip around above his head. Now he whistled again: once, twice, three times.

Marius shook his head up and down as if nodding in agreement and then, as delicately as a ballerina, he rocked back on his hindquarters and raised his front legs up into the air so that he was rearing up. The stallion held the pose for a moment and then Wolfgang lowered his whip to the ground and the horse dropped too, coming back to rest in a perfect square halt.

"Wolfgang!" Francoise yelled. The blond man looked up at her and waved. Then he barked instructions to the stallion in a language that Issie didn't understand, and with a shake of his magnificent head Marius turned from the centre of the ring and headed towards the wooden barrier, his long, floating trot chewing up the ground so that it only took a few strides before he reached the wall. When it looked as if he was going to run into the side of the arena, Marius gave one more arrogant flick of his head, turned and started to trot around the perimeter.

Wolfgang shouted out another instruction and Marius began to canter. His neck was arched flamboyantly and every now and then he would lash out with a Flying Change, throwing his front hooves into the air as if striking out at an imaginary foe.

"He is young; he still has too much energy in him!" Wolfgang laughed as he watched the stallion snorting his way around the arena. He whistled at Marius and the horse slowed down to a trot again as Wolfgang climbed up the rails of the wooden arena, pulling himself up so that a few moments later he was standing next to Francoise.

"He's sooo beautiful," breathed Issie, leaning over the rails, unable to stop looking, mesmerised by the movements of the horse.

"Yes, he is," Wolfgang agreed. "But he is not easy. Of all the stallions I have trained, Marius is the most talented – and the most wild. He can be unpredictable." As if to prove this was true, at that moment Marius suddenly gave a squeal and rose up on his hind legs, his front hooves thrashing wildly in the air.

"I am sorry." Wolfgang frowned. "I should not leave him alone like this during a training session. A stallion must always be watched."

And with that he slipped back over the fence,

shimmying down gracefully on to the sawdust, and jogged across to Marius, who was now standing perfectly still and waiting for him as if butter wouldn't melt in his mouth.

"You see now why I prefer my mares." Francoise smiled. "They are temperamental, yes, but not quite so lethal as a stallion can be." She watched as Wolfgang led Marius out of the ring.

"I must go now, too," she said. "The horses must be fed and prepared for yet another performance tonight. I hope you have enjoyed the show. I will get Rene to show you out."

"Wait!" Issie said, panicking suddenly that Francoise would disappear before she had the chance to ask her the question.

"I mean, I wanted to ask you a question, Francoise, before you go."

"Of course." Francoise smiled. "What is it?"

"Why did Blaze rear when you whistled at her in the paddock the other day?"

Francoise's smile suddenly disappeared. For a brief moment Issie saw the look of shock on the Frenchwoman's face. Then she regained her composure.

"If I startled your mare it was a mistake and I have apologised." Francoise's voice was measured and cool. "It was nice to see you again, Isadora. But I must go now. Please take good care of Blaze. I will see you soon, no doubt."

"What was that all about?" Stella was wide-eyed as they left the stables. "Francoise is definitely up to something. What's her deal?"

Issie shook her head. "I don't know," she said, unable to keep the concern out of her voice. "But I need to find out."

As Kate's mum drove them home that night Issie thought about the way Francoise had reacted. Did she have a secret? And what did it have to do with Blaze?

Issie had been shaken from her daydreams by Stella and Kate asking if she would mind being the one to feed the horses that evening. She had been only too happy to say yes. After Francoise's strange behaviour she had suddenly felt a desperate need to check up on Blaze.

The light was fading and the sky was bruised purple and turning black when Issie finally arrived, later that night, at the pony club. Issie parked her bicycle up by the gates and looked out across the paddocks. Blaze, Toby and Coco had their heads down grazing happily, tearing up fresh chunks of sweet, green summer grass. They all looked up when they saw Issie, and Blaze nickered a greeting, knowing that Issie had come to feed her.

After her last experience in the tack room, Issie knew exactly where to find the light switch and she flicked it on before she entered the room. The bins of horse food were all lined up against the far wall and colour coded so that the riders couldn't get confused. Blaze's pony pellets were in the big blue feed bin, while Toby and Coco were both having chaff and sweet feed from the green and yellow bins.

Issie took the lids off the feed bins and used the scoop hanging on the hook next to the bins to measure out the right amounts into the ponies' feed buckets. Then she took all three buckets over to the tap and filled them with a little water, mixing the feed around with her hands. She smelt a strange, bitter smell rising off the pony pellets as the water mixed in with them, and she screwed up her nose.

Outside the tack room on the other side of the fence she could hear Blaze, Toby and Coco stomping their hooves restlessly. They knew their dinner was coming. "Just a minute!" Issie yelled out to them.

She stacked Toby and Coco's feed buckets on top of each other and tucked them under one arm, picked up Blaze's bucket and tucked that under the other arm and stepped outside. As she walked through the doorway, Issie gave a cry of alarm. There was someone there! No, wait, not someone. In the darkness the shape stepped nearer to her. It was a horse. It was Mystic!

"Hey, boy!" Issie laughed. "Oh, you gave me such a shock." Mystic was staring at Issie now, his eyes were dark with intent.

"What is it, Mystic?" Issie noticed that something wasn't right. Mystic was tense, pawing the ground with his left hoof, shaking his mane and looking agitated.

"Mystic, what's wrong?" Issie was really worried now. Mystic's nostrils were flared and he had a wild look in his eyes. The grey gelding snorted and stomped in front of her. Then suddenly he rose up on his hind legs so that he was towering above Issie. His hooves thrashed in the air perilously close to her head as he lashed out at her.

Issie screamed and panicked, throwing the feed buckets to the ground, leaping backwards and out of the way of Mystic's flailing front legs. "Mystic!" she screamed. "Stop it!"

CHAPTER 9

Issie was shaking with shock. Mystic had just attacked her! In front of her now, the grey gelding was fretting and shifting about nervously, shaking out his mane and stomping his front hooves restlessly.

"Easy, boy," Issie soothed. But Mystic still seemed tense. Suddenly he went up in the air, rearing again. This time, though, instead of rearing over Issie, his hooves thrashed the air above the feed buckets which were now strewn about, their contents scattered in the dust.

Mystic came down hard on the red plastic feed tub, whacking it firmly with his hooves so that it overturned again and the last remnants of Blaze's pony pellets were emptied on to the ground.

Then, almost immediately, the fire left Mystic's eyes. The dapple-grey was trembling and his coat was flecked with sweat, but the darkness had left him and he was his old self again.

Mystic stepped towards Issie, his head lowered as if in apology, his dark eyes were gentle once more. He nickered softly to her and stepped closer still, reaching out his neck and pushing against her, his soft velvety muzzle nuzzling against her arm. It was as if he was saying, "Sorry I scared you like that. Are you OK?"

Issie was confused. One minute her horse was lunging at her with his hooves flying over her head, and the next he was nuzzling her as if they were still best friends. Why had her own beloved Mystic tried to hurt her? It didn't make sense.

She cast her eyes over to the feed buckets which were upturned on the ground in front of her. The hard feed had been ruined. She would have to go back into the shed and fill them again.

"Oh, Mystic! Look what you've done!" Issie shook her head. And then suddenly she understood. This was exactly what Mystic had meant to do! He had never meant to hurt her at all. He had been trying to make her drop the feed buckets...

The horse feed! Issie said to herself. And then she turned to the little grey pony standing quietly now beside her. "Is that it, boy? It is the horse feed?"

She reached over for the red tub that was lying on the ground and picked it up. She remembered now how she had smelt something funny when she had been dishing up Blaze's feed. She stuck her face into the empty bucket and took a deep, long sniff. The smell was still there. A strange chemical bitter scent. What was that?

She put the tub down and went back into the tack room and over to the bins of hard feed where she had dished up the ponies' dinner. Issie opened the blue bin which housed Blaze's food and took another sniff. There was that smell again! She had smelt it before, but what was it?

Now she scanned the shelves above the feed bins where the riders kept their equipment. There were rolls of bandages and packets of gamgee, hoof oil and antibacterial creams, leftover empty tubes of worming paste and a big blue bottle of Showpony shampoo. And then she saw what she was looking for. On the shelf next to the worming-paste tubes directly above the feed bins sat a yellow bottle. The bottle had a childproof cap and a typed label on the front with vet's instructions. In large blue type at the top of the label was the word: SELENIUM. Underneath that, in slightly smallertype,theinstructions read: DIETARY SUPPLEMENT. GIVE 5MLS 2 TIMES A WEEK IN HARD FEED. DO NOT EXCEED RECOMMENDED DOSE.

Issie picked the bottle up and was shocked to discover that it was empty. "But it was half-full the last time I used it," she thought out loud. She squeezed off the childproof cap and took a sniff of the contents. It was the same bitter smell that was in the hard feed. Issie's eyes widened as she realised that someone must have emptied the whole bottle into the feed bin.

Selenium was good for horses and Issie's vet had given her the supplement to feed Blaze, but he had warned her that it was dangerous to give a horse too much. A whole bottle of selenium in her feed would be bound to make Blaze feel really sick.

Issie looked over now at Mystic. The little grey was still pawing uneasily at the ground where the hard feed was lying in the dust.

"I know, Mystic. I'm coming," Issie said, and she grabbed the spade that hung on the wall of the tack room, threw it into the wheelbarrow, and wheeled it over to the scattered feed bins lying on the ground. Carefully she scraped up the pony pellets which were now mingled in with the dust on the ground and dumped the spilt feed into the wheelbarrow. She made sure to scrape all of it up as she didn't want to risk the horses eating any of it by mistake. She went back into the tack room and, using the spade again, she emptied the blue bin which contained Blaze's contaminated hard feed out into the barrow too. Then she dumped the whole wheelbarrow-load in the big green rubbish bins at the front of the clubroom where the horses couldn't possibly reach it.

Watching her over the fence as she worked, Blaze, Coco and Toby kept giving her expectant whinnies. "I know you want your food," Issie shouted back at them as she washed out Blaze's storage bin, "but you'll just have to wait until I've cleaned up here first."

Finally, once she had checked to make sure that Coco and Toby's feed wasn't tampered with, she scooped all three of them up a new meal, giving Blaze a little bit of the same chaff and sweet feed mix as Toby and Coco were having so that she wouldn't miss out on her dinner.

"What do you think, Mystic?" Issie stood in front of the gelding with the feed buckets again and let the little grey inspect them this time. "Is it OK now?" Mystic gave the new feed a quick sniff of approval, then stood calmly by as Issie carried the three buckets over the fence and placed them down on the ground for Blaze, Coco and Toby.

Issie stood for a moment, watching her mare happily snorting and munching her way through the feed. A chill ran down her spine. *What might have happened if she had given Blaze the poisoned feed by mistake?* She didn't like to even think about it. Instead, she focused her thoughts on another question. *Who could possibly have done this? Why would anyone want to hurt Blaze?*

"Thank goodness you were here, Mystic," Issie said, turning around to the little grey gelding standing behind her. But Mystic wasn't there any more and Issie knew better than to bother to look for him. Blaze was safe now, and Mystic had gone just as quickly as he had arrived.

The next night, a second meeting of the secret pony-club gang was called. This time, though, the mood was much more serious in the clubroom as Issie told the others about the poisoned horse feed. Of course she skipped the bit about Mystic, telling the others that she had noticed the strange smell herself and the empty bottle of selenium and had figured out that someone must have put it into Blaze's feed bin.

Everyone was quiet for a long while when Issie finished her story. And then finally Kate spoke: "Well, I think we should tell the police," she said.

"Tell them what?" Dan snorted. "That someone spilt a bottle of supplement into a tub of horse feed? Big deal! That sounds like an accident to me. We need to find someone with a motive, a reason to hurt Blaze."

"I can think of someone," Stella piped up. The others all turned to look at her. "Oh, come on! It's so obvious!" Stella said. "It was Francoise! It had to be!"

She turned to Issie. "You've already found her lurking around the tack room once, and now here she is again. She's the one who cut the stirrup leathers — obviously she meant to hurt you and got poor Annabel by mistake. Now that's failed she's trying to poison Blaze. Issie, it has to be her!"

Issie felt her chest tightening. Could it be true? Was Francoise really trying to hurt Blaze?

"What if it wasn't Francoise?" Issie said. "You're all just assuming it was her. But what if it's not? Francoise has no reason to hurt Blaze or me. Maybe she's not the one who did this, and while we're wasting our time on Francoise the person who is really causing the trouble is still out there!"

"Issie, calm down," Dan said. "I think Stella is right. It's pretty obvious, isn't it? There have been too many strange coincidences since this Francoise turned up. Why is this woman interested in you and your horse? I think there's something fishy going on and you have to face the fact that she's behind it."

"Well, what if she is?" said Ben. "We still can't tell the police. We don't have any proof."

"We'll have to get some." Kate nodded.

"But I keep telling you," Issie was furious now, "Francoise had no reason to do this. What if she hasn't done anything wrong?"

"Issie, I can't believe you are still standing up for her!" Stella snapped back. "After all she's done. If Blaze had eaten that feed she would have been sick. So would Toby and Coco if they had eaten any. So she's putting our horses in danger too! You have to face up to the fact that Francoise is the one behind all of this or other horses may be hurt as well as Blaze."

Issie looked around the room at her friends in disbelief. The room went quiet once more as the five friends stood there, not speaking.

"I think we should take a vote," Ben said finally. "All those who think it was Francoise raise your hands."

There was a brief pause, and then four hands went up in the air. Issie took one last look around the room, and then she burst into tears and ran out the door.

It was nearly dark when Issie arrived home, and Mrs Brown was waiting for her. "I'm glad you're home," she called out to Issie as she walked in through the front door. "I've made roast chicken for dinner and it's ready now."

Then she saw her daughter's tear-stained face, and her eyes which were red from crying all the way home on her bike. "Issie! What on earth is the matter?" She gave her a long hug and then sat her down in a chair next to her at the kitchen table.

"I had a fight with Stella and the others," Issie sighed. "They all think that Francoise is the one responsible for everything…"

At that moment the doorbell rang. "It's nearly eight o'clock! What now? It looks like we will be eating cold chicken for a late supper at this rate." Mrs Brown smiled at her daughter as she got up from the table and went down the hallway to answer the door.

"*Bonjour*, Madame Brown." Isadora heard the voice of Francoise D'arth. "May I please come in? I have something very important to discuss with Isadora."

When Issie saw Francoise's face as she entered the kitchen, she knew immediately that something was very wrong. The dark-haired Frenchwoman looked very grave indeed.

"Would you like some dinner, Francoise?" Mrs Brown offered. "We were just about to sit down to some roast chicken."

"*Non merci*, thank you but no." Francoise shook her head. She was still standing back in the doorway, as if she were afraid to come closer. In her hands, Issie saw that she held a piece of paper.

"Well, then, at least sit down and let me make you a cup of tea," Mrs Brown said, and she gestured for Francoise to take a seat at the table across from Issie. "Now, you said you had something important to discuss?"

"Yes, but, well, I don't know how to begin..." Francoise said.

"Milk or sugar?" asked Mrs Brown.

"I like it black please." Francoise smiled weakly in response to Mrs Brown's question.

"Isadora," Francoise said, "do you remember the day when I first met Blaze, that morning at the pony club when I whistled for her, and she behaved strangely?"

Issie nodded, but didn't speak. Her heart was pounding in her chest.

"It was almost unbelievable," Francoise continued. "For only one of my mares, one of the Arabians of the El Caballo Danza Magnifico knows the sound of my whistle. Only one of my dancing Arabians would know that it is a signal to rear up and to gallop. My mares are trained in this way."

She looked Issie in the eyes. "It was at that moment, Issie, when Blaze responded to my whistle, that I knew who she really was. But it was not enough for me to know. I knew that my word would not be enough for you. So I needed proof."

Out of her pocket now, Francoise removed a plastic bag. Inside the bag were five long flaxen-blonde strands of horse hair.

"I came back the next night and pulled these out from Blaze's mane," Francoise explained. "These hairs contain Blaze's DNA. For the past week they have been at the laboratory being analysed and cross-checked against the hairs of my own dancing mares. They prove without a doubt what I have known in my heart the whole time, ever since I met Blaze."

"What is that?" Issie's mother asked as she put the tea down in front of Francoise.

Francoise gave Issie a look of deep sympathy. It was a look that made Issie feel completely and utterly sick because she knew in her heart now what was coming next. She felt the knot of anxiety that was growing inside her reach around her heart, making it hard to breathe.

"The tests confirmed what I knew," Francoise said. "Isadora, the horse that you call Blaze was once known by another name, her true name. She is called Salome. And she belongs to me."

CHAPTER 10

Francoise D'arth put the piece of paper, which Issie now realised was the DNA test result, down on the table. Issie stared at it. The numbers and words on the page were a blur to her, but she knew that what Francoise was telling her was the truth. It all made sense.

Issie thought back to that moment when she first set eyes on the El Caballo mares, and her shock when she saw how much they resembled Blaze. In the show, the mares had reared up and danced as part of their performance. When Blaze had reared at Francoise's whistle she was performing too, just as she had done when she was an El Caballo mare. Blaze wasn't Blaze at all – she was, what did Francoise call her? Salome. Of course! Issie knew she had seen that name somewhere. It was the same name as the dancer, the one who performed the Dance of the Seven Veils.

Francoise D'arth saw the pained look on Isadora's face and the tears welling in her eyes. She reached out across the kitchen table and took both of Isadora's hands in her own. "I would like to tell you a story," she said softly. "It's the story of the horse that you call Blaze."

Issie nodded mutely and Francoise began. "Isadora, the Arabian horse is a living treasure. In ancient times sultans and kings considered their best horses to be their most precious possessions. But did you realise that above all else, what mattered most to these kings were their mares? These mares were treasured beyond even the great Arab stallions, because their beauty and speed could be passed on again and again in the fine foals that they would bear.

"One such mare was a great beauty called Mahabbah. Legend has it that her beauty was unparalleled. She was a chestnut, just like your Blaze, and most of her descendants today are chestnut too. Mahabbah's bloodline is highly prized and it is from her that many of the mares at the El Caballo Danza Magnifico are bred."

Francoise smiled. "Your Blaze, the mare I call Salome, is descended from royalty. After all, Mahabbah belonged to sultans and was ridden by princesses. Her blood was then mingled with the strength and speed of the modern Thoroughbred. Blaze's dam was the mare Bahiyaa, a direct descendant of Mahabbah. Her sire was the great stallion, Night Dancer, a Thoroughbred also of noble and revered bloodlines."

Francoise looked at Issie, who was too stunned to say anything. "You seem surprised, Isadora." Francoise smiled. "Surely you must have known that Salome was a mare of high breeding?

"Over the years," she continued, "El Caballo Danza Magnifico's stud farm in Spain has grown. There we breed all of the horses that will appear in our show, the Lipizzaners and the Anglo-Arabs. We use the Lipizzaner stallions because of their great power and classical grace, and the Anglo-Arab mare because of her beauty and intelligence. Our mares are all bred to be the best examples of the breed. Yet when Salome was born, I knew she was something special. Her beauty surpassed the others and could be seen even when she was still a leggy foal at her mother's feet. I took it upon myself to train her to join the dancing Arabians.

"It was not an easy task. Salome has a mind of her own, as you have no doubt discovered. But she soon proved to be the cleverest of all my mares – as well as the most beautiful."

Francoise looked grave. "The El Caballo horses travel many hundreds of miles to perform. Our school travels around the world, you know, and almost one year ago we arrived here for the first time.

"It was the night of our first performance. We put the horses in their stalls. In those days we did not have Rene, who now guards the stables, and while all the riders went to dinner before the performance, there was no one left behind to watch over the mares. That was my mistake.

"The thieves took Salome first. They did not realise, I think, that she was my favourite. I believe that they had planned to steal all the mares, not just her. Luckily, we arrived back before they could open the other stalls and so they fled with Salome and left the rest. We did not even realise she was gone until hours later when we opened her stall and saw that she had disappeared.

"Rewards were offered, of course. I would have done anything to get her back. At first, we thought that maybe she had been smuggled overseas. In the right hands, Salome was worth a great deal of money. But these horse thieves did not realise how valuable their prize was. And they did not know what to do with her.

"I wanted to stay and search for her but the El Caballo Danza Magnifico must always keep moving. Our show travels all the time, month after month, year after year. It was impossible for us to remain in one place any longer. Besides, even if we could stay and look for Salome, we did not know where to begin. The thieves could have taken her anywhere. It was futile. I had given up all hope of seeing her again until... until we came back here again, this time to Chevalier Point, and I met you and heard your story. You told me that you had a mare that looked just like mine, and although I didn't dare hope that it might be Salome, I knew I had to meet her. It turned out that it was very lucky that I did."

Issie wiped a tear away roughly with the back of her hand.

"I am sorry," Francoise sighed. "Perhaps not so lucky for you. I did not mean to be cruel. I can see how much Salome means to you."

Francoise gestured at the piece of paper that she had put on the kitchen table. "This is why I had to have proof before I could speak to you about this, Isadora. I know how much you love this mare, and how much Salome also adores you too. You have saved Salome's life. If it were not for you I am sure she would have died. The horse thieves had treated her so badly and she was so very unwell when she came to you that only someone who truly loved her and could win her trust could have saved her life."

Issie smiled.

"However," Francoise's face was stern now, "Salome is not your horse and she is too valuable to the riding school for me to give her up to you. Besides, even if I wanted to give her to you, I could not.

Salome does not belong to me, she belongs to the El Caballo Danza Magnifico, and I work for them. They own her and, as you can imagine, they are looking forward to her return. Salome will once again become part of the Dance of the Seven Veils and our troupe will return to normal once more."

"But you can't! You can't take her!" Issie felt her face flush with anger and pain. "You don't need her. I saw the show. You can do it without her. Blaze is mine. I love her and she loves me. She's my horse and you can't take her from me!"

"Francoise, really, this doesn't seem very fair," Mrs Brown said. "Isadora was asked to be the guardian of this horse and as far as I can see, she has been much more than that. Blaze would not be alive if it weren't for Issie, you've said as much yourself. Isn't there something you can do about this?"

Francoise hung her head. For a moment, she was silent and Issie thought that perhaps, just perhaps, she was reconsidering.

Her hopes were dashed however when Francoise looked up at her again, her eyes filled with steely determination. "I am sorry, Mrs Brown. As I have explained, it is not my choice to make. Salome does not belong to me either, but to El Caballo Danza Magnifico. And she must be returned to the school."

She stood up now and walked towards the door, then she turned and spoke with a voice that was weary with sorrow. "Thank you for the cup of tea, Mrs Brown. It was most kind. I will be back tomorrow with a horse truck at nine a.m. to pick up Salome. I would appreciate it, Isadora, if you could have her ready for me by then? I am so sorry, but it is what I must do. *Au revoir.*"

As Francoise pulled the door closed behind her, Mrs Brown walked across the kitchen and picked up the phone.

"What are you doing, Mum?" Issie asked.

"Calling Tom Avery. I want to get to the bottom of this. If anyone can help us it's Tom," Mrs Brown said.

Half an hour later the doorbell rang again and there was Avery, his face just as grave as Francoise D'arth's had been when she had stood there not long before.

"I've contacted the International League for the Protection of Horses and unfortunately it looks like everything she says is true," Avery told them. "Francoise's paperwork all checks out and Blaze's DNA exactly matches the samples to prove that she is Salome."

He turned to Issie. "I'm sorry, Isadora. I don't think there is anything we can do. It looks as if Blaze is indeed her horse – or at least the property of El Caballo Danza Magnifico. Legally, they have every right to take her."

"But, Tom, there must be something we can do! I'm her guardian. She was given to me and she needs me!" Issie begged him.

"I know, Isadora, I know," Avery said. "If she is truly anyone's horse then she is yours. And if I had ever known this was going to happen, I would never have asked you to be her guardian. I never suspected for a moment that Blaze's real owners would turn up one day."

Avery looked at Issie. "I'm sorry, Isadora, but I cannot see any way around this. When Francoise turns up tomorrow morning you have no choice. You will have to let her take Blaze."

Issie hardly slept that night. Mrs Brown made her hot cocoa and brought it to her room, but it didn't help. she lay quietly in her bed, running through it all in her head, wondering what could be done. As the night shadows flicked across her bedroom walls Issie held her breath and listened. Perhaps Mystic would come to her now and they could save Blaze together. After all, hadn't they always saved her before? Yet Issie knew in her heart that this time it was different. There would be no midnight rescue this time. Mystic would not come. In the morning, Issie and Blaze would have to say goodbye.

It was well after midnight when she finally fell into a restless sleep.

She woke again when the light began to creep over her windowsill. It was a little after seven a.m. and Francoise was due at the pony club at nine. She would have to hurry and get dressed if she was going to cycle to the club grounds to meet her there.

Issie had a shower and dressed quickly in jodhpurs and a sky blue T-shirt, then raced downstairs. Her mum was already there with breakfast on the table – scrambled eggs and toast.

"No, Mum, I can't eat. I'll be late. I need to see Blaze," Issie insisted.

"I know," her mother said. "I'm going to take you to the paddock. Tom is coming too. But please, sweetie, just try and eat a little bit of breakfast before we go. You look exhausted and you need to keep your strength up."

By the time Issie had reluctantly eaten her eggs and Avery had arrived at the house it was nearly 8 a.m. "Time to go, then?" Mrs Brown asked. Issie nodded.

The three of them made the trip in the car to the pony club in silence. There was nothing left to say. Issie was regretting the scrambled eggs, which now seemed to be sitting in her stomach like a rock.

Issie was relieved to see that Francoise hadn't yet arrived when they reached the club grounds. In the far paddock Blaze was grazing peacefully, her long flaxen tail occasionally swishing lazily across her body to whisk away a pesky fly.

Issie was about to call out to the mare when, from behind her, she heard a whistle. Blaze raised her head. Francoise whistled again and this time Blaze returned her call with a shrill whinny, trotting up happily to the fence.

Francoise saw the broken-hearted expression on Issie's face and realised what she had just done. "*Bonjour*, Isadora." Francoise smiled. "We are here too early, I think. Perhaps you might like to catch Salome first and spend some time alone with her before we take her?"

Issie nodded, afraid to speak in case her voice might break and then the tears would start. She left Francoise's side and walked into the tack room. With a shaking hand she reached out and grasped Blaze's halter off the tack-room peg, slung it across her shoulder and set out towards the far paddock. Beneath her, her legs felt as wobbly as rubber, and butterflies churned in her stomach.

Blaze, on the other hand, seemed to have no idea that anything was wrong. To her, it was just another day at the pony club. As Issie approached she nickered a friendly greeting and stuck her head over the gate.

"Hey, girl." Issie tried desperately to smile. "It's OK. You're going on a little trip today."

Blaze nickered again and gave Issie a nudge, using her as a scratching post to reach an itchy spot on her forehead.

"Hey, quit it!" Issie smiled at her. And then her smile dissolved and she was crying, big hot angry tears as she slipped her arm under the pony's neck and slipped the halter up over her nose.

"The thing is, girl," Issie continued, "you have to go with Francoise and I can't come with you. You're going to be her horse now. You don't belong to me – not any more."

The tears were streaming down Issie's cheeks now and she had given up trying to make them stop. Instead, she buried her face deep into the mare's flaxen mane. She breathed in, trying to inhale deeply on her sweet horsy smell, but her nose was so runny from crying she couldn't smell anything. Her hands were clasped tightly around Blaze's neck now as if she never wanted to let go – which she didn't. She could feel the sleek smoothness of Blaze's glossy chestnut coat, and the silky strands of her mane which were tangled through her fingers.

If I just hold on a bit longer, maybe when I look up again they will all be gone and this will all have been a bad dream, Issie wished. She stayed there, with her head buried in Blaze's mane for what seemed like an eternity. But when she looked up again, wiping yet more tears from her red eyes, she could see that the world had not changed. Francoise, Avery and her mother were still waiting for her by the clubroom gates. The ramp to Francoise's horse truck had now been lowered ready to load Blaze.

Issie sniffed and took a deep breath. She wiped her face roughly on her T-shirt. She had made a vow to herself that they would not see her crying. "Come on, Blaze, time to go," she murmured, and she led the chestnut mare up to the waiting horse truck.

Issie watched as Francoise prepared Blaze for her journey, fastening on the padded floating boots and strapping on her dust cover, before putting a hay net inside the truck for the trip. As she worked, she spoke to Blaze gently in French and the mare seemed responsive and calm in her hands.

Finally, Francoise called out an order to her assistant, a young woman who was clearly one of the riders from the school, and the woman stood on the far side of the ramp as Francoise walked Blaze up and into the truck. Ropes were secured and partitions were bolted into place, and then the girl lifted up the ramp and bolted it shut. Blaze was now locked inside the truck ready to go.

Issie looked pleadingly at her mum and Tom Avery. They had been standing quietly watching as Francoise worked. Surely one of them would say something, do something to stop this? Avery walked over to Francoise and spoke to her. Issie couldn't hear what they were saying, but in the end Avery nodded and walked back to where he had been standing, next to her mother under the magnolia trees.

Francoise beckoned Isadora over to her. "We will be here for one more week before we pack up and travel again," Francoise said. "If you want to come and see Blaze once more before we go you would be most welcome. Just give me a call. Until then, *au revoir*."

And with that, Francoise turned and pulled herself up into the cab of the truck. There was a deep rumble as the engine revved into life, and then Francoise waved to Issie out the window as her assistant drove through the gates and down the gravel driveway that led to the main road.

Dust flew up from the tyres on the gravel. By the time it had cleared, the truck was gone. And so was Blaze. And at that moment, Issie forgot her vow and burst into tears.

CHAPTER 11

Issie knew that Blaze was really gone, but when she arrived later that day at the pony club she couldn't help scanning the horizon as if she somehow still expected to see her horse standing there. It was force of habit, she surmised grimly. In the far paddock she could make out the shapes of Toby and Coco grazing happily, but they were alone. Blaze was nowhere to be seen. Issie felt her heart sink all over again when she realised the truth: that Blaze would never be here with them again.

For that matter, Issie would probably never be here again either. She had come to the pony club this afternoon one last time to pick up all of Blaze's gear which was still in the tack room.

"Would you like me to help?" her mum had asked as they pulled the car up inside the pony-club gates.

"No, Mum, I'd rather do this by myself," Issie said. She left her mother in the car and walked across the paddock to the clubroom.

Issie opened the tack-room door and blinked as her eyes adjusted to the gloom inside. In front of her and to the left were the feed bins and the stacks of rugs and muddy covers. To the right hung the bridles and saddles, suspended up on the wall on rows of saddle racks, and among these were Issie's two saddles. There was one made from smooth black leather – a Bates Maestro, which was her dressage saddle. Next to it sat her jumping saddle, which was made out of honey-brown leather and had a flat seat and a well-worn look about it. Issie called them "her saddles" but in fact both of them actually belonged to Tom Avery. Issie still remembered the day he had given them to her when she first rode Blaze bareback to pony club. Now, she guessed, she had no reason to keep them any longer. She would have to give them back.

"I hope you're not thinking of returning those to me," a voice behind her said. "Because my tack room at the farm is full enough as it is."

Startled, Issie spun around to see Tom Avery standing there smiling at her. "Tom! What are you doing here?" Issie said.

Avery looked at his watch. "Team training in half an hour," he said. "I thought I'd better arrive early and get set up before the rabble arrive."

Issie nodded. She had forgotten all about team training. Well, she wouldn't be training any more, that was for sure.

"I was just sorting out Blaze's gear," Issie explained. "Mum and I can drop your saddles back to Winterflood Farm on the way home…"

Tom shook his head. "Isadora, I meant what I just said. I want you to hang on to those saddles for a while longer."

"But, Tom—" Issie began before Avery cut her off.

"You never know, you may still need them," he said firmly, making it clear that the matter was closed. Then he cast his eyes around the room. "Aha – the bending poles – who put them away over there?" He reached across behind the horse covers to pull out the plastic poles. "Why don't you stay and help me train the squad?" Avery smiled at Issie. "I can drop you home afterwards."

"OK," Issie smiled back, "I'll just tell Mum."

Issie was busily pushing the bases of the bending poles into the ground in a nice, neat row when Stella and Kate arrived at the paddock. The girls hadn't seen each other since Issie had run out of the clubroom in tears, and Issie didn't know what to say. So much had happened in just the last few days that it seemed like it was a lifetime ago that they had argued. Issie hadn't spoken to Stella or Kate since then. After Blaze was taken away she had been too depressed to go to school that day. But now she gave her friends a shy wave and Stella smiled and ran over to her, looking puzzled.

"Where's Blaze?" Stella asked. And Issie, relieved to be talking to her best friend again, told Stella the whole story. Then she had to take a deep breath and tell it all over again to Kate, who had come over too when she realised that something was going on.

"But, Issie!" Kate was shocked. "Francoise can't do that. Can she? Blaze is your horse!"

Issie shook her head sadly. "No. She never was. Avery always said that I was only her guardian. She belonged to the ILPH – and I guess she really belonged the whole time to El Caballo Danza Magnifico. It's not Francoise's fault. I mean, Blaze was stolen from her in the first place."

"Issie! There you go again standing up for Francoise. I can't believe it, after all she has done!" Stella was furious.

"No, Stella! Don't you understand? This proves that Francoise couldn't have done it!" Issie said. "That night when I got knocked down in the tack room Francoise was only there to get the hairs from Blaze's mane so she could do the DNA test. She had no reason to cut the stirrup leather. And she had no reason to poison Blaze either – after all, if Blaze was actually her horse then why would she try to hurt her?"

Stella's cheeks were flushed and she was ready to fight back. But as she thought through what Issie was saying, the pink flush turned to embarrassment as she realised that her friend had been right all along.

"All right, all right, so it wasn't Francoise after all. But you have to admit, Issie, that she was acting pretty odd, and I still think she's totally horrible taking Blaze away from you like that. I mean, Blaze is your horse. Everyone knows that."

"The thing is," added Kate, "that if Francoise didn't cut the stirrup leathers or tamper with the horse feed then who else could have done it?"

Issie shook her head. "I don't know. But I'm sure it wasn't Francoise."

"Anyway," Stella said, "I'm sorry, Issie. It was all my fault that we had that silly fight. I should have believed you about Francoise. I am so sorry that Blaze is gone."

"Poor Issie! You must feel dreadful," Kate said. The three friends hugged and Issie felt hot tears welling up. She was brushing them away and hoping no one would notice when she heard voices coming closer.

"Hey, hey, what's going on?" Issie looked up to see Dan and Ben sitting astride their horses with big grins on their faces.

The boys' smiles faded when Stella explained what

had happened to Blaze and unravelled the mystery of Francoise D'arth.

"But, Issie, that's terrible," Ben said. "Who's going to ride now in the Interclub?"

Dan punched him in the arm. "Hey, stupid. What a question! Issie doesn't care about the Interclub. She's lost Blaze. That matters more than any gold shield."

"Hey!" Ben snapped back. "I wasn't being horrible. I just meant that if Issie isn't in the team any more then how are we going to win the Interclub?"

"Well, if you want to win I suggest you get training for a start," Avery barked at them from the clubroom steps. "Come on, everyone, let's get lined up. We've got a busy training session ahead of us and Issie has offered to help out. So let's get started, shall we?"

The riders all lined up in front of the clubroom by the bending poles and Avery walked along the line, adjusting cavesson nosebands here, correcting their positions in the saddle and taking stirrups up a hole or down a hole as he moved along the line.

Morgan and Natasha, who had still been saddling up, joined them now too, and Avery nodded to the girls to get into line before he spoke. "Most of you will have heard about what has happened to Isadora," he said. "Which is very hard luck indeed." He thwacked his left boot firmly with his riding crop. "Still, we have an Interclub to win, and only two more training sessions to go before the competition day, so let's get cracking!"

He turned now to Morgan, who was sitting on Black Jack and looking at Issie with a curious expression on her face. "Morgan, you'll be our new team member now that Isadora is out," Avery said. "We're going to start training today with relay races. Can we all split into two teams please?"

As the riders all splintered off into their teams Morgan, who still looked stunned by Avery's speech, rode over to Issie. She looked extremely worried. "Hey, Issie," Morgan said. "What happened? Avery says you're not in the team any more. Is Blaze OK?"

"What do you mean?" Issie asked.

"Well, if she's feeling sick I'm sure it's nothing that the vet can't fix," Morgan said nervously. "She'll probably just be off her feed for a week or two. It's a pity she won't be well in time for the Interclub." Morgan looked around the paddock. "Hey, where is Blaze, anyway?"

Issie stared at Morgan. "I never said Blaze was

sick," she said flatly. "What makes you think that she's off her food?"

"Yes, where is your little pony, Isadora?" Natasha Tucker trotted up to join in the conversation. "I heard someone say she's run off to join the circus."

"Kind of," Issie said, turning away. She didn't want to talk to Natasha, of all people, about Blaze.

"Really?" Natasha said. "So it is true! Blaze is an El Caballo Danza Magnifico mare? I guess she had good breeding after all. Too good for you, at any rate. Those horses are worth a bomb."

"What are you two talking about?" Morgan was confused now. "Where has Blaze gone?"

Issie shook her head in amazement. "I'm sure Natasha can explain," she said wearily. "I need to help Tom sort out the boxes for the flag races."

Issie spent the rest of the training session sitting in the tack room. Well, actually, if she was honest with herself she was hiding in the tack room. At least, she thought, looking on the bright side, if she didn't have a horse any more there was no more pony club, and no more pony club meant no more Natasha Tucker.

"Issie! We've been looking everywhere for you.

Have you been in here the whole time?" Stella said when she finally found her.

"Ummm, yeah… I was tidying the gear up," Issie lied.

"Anyway, listen!" Stella continued. "I think you're right. It wasn't Francoise at all. It's so obvious really."

"Is it?" Issie said.

"Yes! Think about it, silly. Who can't stand you? Who always wants to beat you? Who would do this sort of thing?"

Issie shrugged. "I don't know, Stella, but if you're trying to cheer me up this is a funny way of going about it."

"It's Natasha, silly! She cut Annabel's stirrups because she thought they were yours. You know she has it in for you. It's, like, just because she's always been the most popular girl at her school, she can't stand the fact that you're the most popular girl at the pony club…"

"What's going on in here, Issie? Come on, let's get going!" Tom Avery's voice interrupted Stella and startled Issie back to reality.

"Let's get the bending poles packed away again, shall we? Then we can go home."

Issie had been unusually quiet as they packed up the car. As Avery drove towards Issie's house, her instructor looked across at her and arched his eyebrow quizzically. "Thinking about Blaze?"

Issie nodded.

"Do you remember the day when you met her?" Avery asked. "My God, that mare was in such a state! Caked in mud, a bag of bones and absolutely terrified, the poor thing. Blaze had been so badly treated when we found her that I knew I needed to find her a very special home. I told you at the time that she was in a bad way and I meant it. She might never have survived if it wasn't for you."

"I still don't understand, I guess," Issie said. "I mean, why you gave Blaze to me."

"Isadora, when I look at you I see myself as a young rider. You have the natural instincts of a horsewoman," Avery said. "When Mystic died I was worried that you might have given up on horses. Issie, you must know that it wasn't your fault that he was killed, but you blamed yourself. I knew the burden you carried and I wondered if you would ever recover. And then Blaze came to me and I knew that you and that mare were meant for each other."

Avery looked hard at Issie. "You couldn't save Mystic, but you could save Blaze. And you did save her, Isadora, you know that, don't you? You should be proud of that. Blaze needed your love – it was your love that made her well again, and it's the reason she has become the amazing horse she is today. If it hurts you now then that is because you loved her so completely."

The car pulled into the driveway outside Issie's front door. Avery parked the car, but before he opened Issie's door to let her out he placed a hand on her arm. "The price we pay for loving horses this much, unfortunately, is that they can break our hearts. But that doesn't mean that we should ever stop caring. Even now you mustn't give up on Blaze," Avery said. "She still needs you."

"But, Tom," Issie protested, "it's over. Francoise has her and they must be leaving town next week. There's nothing I can do."

Avery shook his head. "The bond you have made

with Blaze is impossible for anyone to break, Issie."

He reached across her now and swung open the passenger door. Issie stepped shakily out of the car and Avery pulled the door shut again behind her.

He had driven a few metres down the driveway when he stopped the car and wound down the passenger window and spoke again. "She'll always be your horse, Isadora. The question is – do you have enough faith to still be her girl?"

And with that, Avery floored the accelerator on the Range Rover, leaving Issie standing in the driveway in floods of tears as he drove away.

CHAPTER 12

The signs had already been taken down outside the gates and the trucks were being loaded when Issie arrived at El Caballo Danza Magnifico. As she walked through the main arena there were men up in the rafters above her dismantling the vast lighting rigs.

"Hey! Be careful down there! Does anyone know that you're here?" one of the men yelled out at her as Issie walked nervously underneath them.

"It's OK, Joe – she's here to meet Francoise." Rene, the burly security man, stepped out into the arena and beckoned with his right hand for Issie to follow him down the corridor to the stables.

As they walked down the corridor that ran between the horse stalls Issie could see Francoise at the far end standing in front of the large wooden doors. She appeared to be in a heated discussion of some sort with two of the young stable hands. Issie could only hear snippets of what they were saying.

Francoise was shouting at the boys now and her hands were waving wildly in the air. "You should have known better. Marius has a huge jump in him. The fence was only adequate for keeping the mares. Never a stallion!" Francoise fumed.

The boys responded meekly to this. Issie couldn't hear what they said but it certainly didn't impress Francoise, who threw her hands up in the air in disbelief and stormed off.

She had got halfway along the stable block before she realised that it was Issie at the other end walking towards her. "Isadora! *Bonjour*." Francoise grinned. "I am so glad that you have come."

"Is there something wrong, Francoise?" Issie replied, gesturing towards the two stable boys who were now moving horses through into their loose boxes.

"Pah! Something wrong? Those boys are idiots!"

Francoise groaned, rolling her eyes. "I-d-i-o-t-s!" she stated again.

"Do you know what is the hardest thing for us running a travelling school?" she asked. "Well, I will tell you. The hardest thing is controlling the stallions when they realise that there are mares right next door."

Francoise shook her head. "This is not easy. To control the stallions it is best, of course, if they do not see the mares at all. To keep them apart we put them in separate wings of the stables, and when we graze the horses outdoors when the weather is warm, as it has been lately, we always keep the mares at least two fields away from any stallions. That is the rule here at El Caballo Danza Magnifico. The problem is," she sighed, "some of these young boys they do not bother to learn the rules."

Francoise began to walk back down the corridor towards the wing of the stable where they kept the mares, and she gestured for Issie to walk with her.

"A few nights ago, when the moon was full and the weather was fine, we let the mares out to graze," Francoise continued. "Unfortunately, the boys did not realise this. And so, in the paddock right next door, they put Marius! Can you believe this? Marius! Of all the stallions he is the most powerful, the best jumper. Well, of course he hurdled the fence in a matter of minutes. But it was hours before the stable boys had noticed their mistake. By then he had been in with my mares for such a long time it was chaos!"

Issie felt her pulse quicken. A stallion left wild with mares was dangerous. He could do all kinds of damage. What if Blaze had been in the paddock too? "Are the mares OK?" she asked Francoise, her voice tight with concern.

"*Oui*, Isadora. Yes, I believe they are all OK. It is Salome that we are most concerned about. When we found them in the paddock, Marius was with her. The vet is checking her out once more now. Come, I am sure you will want to see her. And I know she will want to see you." Francoise smiled at Issie and pushed through the large wooden double doors that led at last into the mares' stables.

Next to the third stable door in the row Issie could see a man in overalls, she guessed it must be the vet, putting a vial of blood into a bag on the floor.

"*Bonjour*, Nigel, how is she doing? Has she

recovered?" Francoise said to the vet.

"She's fine," the vet responded. "That bite mark on her neck is healing well and I've given her another antibiotic shot. I'm hoping it won't scar, but at least it will be hidden by her mane," he said. "I've taken some blood to do further tests, but we'll have to wait a couple of days for the results," the vet continued, packing his equipment into the bag. "The mare seems to be fine."

"*Merci. À bientôt!*" Francoise smiled. And then she turned to Issie. "I am so glad you have come. I did not think you would. This must be difficult for you?"

Issie nodded.

"For me also," Francoise said. "It has not been easy because your horse pines for you, do you know that? She has been off her feed anyway and I cannot think what else it could be..." she grinned, "unless she is lovesick for Marius! When I found the two of them together they were quite the romantic couple." She laughed.

"Anyway, Salome will settle in eventually," she added. "But perhaps it is good for her now that you are here once more to say goodbye." Francoise nodded towards the stable doors. "She is in there. Spend as long as you like with her as there is no performance today. We are busy packing. Then come and find me before you leave. I have something for you."

Issie unbolted the bottom half of the Dutch door and ducked down to slip into the stable. Inside, the room was all gloom and shadows. Issie felt the straw bedding scrunching beneath her feet as she moved across the room and flicked on the light switch on the wall.

Illuminated in the far corner of the stall was Blaze. The mare was wearing a silver halter and Issie could see that the shining name plate on the halter read with her name, Salome. Above the name plate, something gold flickered. Issie moved closer to inspect the golden object and realised that it was one half of a golden heart which was threaded on to Blaze's halter. Issie had seen friendship hearts like these at school. The idea was that you wore one half of the heart as a necklace and your friend wore the other half as a symbol that you were best friends for ever.

"Hey, girl," Issie said softly. "Look at you with your pretty silver halter. Don't you look fancy?"

Blaze nickered softly in return and moved around

in the stall now so that her nose was facing Issie. She gave the girl a gentle nudge and Issie felt the warm, velvet smoothness of Blaze's muzzle against her bare skin. The mare nudged again, harder this time and Issie giggled.

"Yeah, yeah, I know, of course I've got you a farewell present," she said, reaching into her pocket and producing a slice of apple.

Blaze took a step closer to Issie and her lips fumbled across the palm of Issie's open hand, searching out the apple, which she munched down eagerly.

"Do you want some more?" Issie asked, pulling another two pieces of apple out of her pocket and palming them to Blaze who eagerly snuffled them up.

As Blaze chewed on the last of the apple pieces, Issie slipped under her neck and around to the other side of the mare so that she could check her wound. Sure enough, there were the teeth marks in Blaze's neck, down low near the wither, hidden by her mane. The vet had applied antiseptic cream and there seemed to be no sign of infection, Issie noted with relief.

"Oh, Blaze! Look at you getting into trouble the

minute I'm not around. What are you going to do when I'm not there to look after you?" Issie murmured. And at that moment she realised the truth. Tomorrow Blaze would be gone, and Issie wouldn't be there to look after her any more. It was really over. Blaze was leaving.

Issie stepped over to the bucket of grooming brushes that were hanging on the wall next to Blaze's untouched hay net. She reached her hand into the bucket and pulled out a body brush. Then she stood back to assess the horse, before beginning to work with gentle strokes, moving the brush over the mare's neck and chest and then down her front legs, sweeping down the delicate tendons over the knee and the cannon bone and down to the pastern.

After a while she stood up again and brushed Blaze's back where the saddle normally sat, brushing over her flanks and rump and down again, and finally working vigorously on her hocks. When Issie had kept Blaze in the paddock at the pony club those hocks were usually muddy from rolling when she brought her in to groom her. But here, at El Caballo Danza Magnifico, the mare was stabled warm and dry so her coat was clean and shiny. She didn't need brushing at all, but Issie wanted to groom her, just one last time.

She worked around to the other side of the horse, taking a mane comb and running it through the fine strands of Blaze's mane. It was so much silkier and less bushy than Mystic's mane had been. *But then Mystic had just been an ordinary old pony,* Issie thought, *and Blaze was a purebred Anglo-Arab with papers to prove it.*

Still, she had loved both her horses equally. When she lost Mystic, she thought that she would never love another horse again. And then along came Blaze, so different to Mystic, so temperamental and haughty. But hadn't she won the mare over? There was a bond between them now; Blaze was her horse. In her heart she always would be. But now, she realised, she had to let her go.

"I'm so sorry, girl, but there's nothing else I can do," Issie said. She flung her arms around Blaze's neck one last time and buried her face in her mane. "It's time to say goodbye," she said.

Issie ran her hand down Blaze's nose, slowly tracing along the thin white blaze that began as a star on the mare's forehead. Issie had named her Blaze because of that white marking on her face, but the horse had a new name now. Issie stepped back to the stable door. "Goodbye, Salome," she said. "I hope they love you as much as I do." And with that, Issie stepped out of the stable and bolted the door behind her.

Blinded by tears, Issie was making her way back out through the sawdust arena when she heard a voice calling out to her, "Isadora! Wait!"

Francoise ran over to where Issie was standing. "I told you to come and see me before you left," she said gently. Then she thrust a small package wrapped in white tissue paper into her hand. "For you," she said. "Keep it close always and do not forget us."

Issie took the package and looked up at Francoise. The raven-haired Frenchwoman had tears shining in her eyes. "I am sorry but I must go now," she said. "There is so much to be done before we leave tomorrow." She smiled at Issie. "I am sure this is not goodbye. So I will say *à bientôt* – see you soon. Until we meet again."

Francoise began to stride across the arena. Then she stopped and looked back over her shoulder. "Do not worry, Isadora. I will take good care of her. I promise you." And with that, Francoise walked away.

Issie watched as she disappeared through the stable

doorway, and then she turned too and headed for home.

It wasn't until much later, when Issie was in her bedroom that evening, that she finally opened the paper package to see what Francoise had given her. Nestled inside the white layers of tissue she saw something gold glittering in the light. Issie picked it up carefully. It was one half of a broken golden heart – to match the broken heart on Blaze's halter.

CHAPTER 13

The weather turned bad the next day and Issie looked out the window and thought about Francoise and her team loading their horses in the pouring rain. A little rain wouldn't stop them of course, Issie realised. Blaze would still be leaving today. She stared out at the dark grey skies, and watched the window fog up with her breath.

"Issie, I've made pancakes!" her mum called from downstairs. Issie didn't usually have time for breakfast. Most days she was too busy charging out the door to go down to the paddock. But there was no horse to hurry off to any more. She padded downstairs, still in her pyjamas, and sat at the table.

"Do you want real maple syrup or the fake stuff?" Mrs Brown asked.

"Fake, thanks, Mum," Issie said. Her mother always asked the question – even though she knew that Issie preferred the taste of the synthetic syrup to the honest maple-leaf version.

"Do you want to go shopping with me today?" Mrs Brown asked as she dished up the pancakes. "You could do with some new clothes and we need to get you some school shoes. I thought we could go to the mall and then get some lunch."

Issie gave her mum a weak smile. "No thanks, Mum. I think I'm going to go down to the River Paddock."

Mrs Brown looked puzzled. "What for?"

"Ummm, there's still some gear in the tack room there and I thought I should clear it up," Issie said unconvincingly.

"I thought all of Blaze's gear was in the tack room at the pony club?" Mrs Brown said.

"Well, most of it…"

"Are you up to something, Isadora?" Her mother arched a brow as she asked the question.

"No, Mum, honest… I need to pack up the rest of my grooming kit and stuff…" Issie paused "…and, well, I guess I want to spend some time alone. The River Paddock is where I first met Blaze…"

Mrs Brown nodded silently. She flipped another pancake in the pan, assessing its brownness on both sides, and then used a fish slice to lift it on to a plate. She carried the plate over to Issie and sat down at the table next to her daughter.

"I used to worry about you with that horse," Mrs Brown said quietly. "After your accident with Mystic I didn't even want you to ride again – full stop. Certainly not on a horse like that. Blaze was so unpredictable. She seemed so highly strung. I was always worried that you couldn't handle her."

"Then why did you let me keep her?" Issie said.

Mrs Brown smiled. "Tom Avery set me straight. We had a little chat and he told me what a born horsewoman you are, that you actually have the talent to take it all the way. Tom says that one day you could be a great rider." Mrs Brown looked at her daughter. "Perhaps even better than he was."

Issie was shocked. She shook her head in bewilderment.

"Anyway, that's what Tom said so don't start arguing with me about it," her mother said briskly, getting up from the table. "And who am I to stand in the way of a superstar in the making? You know I cannot bear horses, Issie. They scare me stiff. But I do love you, and if riding is what you want to do, then you should do it. I know you must be feeling devastated right now. It isn't fair that Blaze has been taken from you. But trust me, somehow we're going to find a way for you to ride again. We're not giving up that easily."

Mrs Brown smiled at her daughter. "Now eat up that second pancake. It's not like you to eat just one!"

It was still raining when Issie set off on her bike to the River Paddock. Her mum had offered to give her a lift but she said she would prefer to ride her bike despite the bad weather. She pulled on her waterproof and boots and set off.

The rain was heavy and by the time she arrived at the paddock her legs, which had been poking out from under the coat, were soaking wet.

On the way to the paddock she thought about what her mum had said. Had Avery really told her mum that Issie was going to be a great rider one day? *Even better than he was?* Avery had ridden at Badminton. Issie would love to be half as good as he was in his day.

She shook her head, dismissing the idea of it. It didn't matter what Tom said. How could she ever be a great rider when she didn't even have a horse? Despite her mum's pep talk about not giving up, Issie knew there was no way her mother could afford to buy her another horse. Natasha Tucker was right — Blaze was too good for her. Horses like her cost a fortune and since Issie's mum and dad had split up, her mother didn't have that much money any more. There was no way she had enough money to buy a horse like Blaze.

Issie parked her bike up next to the turnstile and clambered over the fence, trying not to get her coat caught on the palings. The rain was so heavy now that the whole paddock was blurred in a grey haze. In the far paddock she could make out the dark, wet shapes of horses. Their rumps were turned to face the rain and their heads were hanging dejectedly. The weather was too miserable for them to graze. In the furthest paddock, a small herd of them were sheltering underneath the trees at the edge of The Pines.

The Pines were a cluster of huge pine trees that formed a natural grove at the far end of the River Paddock. Issie had always loved cantering Blaze through the winding paths between the trees on hot sunny days. She looked at The Pines and then cast a sideways glance at the tack room. She was already wet and chilly; the sensible thing to do was to pack up her gear and head home again before the rain got worse. She began to walk towards the tack room, but then she stopped. She changed her mind and set off towards the pine trees instead, walking slowly with her head bent down against the weather.

A trickle of water ran down the back of her neck, slipping sneakily under the waterproof and down her back. She pulled up her collar against the wind and the rain which was now being blown horizontally.

Issie undid the gate between the first and second paddocks and then relatched it and kept walking. She was heading for the corner of the field where the path into The Pines began.

The grass was boggy underfoot so Issie was surprised when she reached The Pines and found that the ground there beneath the trees was quite dry. Sheltered by the branches above, the carpet of dead pine needles remained untouched by the rain. Issie felt the crunch of the needles under her feet and smelt the thick resin scent as she walked along the path between the trees.

She had only gone a few metres into the pines when she heard the sound of hooves. The trees cast dark shadows and she peered into the half-light ahead of her, trying to see. Where was the horse who was making the noise? Her heart leapt as she caught sight of him. The first thing she saw was a dapple-grey shadow. Then the silhouette of a small sway-backed pony came into view. The pony came closer now, weaving between pine trees, trotting in and out of the shadows. And then suddenly there he was in front of her, his dark eyes peering out at Issie from beneath a long, windswept silver fringe.

"Hello, Mystic." Issie smiled. "I should have known you would be here."

Mystic stepped forward now, and Issie reached out a hand to softly stroke his velvet nose.

The grey pony nickered softly. "Oh, Mystic," Issie whispered, "I'm glad I still have you, boy. I'll always have you, won't I?"

She wrapped her arms around Mystic's neck and buried her face deep into the warmth of his thick mane, smothering herself in the smell of horse, closing her eyes and hanging on tight.

"It's not fair," Issie said, her voice trembling. "I miss her so much!"

Mystic nickered again. "Oh, Mystic! You miss her, too, don't you boy?" Issie said.

They stayed there like this for a long time, and as Issie stroked Mystic's velvet-soft dappled neck, she realised that the little gelding seemed in no hurry to go anywhere. Like Issie, he seemed to know that there was nothing he could do this time to help Blaze. And so the pair of them stood there, Issie murmuring to Mystic and the horse nickering softly back to her, almost as if they had their own private language.

After a while the rain seemed to finally ease off a bit. Issie led Mystic over to a big pine stump just off the main path and used it as a mounting block to vault lightly on to the little grey's sway back. Then the pair of them walked together through The Pines, each comforted by the other's company as the rain pattered on the natural canopy above them and the pine needles crackled under Mystic's hooves.

They walked like that all the way through The Pines, and Issie breathed in the tang of wet pine mixed with the familiar, sweet smell of warm horse sweat. She looked up at the black branches above her blocking out the light, making a puzzle of the sky above.

Issie thought about the time she had ridden through here at a wild gallop on Blaze. The mare had been impossible to stop that day, but Issie had managed to stay on somehow. She thought about the time too when Blaze had bolted and jumped the gate between the two paddocks with Issie on her back. That day, she remembered ruefully, she hadn't been so lucky. Avery told her there was an old saying: you need to fall off seven times before you can really call yourself a rider. Well, if that were true, then her time with Blaze had definitely made a rider out of her!

When they finally emerged from the trees, the rain had stopped and it was getting late. Issie guessed it was almost dinnertime. She slid down off the grey pony and gave him a long hug goodbye. "Thank you, Mystic," she murmured.

She walked back across the paddock. At one point she looked back over her shoulder and was surprised to see that he was still there watching her. She gave him a little wave as if to say that she was going to be OK and he didn't have to worry any more, and with that the little gelding stamped a hoof in return, flicked his mane and then set off back into the trees at a high-spirited canter. Issie watched as his grey dapples blurred into the shadows, and then she smiled to herself, turned around and kept walking through the damp grass towards her bike. She was feeling hungry again and it was time to go home.

"Mum! I'm back!" Issie called as she walked in through the front door, peeling off her waterproof and throwing it in the laundry along with her boots before she entered the kitchen. "Mum?"

Issie stood in the kitchen for a moment, puzzled as to where her mother might be. And then she heard her voice in the hallway talking on the phone. "All right, then. Of course. Yes, she's just arrived. We'll come now. Put the kettle on and we'll see you in a minute."

Issie walked through into the hallway just as her mother hung up the phone. Her mum, she thought, had a very queer look on her face. Something was up.

"Put your coat and boots back on," Mrs Brown instructed briskly. "We're off."

"What's going on? Where are we going?" Issie pestered her mum as she pulled her wet coat and boots back on again and clambered into the car.

"You'll see," is all her mother would reply.

And so the two of them drove in tense silence, with Issie occasionally trying to ask again what was going on and her mum just shaking her head and saying, "Wait. Just wait. We're nearly there. It's not far."

It was getting dark as Issie and her mum drove up the tree-lined driveway into Winterflood Farm. As they pulled up into the gravel turning bay, Tom Avery stepped out of his front door to meet them. He was dressed, as always, in jodhpurs and long boots. He smiled broadly when he saw them both. "Come in," he said. "Good timing. We've just made a pot of tea."

We? thought Issie. Who else was here? There had been a strange car, a Peugeot, parked next to Tom's horse truck. Who was here with him?

She stopped and shook the rain off her coat before hanging it on the hook in the front porch, and then followed her mother in the door.

Avery's house was a tiny, old-fashioned cottage with an Aga in the kitchen and a big wooden dining table and chairs taking up the centre of the room. It was into the kitchen that he led them now, and Issie couldn't believe her eyes when she saw who was sitting at the kitchen table. There, right in front of her was a face that she never thought she would see again. It was Francoise D'arth.

"*Bonjour*, Isadora," Francoise said, standing up. "We have just made tea. Would you and your mother like some?"

"Yes, umm, no… I mean… Francoise, what are you doing here?" Issie couldn't help her reaction. The last time she saw Francoise D'arth she was taking

Blaze away and now here she was again, in Tom Avery's kitchen, smiling and offering pots of tea.

"I know, I know." Francoise seemed to read Issie's mind. "It is strange, is it not? I, too, thought that I would never see you again. At least," she added, "not for a very long time. But here we are. The fates have changed their minds."

"But aren't you leaving today?" Issie asked. Her heart was racing.

"*Oui* – yes, I am leaving," Francoise replied. She checked her watch. "In fact, I need to be leaving very soon. The rest of the crew are packed and will have departed already by now. But first I had to bring you something."

Issie remembered the gold heart necklace. "Oh – thanks but... do you mean the necklace? Don't you remember? You already gave it to me. It's very beautiful. I didn't get to say thank you..."

Francoise laughed. "Isadora, do you really think I would come here at this hour in this weather to bring you a necklace?" She wrapped her arm around Issie's shoulder and led her out towards the back of the house. "Listen, our tea can wait." Francoise winked at

Tom. "I have something to show you. Come with me."

As they stepped out the back door, Francoise slipped behind Issie. She reached her hands up so they were over Issie's face, covering her eyes. Then she guided Issie out the door and into the field directly behind Avery's house. Francoise whispered something in Issie's ear and then she pulled her hands away again. "*Voila!*" She laughed.

Issie gasped. There, standing in front of her, dancing nervously and tugging against the lead rope in Tom Avery's hand, was Blaze.

The pot of tea went stone cold, of course. There was a tearful reunion between horse and rider, and laughter and lots of hugs. Finally, Avery pointed out that it was still raining and it was getting dark and they were all getting far too wet, and shouldn't they turn Blaze out for the night in his spare paddock? And so they all went inside again and a fresh pot of tea was brewed and Francoise finally had the chance to explain.

"I had a call this morning from the masters in

Spain who own the El Caballo Danza Magnifico riding school," Francoise said as she sipped her tea, which she took without milk and with a slice of lemon. "Their instructions to me were brief and quite to the point. They told me that Salome was to be brought back to you at once."

"But I don't understand…" Issie was confused.

Francoise gave a perplexed shrug. "Neither do I. All they told me was that someone had paid them for the mare. Handsomely, I assume. Horses such as Salome do not come cheap. She is valuable – but I suppose not irreplaceable. There are some young mares back at the farm in Spain which we have been training for some time now, ever since she was stolen. Perhaps they may take her place. But none will be as good as she was…"

Francoise paused for a moment and then continued. "Of course when they told me that Salome was to be returned to you I called your house immediately to tell you the news – but you were out. It was your mother who arranged for me to bring Salome here. She wanted it to be a surprise."

"Mum!" Issie said.

Mrs Brown beamed at her. "Well, I thought it was my turn to have a secret for once," she said.

Issie grinned back at her mother and then she turned to Francoise. "So who is this person who bought Blaze?" Issie was puzzled.

Francoise lowered her eyes and blew on her hot tea to cool it a little. "They did not tell me who it was, " she said. "What was the term they used? Ah yes… they said to tell you it was an anonymous benefactor!" Francoise laughed.

"And this benefactor… they own her now?" Issie was still confused.

"No, no, Isadora. You don't understand." Francoise smiled. "They bought Salome – Blaze – for you. She is your horse. You own her."

Francoise pulled the papers out of the inside pocket of her gilet. "I have all the paperwork right here including her bloodlines," she explained. Francoise paused, and then smiled. "But we can talk about that later. Right now, all you need to know is that Blaze is your horse – and for good this time."

Issie couldn't help herself. She threw herself across the table and hugged Francoise with delight.

"Hey," Francoise laughed, "you must take good care of her, Isadora. Salome was the star of my stable, and I shall miss her very, very much. But I am sure I shall see you both again."

She stood up and put her tea cup down on the table. "I had better go now. The others have driven on ahead and the weather is so frightful I really should try and catch up…"

"Wait!" Issie felt like she had so many questions still to be answered. "Francoise, please, just one more thing. I need to ask you about that night when I ran into you in the tack room. You told me afterwards that you were there to get Blaze's hairs for the DNA sample…" Issie paused. "I don't know how to ask you this but I have to know. Did you have anything to do with cutting the stirrup leather, the one on Annabel's saddle? Or putting the selenium into Blaze's feed?"

Francoise shook her head. "I am so sorry. When I heard of these things that have happened, I realise now that I should have said something sooner. Perhaps I could have saved poor Annabel…" She looked down at the table as she spoke, "Isadora, I told you that I was at the pony club that night. But I was never in the tack room. I was coming back across the paddock when I saw you in the doorway. There was a woman with black hair, she knocked you down. I saw that you were not hurt so I ran after her, but she was gone too quickly and then I realised that you had seen me, so I ran too and jumped over the fence and drove away."

Issie looked at Francoise. Could it be true? Was there another woman at the pony club that night?

"Isadora," Francoise smiled, "please trust me. I have no reason to lie. I know nothing of the stirrup leather. I did not touch the horse feed. I would never hurt Blaze or any other horse."

Issie nodded quietly. "I know, Francoise," she said. "I do believe you. It wasn't you in the tack room that night, and it wasn't you who poisoned Blaze's feed. In fact, I think I know who did it. Now I just have to prove it."

CHAPTER 14

Natasha Tucker straightened her tie and admired her reflection in the wing mirror of the Mercedes. Today's pony-club rally was the final team training session before the Interclub Gold Shield and all the riders were in full uniform so that Avery could check their turnout.

"Mum," Natasha scowled as she cast her eye over her palomino mare, "I asked for Goldrush to have an odd number of plaits and you've gone and done evens again!"

Mrs Tucker stuck her head out of the door of the Mercedes and rolled her eyes at Natasha. "Maybe

399

you'd like to try getting up at six in the morning to groom Goldrush yourself?" she responded.

"Uggh. No thanks," Natasha groaned. She looked across at the group of riders saddling up under the spread of a large plane tree. One of them was laughing and chattering away as she brushed out the long flaxen tail of her pony. Natasha took a second look at the girl and the horse. "I don't believe it!" she said.

"What now?" her mother asked with an air of resignation in her voice.

"Isadora is here and she's got her horse back!" Natasha said.

The news of Blaze's return spread like wildfire through the pony club that day. Issie knew it would. She also knew, after her conversation last night with Francoise, that not everyone would be pleased to see Blaze was back. If Francoise was not responsible for Annabel's accident or for Blaze's poisoned horse feed, then the real culprit was still here at the club.

When Francoise told Issie that there was another woman in the tack room that night, the pieces of the puzzle suddenly fell into place. "I think I know the reason that Annabel's stirrup leather was cut," Issie told Stella and Kate. "I think I know why they did it. And I also know who did it — it was the same person who poisoned Blaze's horse feed."

"Well?" Kate said. "Come on. Who was it then?"

"I can't say yet. I want to be sure that I'm right before I start accusing anyone," Issie said. She looked serious. "You must promise me that you'll both be careful and make sure to check your gear today before you ride. Whoever caused those accidents is still out there. I can't explain it yet, but I'm pretty sure that now Blaze is back we may all be in danger."

"Shall we tell Dan and Ben?" Stella asked.

Issie nodded. "They need to keep a close eye on their horses."

"What about Natasha and Morgan?" Kate said.

"No," Issie said firmly. "Don't tell them."

"But they might be in danger too!" Stella squeaked.

But Issie shook her head. "No, I don't think so," she replied quietly.

When the girls lined up with the rest of the squad for

the training session all eyes were on Issie and Blaze.

"Excellent!" Tom Avery said as he addressed the team. "Now, as you can all see, Isadora has Blaze back."

He turned to Issie and gave Blaze a cheerful slappy pat on her neck. "How is she feeling, Issie?"

"Great, Tom!" Issie smiled. "She's fine – I think she's just happy to be home again."

"Excellent," Avery said. He turned to the lineup of riders now and gave his right boot a resounding whack with his riding crop to get their attention. "Right. With Isadora and Blaze back in the team we're going to have to do some reshuffling," Avery said blithely. "Morgan, you will be team reserve again."

Issie looked across at Morgan. She glared back at Issie, her eyes blazing with anger and then looked away.

"Hold on a moment, Tom!" a voice called out from the clubroom steps. Araminta Chatswood-Smith came striding across to where Avery stood addressing his team. "Are you telling me that you're dropping Morgan from the team just because your star rider is back again? That doesn't seem very fair, does it?" Araminta's voice was steely and cold.

"I agree, Minty," Avery said. "It's rough on Morgan, but I can't leave Isadora out either. She was originally selected to ride and now that she can ride, I have to put her back in the team."

"All the same," Araminta fumed, "my daughter has trained hard for this team. Riding in the Interclub Shield is very important to me."

"Important to *me*?" Avery repeated her phrase. "You mean important to *Morgan*, don't you? Who exactly are you talking about here, Minty, because it strikes me that you might be confusing your own ambitions with Morgan's wishes."

"I'm doing nothing of the sort," Araminta harrumphed. "Morgan is desperate to ride in the Interclub Shield. I think you need to reconsider your decision."

"And I think you need to leave the team selection up to me," Avery said. "Listen, Minty, I'm sure she'll get the chance to ride in the Interclub. Next year…"

But Araminta wasn't listening. "Come on, Morgan, training is over!" she snapped at her daughter, and she stormed off in disgust.

Morgan looked a bit bewildered. She watched her

mother stomping off towards the horse truck, and then shrugged her shoulders, gathered up her reins and clucked Jack on, trotting off after her mother.

"Tom, maybe I shouldn't be in the team..." Issie began.

"Nonsense, Isadora. You're in the team and that's final," Avery said calmly. "There'll be no further discussion on the matter."

"Now, everyone, we're doing rider on the flat training today. The winner of this event gets three big points for the team, so everyone spread yourselves out around the arena and walk on with a loose rein to get them warmed up. Let's start thinking about our position in the saddle, shall we?"

At the end of the day as Issie unsaddled Blaze she thought about the past few weeks and everything she had been through. She had lost her horse and now she had her back. After that, a little thing like the Interclub Shield shouldn't really matter much to her at all. Yet she still found herself thrilled with the idea of being in the team and she felt butterflies in her tummy even thinking about the competition. The Interclub was this weekend. They had just a few more days to prepare. She slid the stirrup leathers up on her saddle and undid the girth, then moved around to the other side of her horse and slid the saddle off.

As she slipped the bridle over Blaze's ears she spoke softly to her. "Now that you're back we have a competition to win," she told her. "Are you ready, girl?"

Blaze nickered in reply and Issie laughed. "Yeah, me too!" she said.

With the bridle hanging down from her shoulder and the saddle slung over her right arm she walked over to the tack room. The team would all be leaving their horses and gear here until the day of the Interclub rally so that they could fit in one more training session before the event.

In the tack room, Issie slid her saddle on to the wooden saddle horse. She thought about the training session today and how furious Araminta had been when her daughter hadn't made the team after all. Araminta's fury had only confirmed Issie's suspicions.

It was more than a coincidence, Issie thought, that

all these accidents had started happening after Araminta arrived at the pony club. Issie had seen some pushy pony-club mums before but this was extreme. It was scary how much Araminta wanted Morgan to ride in the Interclub. Was she really so determined that she would go to any lengths to get rid of anything that stood in her way? Did that include sabotaging other riders who were chosen ahead of her own daughter? Issie remembered Francoise describing the stranger in the tack room that night as "a woman with dark hair". It all made sense. It had to be Araminta.

Issie looked around the tack room. If Araminta was causing the accidents would she give up now? No. Araminta wasn't the sort to give up. She would make one last effort to get rid of the competition and get her daughter in the team. Only this time, Issie would be ready for her.

That evening, after her mum had gone to bed, Issie snuck down to the kitchen and packed her backpack with everything she would need. She had a silver

Thermos filled with the leftover soup from dinner in case she got hungry. Her mum had bought her a new torch for school camp, and she put that in too, checking the batteries to make sure they still worked. She also borrowed her mum's mobile phone just in case, and put in the throw rug off the sofa to snuggle under if it got cold. Then she strapped her backpack on to her back, grabbed her bike out of the garage and set off.

As she cycled along the backstreets that led from her house to the pony club, she began to wonder if what she was doing wasn't a little mad. Perhaps Annabel's stirrup leather had really been an accident after all. And was she sure that someone had tampered with Blaze's feed? Even if Araminta really had tried to sabotage the team, that didn't mean she would be back tonight. Issie was beginning to have real doubts about her plan. Then, as she parked her bike up by the pony-club gate, she saw a silvery shadow in the nearest paddock and heard a low whinny calling out to her. Mystic was here!

The little grey came closer, tossing his mane and snorting. He seemed distracted and nervous, Issie thought, and she realised that she had made the right decision to come to the pony club tonight. If Mystic was acting like this then something had to be wrong. The grey gelding trotted over to Issie, snorting and quivering with tension.

"Easy, boy," she soothed, although she knew that she was just as nervous as he was, and she was saying this mostly to calm herself down. Issie peered out into the blackness of the horizon. She could just make out the shapes of the horses grazing in the far paddock.

"Mystic, you go keep close to them," she whispered to her horse. "Look after Blaze. I'll be all right here by myself."

Mystic seemed to understand her instructions. He wheeled about instantly and cantered off, his head held high. Issie watched him blurring into the shadows as he reached the other horses. She heard another horse, perhaps it was Blaze, calling back to him, her soft whinny carrying clearly in the crisp night air.

Issie looked back at her bike. It was too obvious to leave it here leaning up against the fence. She didn't want anyone to know that she was already here. But it was too heavy to lift over the fence and she didn't have a key to the paddock gate. She would have to hide it somewhere.

She decided to shove it into the hedge on the other side of the gravel driveway by the club gates. It turned out this wasn't as easy as she thought, but eventually she found a gap and with a little effort she managed to wedge the bike into the hole. She hunted around and found a couple of branches to prop in front of it to hide it completely. Satisfied with her work, she walked back to the pony-club gate, climbed the rungs, swung herself over and headed for the clubroom.

She found her way to the tack room easily in the dark without even having to resort to the torch in her backpack. *I've been sneaking about here so often I can find my way in the dark*, Issie thought to herself. She found the tack room key easily this time too and opened the door.

It was pitch black inside and she reached for her torch. She didn't want to switch the light on in case someone saw it and got frightened off. She turned on her torch briefly to make sure that she'd locked the door again after herself. Then, once she was inside with the door shut behind her, she turned it on one more time to find a spot just behind the saddle horses where she could snuggle down in her blanket and take out her Thermos of soup for a midnight feast while she waited.

It wasn't the most fun way to spend an evening, Issie thought as she tried to get comfy, sitting here alone in the pitch dark, in a creaky old tack room. She curled up under the blanket for a bit, and then got bored and filled herself a cup of soup. Luckily her mum had just made a big pot of homemade chicken and vegetable that night, which was her favourite. She wished she had packed some juice and maybe a chocolate bar as well. She put the lid back on the Thermos and settled down to wait.

Issie must have dozed off so she wasn't sure what time it was when she heard the sound of footsteps outside the tack-room door. The noise instantly woke her up and she panicked, fumbling around underneath the blankets to find her torch.

There was the sound of keys in the lock. She threw the blanket off and crouched down low behind the saddle horses and waited.

The door opened. Issie looked up between the saddles and saw the figure of a woman, her long hair silhouetted against the night sky. The woman reached up for the light switch and just as she did, Issie stood up from behind the saddle horse. As the lights came on there was a moment of stunned silence as Issie finally stared the mystery in the face.

"It's you... But why...?" Issie found herself too dumbstruck to finish her sentence. She looked at the dark-haired figure standing opposite her. Not a woman, as she had thought, but a young girl, just like her. It was Morgan Chatswood-Smith.

CHAPTER 15

Issie couldn't believe it! Morgan? Illuminated by the tack-room light, Morgan stood in the doorway. When she saw Issie she froze to the spot in shock. Then her face turned dark with anger and she glared at Issie. It was the same look Morgan had given her when Avery had thrown her off the team in favour of Issie.

Issie's face looked just as shocked as Morgan's at first. She had been expecting Araminta to walk through the door. After Araminta's furious outburst during training, Issie had been convinced that she was the one responsible for sabotaging Annabel and trying to poison Blaze.

Issie realised now that she had been thinking about

this all wrong. She began to play back the events of the past months in her mind. When Francoise had said she saw a woman with dark hair in the tack room that night, Issie had assumed the woman was Araminta but it could easily have been Morgan. And then there was Blaze's poisoned feed. Of course! When Issie talked to Morgan at team training she had instantly assumed that Blaze wasn't there because she was sick. *She must have thought that her poisoned horse feed was the reason for Blaze being off the team*, Issie thought.

It was all making sense now. "Have you been doing all of this, Morgan?" Issie asked. "Was that you in the tack room that night? Did you cut Annabel's stirrup leather? Poison Blaze's feed?"

Morgan nodded.

"But why?" Issie asked. "Morgan, why? Do you really hate us all that much? You could have killed Annabel! You could have hurt Blaze too!"

As Issie said this, the dark expression on Morgan's face crumpled into one of total misery and she burst into tears. "Stop saying that! I know that now! I never meant to do it. I didn't want to hurt anyone. I just wanted to ride in the Interclub so badly.

All I could think about was making the team…"

Issie shook her head. "But why hurt Annabel? What did she ever do to you?" she asked.

Morgan's voice was shaky. "I never meant to. I thought if Annabel couldn't ride then Avery would put me in the team. I just wanted her to get a fright. I never thought she'd end up in hospital. And then, after all that, Avery didn't put me in the team anyway. He picked stupid old Natasha instead.

"Anyway, I decided that if one of the horses got sick then he wouldn't have any choice – he would have to make me a team member. I was the only reserve left. So I put the selenium in the feed. When Blaze didn't turn up for training that day I thought she must have been sick because of what I did to the horse feed, and then I got worried that maybe Blaze was really sick and I didn't mean to hurt her and it was all my fault and the whole thing was such a mess, but it was too late by then and I couldn't stop it…"

Morgan's sobbing made it hard for her to speak.

"Hey, calm down. It's OK," Issie said. "I get it. You didn't mean to do it. Things got out of control. But I just don't understand. Why would anyone want to be in the team that badly?"

Morgan pushed her dark hair back off her face and wiped her eyes roughly with the sleeve of her jumper. "Of course you don't understand!" she snapped at Issie. "You don't have your mum pushing you all the time, telling you that you have to be a great rider like she was."

She took a deep breath, trying to calm down before she spoke. "Do you have any idea what it's like for me being the daughter of 'famous rider' Araminta Chatswood-Smith? It's awful! All I ever hear about is how great my mum was and what a star she was in her day. No one ever really wants to know me – they just want to talk about her." Morgan took another deep, quivery breath. She was still crying though and big tears rolled down her cheeks as she spoke.

"The worst of it is that I always disappoint Mum," she said. "I try my best. I really do. But I'm not as good as her. I get scared on the showjumping course, Issie. I don't think I can ever ride over big jumps like she did when she was a girl. I don't think I'm good enough. And then I came here and all she could talk about was how 'back in her day' she had been on the team that won the Interclub Shield. And I started thinking that if I could make the team and help win the shield too then maybe I would finally be as good as she was."

Morgan looked down at her boots. Her voice turned very quiet now. "All I ever wanted was to be on the team. I just wanted to make her proud of me."

There was a long time where neither girl spoke and all that could be heard was Morgan blowing her nose and making little damp sniffy noises as she tried to stop crying. And then Issie spoke. "You realise that Annabel is in hospital because of you?" she said. "And Blaze could have been really sick too if she'd eaten that horse feed."

Morgan nodded. "I know. I am so sorry. I never wanted to hurt Annabel or Blaze. I just got so, well, obsessed about winning and making the team. I went a little crazy."

"Why did you come here tonight?" Issie asked.

"I was going to steal some of the gear," Morgan said. "I figured if you couldn't find your saddles and stuff then you wouldn't be able to ride and Avery would have to put me back in the team at the last minute."

Issie nodded. Despite everything that Morgan had done, as they stood there together in the tack room it was hard not to feel sympathy for her. All she had wanted to do was to please her mother, to live up to her expectations. Maybe, Issie realised, having a horsy family wasn't all it was cracked up to be.

"I'm really sorry, Morgan, honestly," Issie said, "but I have no choice." She reached into her backpack and pulled out her mobile phone.

"Are you calling the police?" Morgan snuffled miserably.

"No, I'm afraid it's worse than that," Issie said. "I'm calling your mother."

When Araminta Chatswood-Smith arrived at the pony club that night she found the two girls in the tack room cuddled up under the blanket together, sipping the last of Issie's soup and talking about ponies. Morgan had even been laughing at one of Issie's stories, but now with the arrival of her mother the smile quickly left her face.

"What is going on here?" Araminta demanded. "What

are you both doing here in the middle of the night?"

"What will I tell her?" Morgan whispered to Issie as her mother stood in the doorway glowering at her.

"Tell her the truth," Issie whispered back, giving Morgan's hand a squeeze in support.

Morgan reluctantly got up from behind the saddle horses. "Mum," she said, "I... I... need to tell you something..."

As Morgan unfolded the whole sorry story, her mother sat quietly, her mouth set in a grim line, her arms folded across her chest. She didn't interrupt or ask any questions as her daughter spoke, she just listened. When Morgan had finally finished – she was in tears again by this time – Araminta Chatswood-Smith unfolded her arms and wrapped them tightly around her daughter in a huge bear hug.

"Oh, Morgan, what have you done?" she said softly. She kept her daughter in a tight embrace, pressing her cheek hard against her dark hair as Morgan snuffled and wept in her arms.

She sat like that for a moment, thinking carefully before she spoke again. "You are in a lot of trouble. You know that, don't you? What you did was a terrible,

terrible thing. What were you thinking?"

"I just wanted you to be proud of me," Morgan muttered under her breath.

"Proud?" Araminta boggled. "For pity's sake!" Then she saw the look on Morgan's face and the tears streaming down her cheeks and she took a deep breath before she spoke again. "This is my fault as much as it is yours. I never thought about how hard I was pushing you. I thought I was helping you, but I can see now that I was putting too much pressure on you."

She reached out her hand and wiped away the tears on Morgan's cheek. "You don't have to be a famous rider to make me proud. You don't have to make the team and you don't have to win. I know you are not me — and you don't have to be. You just have to do your best and be happy. OK?"

Morgan nodded.

Araminta sighed. "I know it can't be easy being my daughter. But it was the same for me too, you know, when I was growing up. Once I became a famous rider, horses were suddenly a serious business. All I ever cared about was winning. I was so focused for so long that I guess I forgot that horses were supposed to be fun." She smiled down at Morgan. "Maybe you can help me remember?"

Morgan smiled back up at her mother. "Thanks, Mum. I'm so sorry."

"I think you owe a few other people more than just an apology," Araminta said. "What you did to Annabel was a terrible thing. You'll have to go and see her and her parents and tell them everything. If they wish to refer the matter on to the police, well, we'll have to deal with that. They have every right to be furious after what happened.

"And," she sighed again, "I need to do some apologising too. Poor Tom. I was completely out of line when I yelled at him at the team training the other day."

She turned to Issie now, who was quietly packing her Thermos, blanket and torch back into her backpack for the trip home. "Isadora, my daughter and I owe you an apology too, for the dreadful business with the horse feed."

Morgan nodded. "I'm so sorry, Issie. When I think that I could have hurt Blaze I feel so awful…"

Issie stopped packing her backpack. "Honestly, it's OK," she said. "I think I do understand now, Morgan – and I'm just glad it's all over." She smiled at Morgan.

"You want to be friends?" she asked.

Morgan looked so grateful that Issie thought she was going to burst into tears all over again. She flung her arms around Issie and gave her the hugest hug. "Yes, thank you," she whispered. "Friends for ever!"

At the secret meeting of the pony-club gang the next night, Issie told the others everything that had happened. She had to tell the story several times because Stella kept interrupting. "Honestly! Why would anyone want to be in the team that badly?"

"Oh, come on, Stella!" Kate said. "Remember how you reacted that time when you thought you hadn't made the team?"

Stella nodded. "Yeah, but I didn't go around doing crazy stuff."

"She's not crazy," Issie said. "She just got a bit freaked out because her mum was pushing her so hard and she made a few bad calls."

"One of which landed Annabel in hospital," pointed out Kate.

"Has Morgan spoken to Annabel yet?" asked Dan.

Issie nodded. "Her mum took her around to Annabel's house today and Morgan had to apologise to Annabel and Mr and Mrs Willets. They were really angry. But Mr Willets said it meant a lot that Morgan had come forward herself and been brave enough to tell them. Morgan offered to help look after Eddie too until Annabel got better, and Araminta told Annabel that she would give her private lessons every week for the rest of the year to help make up for what Morgan had done."

"Wow," Stella grinned, "private lessons with Araminta Chatswood-Smith! I wish I had broken my leg!"

The others all glared at her and Stella stopped grinning. "Well, you know what I mean," she grumbled.

"Anyway, it's all cleared up now," Kate said. "And just as well. There are only two days left before we have to ride for the Interclub shield."

"Oh, who cares about that dumb old Shield now," Stella said. "Haven't we all learnt our lesson from this? It's stupid to get all worked up about a silly old competition. In fact," Stella said grandly, "I don't even care if we win the Interclub any more."

The whole room went quiet and everyone looked at Stella completely stunned.

"Just joking!" she laughed. "Come on! We've got time tonight for a few more practice runs with the bending relay. Last one to their pony has to pick up all the flags for the flag race!" And she raced for the clubroom door with the others tearing after her, all of them pushing and giggling as they tried to be the first ones to get there.

CHAPTER 16

On the morning of the Interclub Shield, the girls watched as the teams arrived at the showgrounds, turned out in their club colours.

"That's Westhaven!" Kate said, pointing to a rider on a striking chestnut wearing a gold jersey and black tie. "And there's Mornington," she said, nodding towards a young girl on a grey dressed in a sky blue jumper and white tie. Red with a black tie was St Johns and there were purple jerseys with gold for Garnet Ridge.

"Ughh, those poor riders at Garnet Ridge. The purple jumpers they have to wear are awful." Stella pulled a face. "I think I like the Marsh Fields colours the best."

"Traitor!" laughed Kate.

"I am not!" said Stella. "It's just that emerald green with a light green tie would be really good with my hair."

"Actually, Blaze would look really good with the Marsh Fields colours too," Issie said. "Maybe we should all swap teams now!"

"I'm sure Avery would be thrilled," said Kate. "Swapping teams to join our archrivals just because you like their colours better!"

"Oh, well, too late to change anyway, even if we wanted to." Stella checked her watch. "Rider on the flat starts soon and Avery told us all to meet him at exactly ten minutes to nine for the team briefing – which is now!"

Signs had been erected in the showgrounds so that each team had a designated warm-up area. Next to the sign marked CHEVALIER POINT, Avery was busily gathering his squad together. Issie looked at the rest of her team admiringly. They had all spent hours prepping their horses, getting up way before dawn to plait manes and tails, whiten socks and oil hooves. The chestnuts, browns and bays – Blaze, Coco, Toby and Max – all had chequerboard patterns brushed perfectly on to their rumps to show off their shiny coats. Dan was groaning about how much effort it had taken to get all of the green grass stains off Kismit's pale grey hocks.

Even Natasha, who was now yawning melodramatically, seemed to have actually got up early to help her mother get Goldrush prepared. Goldrush was one of those palominos with a dark, sooty-coloured muzzle and Natasha had brought out her features by rubbing a damp cloth with a little Vaseline gently on her nose and around her dark eyes. Goldrush looked so pretty with her long eyelashes it was almost like she was wearing mascara.

"Splendid!" Tom Avery said as he assessed them all, moving along the line of riders, checking their girths and nosebands.

"Dan, I think you can take your stirrups down a hole please for rider on the flat," Avery commanded as he cast an eye over everyone's stirrup length and position.

"Now," Avery smiled, "I've got a couple of helpers today." He turned to Araminta and Morgan, who had been standing back by the Range Rover watching all this time. "Come on, ladies, front and centre!" Avery instructed, beckoning Araminta and Morgan to come over and stand next to him.

"Right," he said, "Minty is going to be giving you all some last-minute coaching with the rider on the flat class, and Morgan is going to help with setting up practice jumps and the games. I'll be wandering around and keeping an eye on you all throughout the day and helping out where and when I'm needed."

As Avery talked on, Morgan, who was standing shyly next to her mother gave Issie a little wave and Issie smiled and waved back.

"Right, then, let's get all these ponies moving on a twenty-metre circle and start warming up so that Araminta can give you a bit of advice on the rider classes," Avery said. "Find yourself a space and work them on a loose rein at a medium walk."

He turned to Araminta. "They're all yours, Minty."

"Thanks, Tom," she said, "for everything. I'm so sorry about what I said to you the other day."

Avery shook his head. "You've already apologised, Minty – no need to say any more about it. It's great to have you back at Chevalier Point."

Araminta smiled at him. "Well, I'd best get out there and give them some pointers then. We want our team to win!" She laughed and strode off to the centre of the ring, instructing the riders as she went: "Come on then, let's take up the reins and get them collected, everyone. We have work to do!"

Issie was about to join the other riders, but first she trotted Blaze up to say hi to Morgan, who was arranging some painted rails into a practice jump. "How are things?" she asked.

"Good. Really good, actually, thanks," Morgan said. "Mum has been great. Can you believe that she even suggested I should take the rest of the summer off and decide if I really want to ride, because she felt so bad about pressuring me?"

Issie was shocked. "Are you going to do that?"

"No way!" Morgan grinned. "I still love riding more than anything. I guess I didn't realise that before now. It's weird but, well, once Mum told me I didn't have to do it to make her happy, everything changed. It was like the weight lifted off my shoulders. Jack has been going really well since then too. He's jumping brilliantly and I'm going to start doing some extra training sessions with Annabel soon – the doctor says her leg will be fine to ride in a couple of weeks. And guess what? Jack and Eddie really like each other! They're best friends. Whenever I go down to the paddock they're always hanging out together!"

Issie laughed.

"You'd better get going. You've only got a little while before the first event and you need to warm up," Morgan said. She looked wistfully across at where her mother stood, instructing the riders as they trotted in a circle around her.

"Do you wish you were riding today?" Issie asked.

"Yeah, I do," Morgan confessed. Then she brightened up and smiled. "Maybe next year I'll make the team." She saw a worried look pass over Issie's face. "Don't worry." Morgan laughed. "I'm ready to earn it this time. I've got the whole year to get training."

Morgan gave Blaze a hearty pat on her neck. "Good luck, Issie," she said. "I really want to see your name engraved on that gold shield." She laughed. "But no pressure, right?"

"Right!" Issie laughed too.

"Canter on!" Araminta Chatswood-Smith commanded. Issie, who had just joined the others riding on the circle, gathered up her reins in preparation, sat heavy, put her legs on a little and pushed Blaze into a graceful canter.

"Very good, Isadora," Araminta said. "Now, I'm going to let you in on an old show-riding trick. It's not cheating, exactly, but it will make the judge think you are a marvellous rider. Now, remember, the judge is going to be standing in the middle of the ring, so he can only see your inside leg. You need to keep that inside leg completely still. I mean completely. If you need to kick your horse on then use your outside leg. That way the judge cannot see you and you will look like you are doing absolutely nothing to make your horse perform perfectly!"

"Excellent, Stella, excellent," Araminta said. "Hands up a little and totally still please, and don't drop your shoulder in, stay nice and upright. Imagine there is a thread running through the centre of your body and up and out through the top of your helmet, pulling you up from above so that you are sitting upright and perfectly straight. Lovely! You all look marvellous!"

Araminta's lesson came to an abrupt halt a few moments later as the riders were called into the ring by the judge. Issie tried to remember Araminta's advice as she warmed Blaze up, finding a clear space among the other riders.

In each event riders were competing for first, second and third place ribbons – with team points to match. Riders got three points for first, two for second and one point for third. The results would then be tallied on the scoreboard and at the end of the day the team with the most points would take home the Interclub Gold Shield. Every single point mattered. If one of the Chevalier Point riders could win rider on the flat today then the team would be off to a flying start.

"Prepare to trot and... trot on!" ordered the judge.

Issie gave Blaze a wee nudge with her outside leg and tried to keep her position completely still. Blaze had been going beautifully since Francoise had given her back. Issie figured her mare must have had some extra schooling during her stay at El Caballo Danza Magnifico.

Now, as Issie asked gently with her hands, Blaze flexed her neck gracefully, dropping neatly on to the bit. She lifted her legs gaily as she trotted around the ring, her paces as precise as a prima ballerina. "Good girl," Issie murmured under her breath.

It was one of those days when Blaze could do no wrong. When Issie asked her for a canter, she responded perfectly. When the judge called them into the centre of the ring and asked Issie to do a figure of eight for him, Blaze was a dream. She even did the rein-back at the end and stood at a perfectly square halt as Issie nodded her salute to the judge.

When the winners were called into the ring to accept their sashes, Blaze and Issie were first – followed by two riders wearing the emerald green vests of Marsh Fields.

As they cantered the ring for a victory lap with their ribbons tied around the horses' necks Issie looked over to see Morgan and Annabel standing together, both of them grinning and clapping like mad. Her mum was standing next to them, chatting happily to Araminta Chatswood-Smith and absolutely beaming with pride.

The scoreboard at the end of the showgrounds was chalked up with the first points of the day. "Three for us, and three for Marsh Fields. I get the feeling this is going to be close," Dan muttered.

He was right. For the rest of the morning the teams were neck and neck on the leader board. Chevalier Point got another two points for rider over hurdles – Dan and Kismit came second in this event with a beautiful clear round.

There was fierce competition in the jump-off against the clock, and the best of the Chevalier Point riders in this event was Kate who came third on Toby, putting another point on the board.

By the time they stopped for lunch the scores really couldn't have been closer. Chevalier Point was in the lead – but only just. The team had seven points on the board while Marsh Fields were uncomfortably close with six.

After everyone had eaten lunch, Avery gathered the team around to talk about their strategy for the afternoon's competition. "We've only got two events to go," he said. "The team flag race and the team bending relay. I've figured out the running order for the team races," Avery continued. "Stella, you'll go first. Coco is a whiz at games and you'll get us off to a flying start." He turned to the rest of the team. "Kate, I want you to follow Stella and Coco. Then can we have Dan, please, and then Ben, and then Natasha. And finally… Issie, I'd like you to be the last rider in the team."

Issie nodded. The butterflies that had suddenly begun to flutter in her stomach made her wish she had never eaten that second helping of her mum's chicken pie at lunch.

As the teams lined up, she surveyed the competition. The Marsh Fields team looked particularly lethal, all of them on compact, perfectly groomed ponies who looked like they meant business. Surely they would be the team to beat.

"On your marks... get set... go!"

The starter's gun sounded and there was a whoop of excitement as the first six riders charged out and broke into a mad gallop. Stella hauled Coco up at the first pole and snatched at the flag. The rubber band holding the cotton handkerchief to the pole gave away easily in her hands and she gripped it triumphantly, spinning Coco around and kicking her on. She rode back hard towards the oil drum with the wooden box on top that stood at the end of the row of poles at the finish line.

"Come on, Stella!" The Chevalier Point team were screaming their lungs out.

Stella deftly threw the first flag into the wooden box and there was a soft "clunk" as the flag landed in the box.

With the first flag away, Stella raced back to grab the flag from pole number two. She was in the lead – but only just.

"That girl from Garnet Ridge is really fast," Issie said, pointing out the rider on the row of poles at the far end on a zippy little bay.

By the time Stella had grabbed the flag off the last

pole and was racing back to the finish line, the girl from Garnet Ridge had gained on her and passed her. Garnet Ridge had taken the lead and their second rider was already up and racing.

The Marsh Fields team was also very quick, and as Stella crossed the line and Kate set off, the second rider from Marsh Fields also kicked his horse on and set off too.

"Go, Kate! Go!" Issie yelled. The butterflies in her stomach had been replaced by a sick feeling of dread. Kate wasn't the fastest rider on the team and everyone knew it. They were already a length behind Garnet Ridge. They couldn't afford to lose any more ground.

"Come on, Toby," Issie muttered under her breath. To her amazement and everyone else's, Toby seemed to be holding his own so far. Kate had wisely decided to go for the nearest flag first – riders were allowed to collect the flags in any order they liked. Kate's decision to begin with the closest pole meant that Toby's lanky Thoroughbred stride was kept to a canter at first and Kate managed to turn him easily around the poles. As she moved on from flag one to two, three, four, five and six Kate kicked Toby on to lengthen his frame.

Now the big bay was in full gallop, his stride swallowing up the ground.

"Go, Kate! Go, Toby!" the team screamed. Kate galloped back hard with the last flag and threw it wildly at the box on top of the barrel. Miraculously, it went in!

"Go!" she instructed Dan as Toby raced past him. "Go!"

Kate heaved on Toby's reins but she was halfway down the field before she could pull him to a stop and come back to join the rest of the group.

"That was amazing!" Stella beamed at her.

"I know!" Kate beamed back. She gave Toby a big slappy pat on the neck. "We've been doing extra practice. Wasn't he brilliant?"

Toby's quick pace had put the Chevalier Point team into the lead and now Dan and Ben both managed to maintain it. Incredibly, none of the riders from Garnet Ridge, Marsh Fields or Chevalier Point had dropped a flag so far. Riders from the three other teams had dropped their flags. Sometimes when they missed the box the flag still landed safely on the barrel top. Then, all the rider had to do to save the day was ride back to the barrel, snatch up the flag and deposit it in the box. But if they missed the barrel entirely and the flag fell on the ground it was a disaster. The rider would have to dismount and pick it up, then get back on again before throwing the flag in the box. By the time they were back in the saddle the rider would have lost valuable time and the other teams would be in front.

Marsh Fields, Garnet Ridge and Chevalier Point were clearly out in the lead by the time Natasha and Goldrush set off from the starting line.

"Go, Natasha! Go, Goldrush!" the Chevalier Point team yelled. Natasha, her face set in stony concentration, kicked Goldrush on, galloping the full length of the field to grab her first flag.

The palomino was quick on the turns and Natasha grimly hung on to the lead as she raced across the line a whole length ahead of the Garnet Ridge and Marsh Fields riders. As she threw the last flag in the box and pushed Goldrush on for the final strides over the finish line, she yelled out to Issie, "Go! Now!"

The screams of her team mates rang in her ears as Issie crossed the line and galloped her way to the far end of the field to take her first flag.

At the furthest pole, Issie pulled Blaze up and

reached out to grab the flag. She felt the soft cotton fabric with the hard pebble sewn into its hem. Her hand tightened around it and pulled hard and the flag came loose. They raced back down the field, Issie leaning low over the barrel as they turned at the end, chucking the flag smartly into the box.

As they did the same on poles five, four and three, Issie felt her nerves vanish. She looked across at the riders from Garnet Ridge and Marsh Fields. She was about a length in front of both of them. All she had to do was keep her lead and her team would win. She snatched the flag off the second-to-last pole and kicked Blaze on, circling around and throwing the flag at the box on top of the barrel. But there was no "clunk" as the flag hit the bin.

"Issie!" the cry went up from her team mates. "Issie! You've missed it!"

Issie pulled Blaze up hard. She had totally missed the box and the barrel – the flag was on the ground!

She spun the chestnut mare around and flung herself out of the saddle, scrabbling around in the grass, snatching up the flag off the ground. Without hesitating she vaulted back up on to her horse, taking a moment to find her stirrups as Blaze danced nervously. Then she pulled the mare right up close to the barrel and dropped the flag carefully into the box. One more flag to go!

The mistake had been costly though. By now the other two teams had taken the lead. Marsh Fields was clearly in front by at least a length and the other rider from Garnet Ridge only had one flag to go as well. Issie kicked Blaze on. She had to make up time on the last flag!

She reached the last pole in just two strides and spun Blaze around with one hand on the reins as she reached out to grab the flag with the other. She felt the flag come away in her hand. And then she was racing back as hard as she could for the finish line. She gripped the pebble inside the soft cotton in her hand. *Must get my timing right this time*, Issie thought as she galloped down on the oil drum. She pulled Blaze up and threw the flag precisely at the box. This time it went in and Issie waited until she heard the "clunk" and then galloped home across the finish line.

She had made up some ground on the last flag but it wasn't enough. Her mistake with the second-to-last flag had cost her team dearly. They had lost.

CHAPTER 17

They had lost. And it was all Issie's fault. "Oh don't be a drama queen!" Stella snapped at Issie when she told her this. "We haven't lost at all! We still came second. That's two points!"

Kate agreed, "That's right. Marsh Fields won so they got three and we got two. Which means that now both teams have nine points. We haven't lost yet."

"All the same," Issie groaned, "if it wasn't for me… maybe you should go last in the bending race, Stella?"

"No way!" Stella said. "I like going first. Last is way too much pressure!" She smiled at Issie. "You just had some bad luck in the flag race. The bending relay will be different."

"I hope so," Issie said ruefully.

If the butterflies in her stomach had been churning before, now they had formed a tight, fluttery knot that seemed to be making it impossible to breathe. Issie felt her hands clammy and damp on the reins. She wiped them on her jodhpurs. The team was lining up now for the bending relay. The final event of the day. If Chevalier Point won this, they would take the shield home. If they lost, Marsh Fields would be taking it home again for the third time in a row.

Behind the starting line, Tom Avery lined his riders up, working his way along the queue with last-minute advice for each of them. When he saw the look on Issie's face his smile faded. "Something up?" he asked.

"I don't think I can do it, Tom. I think Stella should go last," Issie ventured.

"Coco and Stella are quick," Avery said. "But Blaze is the fastest horse on the team."

"But if we lose the bending relay, we lose the shield," Issie protested.

Avery smiled. "Isadora, you need to start having a little faith in your horse – and in yourself."

He leaned in closer and whispered to her now, "You are one of the most talented riders I've ever taught, Issie. Don't let fear make you underestimate your abilities. You don't even know your true potential. But I do. I can see the rider that you will become..." Avery paused "...Anyway, I don't think your mysterious benefactor would be very pleased to find out that he moved heaven and earth to get your horse back, only to have you lose your nerve over a silly bending game."

Issie looked at Tom. Her benefactor? What did he mean? Was it possible that Blaze's return had something to do with Tom Avery?

She wanted to ask him more, but there wasn't time. Not now. The relay was about to start. Stella and Coco were already lining up at the start line.

"Issie?" Avery was standing there still, waiting for her answer. "Are you ready to do this?"

Issie nodded. "I'm ready," she said. And she gathered up Blaze's reins and took her place at the back of the lineup.

"On your marks... get set... GO!"

At the starter's gun the first row of horses and riders catapulted forward like racehorses from a gate and began weaving between the bending poles. Stella and Coco started well, but so did the rider from Marsh Fields – a girl on a rose-coloured roan, who whipped through the poles like wildfire.

By the time Stella reached the line and handed the baton to Kate, Marsh Fields were already ahead by a length.

"Go, Kate!" Dan, Ben and Natasha were yelling as Kate set off winding Toby through the poles.

Issie was at the back of the group, circling Blaze to keep her calm. The mare was so excited about the race she couldn't stay still. "Steady, girl, steady now," Issie soothed as Blaze danced beneath her. She was flicking her head trying to loosen Issie's grip on the reins. There was already a froth of white sweat on her neck and her nostrils were flared wide as she breathed hard. Issie held on as Blaze suddenly spooked, shied to one side and let out a low snort.

"Are you OK?" Ben asked as he watched Issie trying to control the Arab mare.

"Yeah," Issie said uncertainly, "Blaze is just a little nervous."

"Go, Dan!" Kate shouted as she charged back across the line. Toby had done well on the bending race, but he wasn't as fast as the Marsh Fields team who were now two lengths ahead.

"Go, Dan, go!" the team screamed as Kismit tore through the bending poles. At the last pole the flea-bitten grey made a tight turn, gaining a little on the Marsh Fields rider. By the time Dan crossed the line and passed the baton to Ben they were only one length behind.

Ben kept up the pace when it was his turn, riding like a speed demon. But so did the Marsh Fields rider, a boy on a brown mare. Not only that, Issie could see the Westhaven rider gaining on them too.

"Natasha!" Ben yelled as he thrust the baton into her hand. Natasha paused for a moment as she fumbled to get the baton out of Ben's fingers and then she clucked Goldrush on into a fast canter and set off through the poles.

Issie was up next. On the starting line now she tried to calm Blaze down. But the mare refused to stay still, dancing and snorting underneath her. "Easy, girl, it's OK," Issie cooed. She kept a tight grip on the reins as Blaze fought for her head. She wanted to go, but if she broke across the line too soon, the team would be disqualified. Issie had to hang on and try to keep her calm.

"Go, Natasha!" Ben and Dan were screaming now. The palomino rounded the last bending pole and headed back, weaving in and out of the upright plastic rods.

Issie was forced to turn Blaze so that her hindquarters were facing the start line to distract the mare and calm her down. "Wait, girl. Waiiitt…"

Issie spun Blaze around to face the poles just as Natasha raced over the line to hand her the baton. Issie reached her hand out. She felt the smooth wood of the baton with her fingers. It was almost in her hand when suddenly Blaze reared up. The chestnut mare went up on her hind legs, her front legs thrashing wildly in the air.

As Blaze reared over her Natasha squealed in fear and nearly dropped the baton.

"Blaze!" Issie shouted. She could feel herself slipping back in the saddle as Blaze went up, but she fought to hold on, gripping hard with her legs and grasping desperately at Blaze's mane with one hand. With the other hand she reached out in midair and made one last snatch at the baton.

Natasha, who was cringing away from Blaze's hooves, managed to keep her arm sticking out far enough for Issie to wrap her fingers around the wooden bar.

Issie felt her fingers close around the smooth wood. She had it!

Blaze brought her front legs down, and as soon she hit the ground Issie kicked her on towards the poles. "Go, Blaze!" she shouted at her horse, "Go!"

Issie looked to her right where the rider from Marsh Fields, a girl on a jet black gelding, was a full length ahead of her. The rider from Westhaven was right beside her too. If Issie wanted to win she had no choice but to ride as hard as she had ever done in her life.

Lying low over Blaze's neck, she kept a tight grip on the reins to guide her horse and urged her on with her legs and hands. "Let's go, Blaze!" she whispered hoarsely. Her heart pounded in her ears as she looked ahead down the row of poles. No more mistakes now. She couldn't afford to make any after a start like that.

Issie hung on and tried to get her horse into a rhythm as they slalomed down through the poles.

When they hit the final pole Blaze pivoted the turn at a gallop and as Issie leant over to try and keep her balance she thought that both of them might lean too far and fall. But Blaze kept her footing and the tight turn gained them some ground. As they wove back through the poles there was less than half a length between Issie and the Marsh Fields rider. Then Blaze inched forward and they were running next to each other. Blaze gave a snort of defiance as she eyed up the black gelding next to her and Issie felt the mare beneath her give a burst of speed.

The finish was ahead of them now – just one more pole to go. Issie leant low and hung on as Blaze gave a final surge and galloped across the line. She was almost half a length ahead of the black gelding. They had won.

When Issie thought back afterwards, it was hard to pick her favourite moment that day. There was the excitement of crossing the line with her team mates screaming and whooping so loud she had wanted to let go of the reins to cover her ears. Then they all stood there and watched with enormous grins on their faces as the scorekeeper wrote up the final tally on the board. Marsh Fields eleven points… Chevalier Point twelve!

The best of all though, she decided, was when she and Blaze stood before the judges with the rest of their team and had their red sashes tied on. Then Issie took the shield in her hands and rode out in front as the whole team did the lap of honour, cantering around the field with their red ribbons flapping around their ponies' necks.

There were more awards too at the pony-club rally the following weekend when the six riders came forward to accept their certificates in front of all the other Chevalier Point riders. The shield was presented to them again – this time with their names engraved on their own miniature gold shield.

"It will hang in our clubroom for the rest of the year," Avery had told them. "And the year after that too, I hope." He smiled at them. "Now that we have it back, I have no plans to let Marsh Fields or anyone else win it from us again."

Issie, Kate and Stella spent a long time at the clubroom that evening after the other riders had gone home, looking at the shield and re-enacting the moment when they had won.

"And what about when Blaze reared up?" Stella said. "Honestly, I never thought we would win at that point. I thought Natasha was going to drop the baton for sure."

"I thought she was going to hit Issie with the baton when I saw the look on her face," laughed Kate. "It's just as well you won, Issie – Natasha would never have forgiven you otherwise."

Issie smiled. "I can't believe it's all over," she said.

"Over? Hardly," Stella replied. "The Interclub Gold Shield might be over but the summer holidays have only just started. School is finally out and we can ride every day now. I can't wait."

Issie couldn't wait either. Especially now that she finally had a horse of her own to ride. "You're really mine now, Blaze. No one can take you away from me again," she told the mare as she let her loose in the paddock that evening.

The chestnut Arab nickered back her approval, and then she nudged Issie once more with her nose in the hope of maybe getting one last carrot.

"Sorry, girl," Issie giggled, "they're all gone. You ate the last one."

With this news, Blaze set off at a high-stepping trot, and Issie began to walk back in the other direction towards her mother who was waiting for her in the car.

"All right, then?" her mum asked as Issie got in.

"Yep," Issie beamed.

"I told you everything would work out fine, didn't I?" her Mum said. "It looks like your horse is back where she belongs."

Tomorrow was the first day of the school holidays and Issie had the feeling that this was going to be the best summer ever.

STACY GREGG

PONY  CLUB SECRETS

Book Three

DESTINY and the Wild Horses

Issie goes mad when she finds out she'll be staying with
her aunt for the summer. What about the dressage
competition she and Blaze have been training so hard for,
and her friends at the Chevalier Point Pony Club?

When she finds out Blaze can go with her, and she'll be
helping to train movie-star horses, Issie's summer starts to
look a whole lot more interesting...

HarperCollins *Children's Books*

Sneak preview...

Avery slapped his riding crop against his long brown leather boots to get their attention. "With the dressage test approaching this weekend I think you're all ready for some more advanced schooling," he said. "Does anyone here know how to do a Flying Change?"

Without hesitation a hand shot up amongst the riders.

"Ah, Natasha. Of course. Please come forward for a moment," Avery said.

Natasha cast a glance at Issie as she rode her new horse Fabergé past her to stand at the front of the ride.

"Now, Natasha here is going to demonstrate a Flying

Change," Avery said. "As you all know, a Flying Change is when we ask our horse to canter with a leading leg, and then we ask with our aids and make the horse change legs in midair." Avery paused. "You might have seen this on your Olympic dressage videos at home. It looks a bit like the horse is skipping, doesn't it?"

"Anky makes it look really easy when she does it on Bonfire," Stella said.

"Well then, let's see how easy it really is, shall we?" Avery said. "Right then, Natasha, why don't you work your horse around the arena at a canter and then ride a Flying Change through the middle of the school to show us how it's done?"

Natasha set off on Fabergé with a look of grim determination on her face. She cantered the rose-grey around the arena and then turned him down the centre to begin her Flying Change. In the middle of the school Natasha gave Fabergé a big kick with her heels. Nothing happened. She looked exasperated. Poor Fabergé looked confused.

"Try again, this time with nice, clear aids. You don't need to kick your horse! Just put that right leg forward on the girth," Avery instructed.

Natasha rode around and down the centre line again. This time though she ignored Avery's advice and gave Fabergé an almighty boot with her right leg. Fabergé shot up like a rocket, putting in a vigorous buck. Natasha gave a yelp of horror as she flew over Fabergé's head and sailed through the air, coming down in a heap on the sandy surface of the arena. Fabergé gave a terrified snort and cantered off across the arena.

Dan and Ben quickly clucked their horses and rode after him while Natasha stood up grumpily and dusted herself down.

"Are you all right?" Avery asked her. Natasha, who was bright red in the face, nodded quietly. "He's a very sensitive horse. If I were you I'd master the basics on him before you try a Flying Change again," Avery said kindly. Then he gestured to Issie. "Isadora, why don't you give it a try on Blaze? Remember, you need to move your right leg to the girth."

"Good girl, c'mon," Issie clucked to Blaze as she set off around the perimeter of the arena. As she rode down the centre line in a canter she sat tall in the saddle and tried to think about arranging her legs into the correct position. Right in the middle of the arena,

Issie did exactly as Avery had instructed – she moved one leg forward and the other leg back and squeezed hard. Beneath her she felt Blaze rise up and throw out her front legs like a school girl skipping down the street – a Flying Change!"

"Textbook stuff! A very nicely executed Flying Change!" Avery was pleased. "Excellent. Now – who's going to give it a go next? Dan? How about you?"

In the end, Issie was the only rider that day to master the Flying Change. "It's not as easy as it looks," Stella had grumbled as they untacked the ponies.

Issie had nodded in agreement with her friend, but the truth was that to her it had been easy. It was as if she only had to think about what she wanted to do and Blaze would respond. OK, so there weren't any fancy Flying Changes in their dressage test this weekend. Still, Issie felt certain for the first time ever, that she and Blaze stood a really good chance. They might even actually win.

"Mum! I'm home! I did a Flying Change today!" Issie

charged in through the front door without pausing to take off her riding boots.

"Isadora! You'd better not still have your muddy boots on!" her mother yelled back from the kitchen.

Issie stopped dead and ran back to the laundry, stripping off her boots and socks before running back to the kitchen to find her mother.

"You can tell me all about it while you eat your dinner," her mother said. And so, between mouthfuls of potato salad, Issie told her mum about Natasha and the Flying Changes and the dressage series that was starting on Saturday.

"Blaze is going so perfectly. This is going to be the best summer I've ever had!" Issie said.

Mrs Brown didn't say anything. She just looked down at her plate and gave her quiche a distracted poke with her fork.

"Mum? What's wrong? You've hardly said anything since I got home," Issie said.

"Issie, I am afraid I've got some, well, it's not bad news really. I mean it's good but it's not good…" Mrs Brown hesitated. "Issie, I've been invited away on a conference for work. They're going to fly me

there and pay for accommodation – the whole thing.
I'll be gone for two weeks."

"That's great!" Issie said. "When?"

"We leave on Friday," Mrs Brown said. "That's why
I wanted to talk to you tonight about the holidays."

"What do you mean?" Issie said.

"Sweetie, I can't leave you here by yourself. If I'm
away for two weeks then who would look after you?"

"Cool. I can go stay with Stella!" Issie said.

Mrs Brown shook her head. "There's something
else, Issie. I got a phone call last night from your Aunt
Hester. It turns out she's had a bad fall off one of her
silly horses and broken her leg."

"Aunt Hess? That's terrible! Is she ok?"

"She's fine," Mrs Brown sighed. "But she can't
possibly look after that farm of hers. She has Aidan to
help her but it's not enough…" Mrs Brown paused.
"…and so I suggested that you could go and stay with
her until she gets better again."

"Me?" Issie squawked.

"Sweetie – it's perfect! You can stay with Hester
while I'm away and she needs your help so it suits
her," Mrs Brown explained. "Besides, you've never

been to the farm before. Hester has loads of ponies and all those other animals that she trains. You'll adore it there."

"But, Mum! Blaze and I have been working so hard for the dressage competition," Issie sighed.

"I know, honey. But I can't see any other way," Mrs Brown said firmly. "I've already asked Aidan if he can drive through to get you. He's going to be here on Wednesday morning."

"But it's Monday now! When were you going to tell me this? What about Stella and Kate? What about my holidays? What about Blaze?"

To be continued...

STACY GREGG

PONY CLUB SECRETS

Book Four

Stardust and the Daredevil Ponies

Issie has landed her dream job – handling horses on a real film set! And with a group of frisky palominos to deal with, Issie's pony-club friends get to help out too.

What is spoilt star Angelique's big secret? Could this be Issie's chance for stardom?

HarperCollins *Children's Books*

STACY GREGG

PONY  CLUB SECRETS

Book Five

Comet and the Champion's Cup

Issie's aunt needs experts to help run her summer riding school. The perfect way for Issie and her friends to spend the holidays! Issie forms a special bond with Comet, a feisty pony with the talent to jump like a superstar. But can she train him in time for the Horse of the Year Show?

HarperCollins *Children's Books*

STACY GREGG

PONY CLUB SECRETS

Christmas Special

ISSIE and the Christmas Pony

Issie has always wanted her very own pony, and perhaps this Christmas her wish will come true. But can Issie find her dream horse in time to join her best friends at pony camp? Discover how Issie found her perfect pony Mystic – and how a little magic helped them to stay together forever.

HarperCollins *Children's Books*

STACY GREGG

PONY  CLUB SECRETS

Book Six

Storm and the Silver Bridle

Issie is heartbroken when her foal, Nightstorm, is stolen in the middle of the night. Her journey to rescue Storm takes her to Spain where she enlists the help of El Caballo Danzo Magnifico.

But can Issie outwit Storm's kidnappers? And is she brave enough to compete in the ultimate riding race, the Silver Bridle?

HarperCollins *Children's Books*

STACY GREGG

PONY  CLUB SECRETS

Book Seven

Fortune and the Golden Trophy

This season Issie and friends are competing for a new prize – the Tucker Trophy. And Issie has to train the doziest Blackthorn Pony she's ever seen into a winner. That is if she can keep him awake!

Meanwhile, someone is sabotaging relations between riders and the nearby golf course... Could pony club itself be under threat?

COMING SOON!

HarperCollins *Children's Books*